What they're saying about Jim Michael Hansen's
NIGHT LAWS

"Hansen's got what it takes to make your heart pound."

—Angie Cimarolli, BOOK PLEASURES
www.bookpleasures.com

"What a ride! . . . [*Night Laws* is] a story that you will long remember after putting the book down, and I give it my highest
recommendation."

—BOOK REVIEW CAFÉ
www.bookreviewcafe.com

"[A] well-plotted thriller that knows its audience and gives them
what they want in spades. It's an airport read, a high-concept
thrill-ride, the kind of popular thriller you can pick up, read,
enjoy and put back down again."

—Russel D. McLean, CRIME SCENE SCOTLAND
www.crimescenescotland.com

"*Night Laws* is fast paced and well plotted . . . While compari-
sons will be made with Turow, Grisham and Connelly, Hansen
is a new voice on the legal/thriller scene. I recommend you
check out this debut book, but be warned . . . you are not going
to be able to put it down."

—Aldo T. Calcagno, CRIME SPREE MAGAZINE
www.crimespreemag.com

"*Night Laws* . . . spells action with a capital 'A' and maintains a
furious pace. The glimpses into the killer's mind and the intelli-
gent countermoves made by the protagonists are enlightening
and provide grist for nightmares and suspense. We rated this
book at five hearts."

—Bob Spear, Editor, HEARTLAND REVIEWS
www.heartlandreviews.com

"This is a gritty crime novel that grabs your attention in the first few pages . . . Jim Hansen has created characters and details that are three-dimensional and vibrant . . . [T]urn off your crime thrillers on television and tune-in to this book."

—Kathy Martin, IN THE LIBRARY REVIEW
www.inthelibraryreview.com

"In this work, Jim Michael Hansen works every angle that a thriller read should have. Skillfully, he defines his characters. . . . His twists and turns are mind-boggling bringing you to one level of suspense, whipping you around to fear and anger, plunging you into frustration and horror, and leaving you in a heap of reading ecstasy. *Night Laws*, in my humble opinion, is a Masterpiece . . ."

—Shirley Priscilla Johnson, Senior Reviewer,
MIDWEST BOOK REVIEW
www.midwestbookreview.com

"[A] fine blend of the taut narrative style reminiscent of the Alex Cross novels of James Patterson and of the plot theme reminiscent of Michael Connelly's Harry Bosch series . . . tensed action of the first order, culminating in a nail-biting, spine-chilling finish. . . . *Night Laws* is recommended, very highly recommended." [Rating: 5 bolts]

—Nayaran Radhakrishnan (Author of *A Fiction of Law*),
NEW MYSTERY READER MAGAZINE
www.newmysteryreader.com

"With ease, Hansen guides us up into the world of the wealthy lawyers and all the way down to the gutters of the ugly urban decay. . . . His no-nonsense style creates well-rounded lifelike characters. He grabs the reader's attention and does not let go until the last page. This read is a great roller coaster ride worthy of John Grisham's *The Firm*."

—Andrei V. Lefebvre, QUILL PEN
www.quill-pen.net

"*Night Laws* is a terrifying, gripping cross between James Patterson and John Grisham. A police procedural infused with legal overtones, Hansen has created a truly killer debut. The characters are compelling, the research dead-on, and there's just a touch of humor to take the edge off one of the grisliest serial killers in recent memory."

—J.A. Konrath, bestselling author of
Whiskey Sour and *Bloody Mary,* www.jakonrath.com

"The author has woven a pattern of intrigue and realism that leaves the reader's heart pounding. He brings his knowledge of lawyers and the law into the dark world of a sociopathic character. Even today, as I drive the familiar streets of Denver, I find myself reliving scenes from *Night Laws* all over again. Mr. Hansen's *Night Laws* is a read you will not soon forget!"

—Katherine Shand Larkin, Esq.
Jackson Kelly PLLC, www.jacksonkelly.com

"*Night Laws* is a creepy, scary, nail-biting read. Jim Michael Hansen and homicide detective Bryson Coventry deliver a one-two punch."

—Sarah Lovett, author of *Dangerous Attachments,*
Dark Alchemy, Dante's Inferno, Acquired Motives, and
A Desperate Silence, www.sarahlovett.com

"*Night Laws* takes the legal mystery fan on a brand new thrill ride through the Mile High City. Look out Grisham, Jim Hansen is re-inventing the genre."

—Evan McNamara, award-winning author of
Superior Position and *Fair Game,* www.evanmcnamara.com

"The electrifying pace of Jim Hansen's first novel is almost stunning. It grabs you on the first page and really takes you for a ride. Set in the Denver legal community, *Night Laws* is a crime story about several murders with mysterious links to a highbrow Denver law firm. But the artfully disturbing details of this lurid page-turner quickly take you into the dark pit of the deviant criminal mind. And like a David Lynch movie, it gives you the uneasy feeling that you now know more about the dark side than you really should."

—K. Preston Oade, Jr., Esq.
Partner, Holme Roberts & Owen LLP, Denver, Colorado
www.hro.com

"Jim Hansen has captured the intrigue and excitement of a major criminal investigation and has looked into the soul of the serial offender."

—Lt. Jon Priest, Homicide Unit, Denver Police Dept.;
Criminal Investigation Expert Consultant for Court TV (*I, Detective*)
www.CourtTV.com

"A thrilling page-turner that grips a hold of you and doesn't let up. Jim Michael Hansen delivers a chilling read in *Night Laws* that rivals Diehl, with a villain so evil you'll think twice about going out alone. This story will stick with me a long time to come, leaving me waiting for the next book in the series."

—Patricia A. Rasey, award-winning bestselling author of
Kiss of Deceit, Eyes of Betrayal and many others
www.patriciarasey.com

"Fast-moving, sharp storytelling, likeable characters who talk like real people, a page-turner all the way to the end."

—Shelley Singer, author of the Jake Samson detective series
and the Barrett Lake mystery series, www.shelleysinger.com

"Edgy, but witty, with regular, vivid turns of phrase, *Night Laws* and Jim Hansen rock. Check it out. Hansen deserves to be on your To-Be-Read list."

—Mark Terry, author of *Dirty Deeds, Catfish Guru* and
Show Business is Murder (Murder at the Heartbreak Hotel)
www.mark-terry.com

NIGHT
LAWS

A NOVEL

Jim Michael Hansen

DARK SKY PUBLISHING, INC.
Golden, CO 80401

Dark Sky Publishing, Inc.
Golden, CO 80401
www.darkskypublishing.com

Copyright © 2006 by Jim Michael Hansen
www.jimhansenbooks.com
www.jimhansenlawfirm.com

ISBN 0-9769243-0-7

Library of Congress Control Number: 2005905750

Cover photography by Sami Sarkis / Getty Images

10 9 8 7 6 5 4 3 2 1

Printed on acid-free paper
Made in the USA

Dedicated to
Eileen

And with many special thanks to

Lieutenant Jon Priest and Sergeant Mike Fetrow, Homicide Unit, Denver Police Department, for generously sharing their years of experience and for answering my many technical questions.

The many authors, book reviewers and others who generously and selflessly devoted their time to review this book.

You, the reader, for trusting me enough to let me sit behind the wheel and take you for a ride. I can only hope that you like bumps, are fascinated by scenery high and low, don't mind sudden starts and stops, will wake me up every now and then, are not a backseat driver, and that you meet a few people to love and hate along the way. Other than that, all I can say is wait for the book to come to a complete stop before getting out.

A few special persons for generosity, encouragement and contributions beyond measure: Anne K. Edwards, Geraldine Evans, J.A. Konrath, Cathy Langer and Nancy Tesler.

Chapter One

WITH A CUP OF COFFEE IN HIS LEFT HAND and the envelope in his right, Bryson Coventry followed the young attorney down the spacious corridors of Holland, Roberts & Northway, LLC, absorbing the undeniable presence of power and money. They passed a small pencil sketch of a cowboy fighting to stay on a horse, an incredibly good piece that almost vibrated right off the wall. Coventry slowed just enough to look at the signature: C.R. He pointed it out to Detective Shalifa Netherwood, walking beside him, and said, "That's an original Charlie Russell."

She glanced at it without breaking stride. "Is he somebody?"

"Was, he's dead now."

"We're almost there," the lawyer—Kelly Parks—said over her shoulder. She was two steps ahead and speeding up.

Even packaged as she was, in an ultra-conservative gray ensemble, Coventry couldn't help but notice the sway in her step and found himself fighting to not stare. She wore her hair down and long, as if she might be someone caught up in a world just a little too stuffy for her basic nature. For some reason he pictured her as one of those pent-up weekend warriors, maybe with a little tattoo of a rose on her ass or shoulder. No, not the shoulder, it would be the ass, where it wouldn't jeopardize her job.

Inside the office the women sat down while he stood for a second to get his bearings. Diplomas, bar admissions and awards jammed the walls, all very sterile and politically correct.

"If it were up to me, I'd take them all down and put up a few good paintings, but they give the clients a sense of security," Kelly Parks offered, waiting. "Please, have a seat. Someone's dead," she added with just the touch of an edge, an invitation to proceed, a tone that suggested that she'd help if she could but the day was moving forward.

HE FOUND A MATCHING LEATHER CHAIR next to Shalifa's, the color of earwax, a real ugly piece, and eased down into it. It felt great, a real surprise, soft but supportive. "Right, sorry," he apologized. He guessed that she was twenty-eight or twenty-nine, with a no-nonsense harried look that probably came from billing ungodly hours and kissing way too many asses, all in the name of someday getting a partnership vote somewhere above the line, or keeping it if she already had it.

He frowned, then opened the clasp of the envelope that he'd been carrying for the last twenty minutes, pulled out the pictures of D'endra Vaughn's dead body, and one-by-one neatly placed them on the desk in front of her. He watched the reaction on her face and detected a pause as she processed the information, and noted that she made no effort to stack them up or look away.

Coventry waited for her eyes then held them: "Her name is D'endra Vaughn, twenty-two years old, an elementary school

16

teacher. She was killed Saturday evening, between eight and eleven. We're trying to find the man who did it and that's why we're here." He placed two more pictures on the desk, depicting a smiling, happy, young woman. "This is what she looks like when she's not dead."

Kelly Parks preempted the obvious question. "I don't know this woman. I've never seen her before in my life."

Coventry studied her voice, found no lies, rose out of his chair, walked over to the window and looked down. On the edge of her desk he spotted a business card holder, took one of her cards, glanced at it, the direct phone number in particular, and wedged it in his front shirt pocket behind the chocolate. He wore jeans, a gray sport coat over a blue cotton shirt, and no tie. "Nice view," he said looking down.

"The window's my favorite part," she said, looking again at Shalifa and then back to him. "It's real handy in case you get the urge to jump. Everyone in the firm gets one. I don't know the dead woman, so I'm sitting here wondering what's going on."

He put on a serious face, to stress the importance of the situation. "The victim had a cell phone and it's missing. We're assuming at this point that the man who killed her took it. All this is confidential, by the way. In any event, it turns out that a call was made from that phone, yesterday, at 3:34 in the afternoon, roughly eighteen hours *after* the woman's death. Here, let me show you." He reached into the envelope, fumbled around, then pulled out a phone log and pointed to the last entry on the second page. "Do you recognize the number?"

"I assume that you know I do."

She looked at him, obviously confused, waiting for an explanation.

"That's your direct work number?" He was sure, but wanted her to confirm it anyway, just in case she'd changed offices or something.

She nodded. "It is."

"No one else in the firm has that number, correct?"

"No . . . I mean, yes, that's correct. It's a direct line to my desk," she said. "What's going on?"

"That's what we're trying to find out."

"I don't . . ."

"Did you get that call yesterday?"

"No, yesterday was Sunday. I didn't even come in."

"Not even for a few minutes?"

As if to prove her point, she added: "I almost never work Sundays, there'd be no reason . . ." She screwed up her face in thought. "Yesterday I shopped at Cheery Creek, bought a few books at the Tattered Cover, paid some bills, washed the laundry, and did some other equally earth-shattering stuff."

"Have you checked your messages this morning?"

"Yes, I always . . ."

"And?"

"And no messages from Sunday, if that's what you're getting at."

Coventry moved away from the window and studied one of the diplomas on the wall. "You went to Case Western Reserve in Cleveland," he said. "I have a friend who went to Ohio State."

"It's huge," she offered.

"That's what he said. *Lots of women*, I think, were his exact words."

"Oh, him. We've met a few times." She smiled, slightly crooked, oddly sexy. It reminded him a little of the woman in that movie with Al Pacino, what the hell was the name of it? The one where he was a cop, the woman was a blond, a shoe salesman, and her past lover kept killing her new boyfriends. He shook his head; it'd come to him later when he could care less.

He estimated her white blouse to cost fifty dollars, the wool-blend suit three hundred, the shoes one-fifty. She looked like she drove a Lexus and had a standing February reservation in Los Cabos. Economically way out of his league. No wedding ring or pictures of guys on her desk, though. That was worth something.

"So if you didn't get the call, could someone else have taken it?" he questioned.

She shook her head. "There'd be no reason to, it wouldn't be for them. What probably happened is, someone called my office, it rings two or three times, and then transfers over to the voice mail system. Then, they hang up before the beep. Maybe they hung up because they realized they had the wrong number. Have you considered that?"

"But then they'd call the right number and it'd be on the log."

"Oh, yeah. Right."

"MAYBE IT WAS A CLIENT OF YOURS," he suggested, getting to the point, one of his two main theories in fact. "He's scared to death at what he did and wants to negotiate a surrender, so he calls you." He paused, to let it sink in, then added: "We'd be interested in that, if that's the case. It'd be in everyone's best interest. Cooperation can mean a hell of a lot at this stage. Later, you don't get ten cents on the dollar."

She shook her head and let out a quick nervous chuckle, as if contemplating the absurdity of the thought. It sounded genuine. "No, sorry. I only do civil law, no criminal work."

"Really?"

"God, no," she said, her mouth growing crooked at yet the second absurd thought in a row. "I wouldn't know a habeas corpus from a café latte." As an explanation she added, "Most big firms like this one don't do criminal work. You don't want a CEO sitting in the lobby next to a car thief."

"What? The car thief might not come back again?" She laughed, and he added: "So he's not a client?"

"If he is . . . no," she confirmed. Then, as an apparent afterthought: "Even if he was, I wouldn't exactly have the liberty of blurting out a name. That kind of thing is privileged. Lawyers take that stuff seriously. There are rules."

Coventry nodded.

She added: "Even calling a lawyer who declines representation is privileged. It'd be a breach of ethics for me to even confirm that a phone call was made, even if I didn't take the case."

"We're not trying to get you in trouble."

He walked back over to the window and looked down, seeing toy cars, people dots, all moving slowly and rhythmically and even sanely from this far up. "Let's talk about what this phone call may or may not mean for a moment. First, we were thinking that he might be a client and we could work something out. I'm still not totally convinced that isn't the case."

"Like I said . . ."

"What I mean is, you might not even know it yet. It's possible he could be a friend, or a friend of a friend. Someone who may know you're not a criminal lawyer, but thinks you can find him one and keep your mouth shut. Maybe even someone you haven't seen in a long time."

She thought about it, getting a distant look, then shook her head. "Technically that's possible, but I just don't see it, personally. It doesn't feel right."

"Do you know someone named Aaron Whitecliff?"

"No."

"Ever hear that name before?"

"No, never. Who is he?"

"Maybe from your past?"

"No, I'd remember. It's one of those names where you get a visual image, white cliffs and all. It would have stuck in my mind."

"OKAY, WELL THEN, LET'S TALK ABOUT the second possible explanation for the call," Coventry said. "We're thinking that the phone call may be a message to you, or to us. It may be his way of saying he's playing a game and you're in it."

She laughed, absurd. "That's nuts."

He looked at her, waiting.

"Look, on a conceptual level, I can see your reasoning," she said. "But I don't know the dead woman, I don't know any crazy people, I don't have any enemies, I don't owe anyone any money, and I floss every night. This whole thing just isn't me, there's no way."

"Well, then, how do you explain the phone call?"

She paused, then said: "I don't know, maybe he tried to call someone else, got a wrong number, then decided to call the right number later from a land line. There's probably a good explanation, if you look hard enough."

He narrowed his eyes. "Even if you don't know him, that

doesn't mean he doesn't know you. I don't want to sound melodramatic, but the sick reality is there are a whole lot of guys out there on the hunt. They pick you out when you're strolling down the street or sitting in a restaurant. You remind them of their third-grade teacher or they just like the way you wear your hair. They follow you around and find out who you are, where you live, what your routine is. They spend their free time in your shadows and lie awake in bed at night making up little fantasies."

She looked like a spider just crawled up her leg. "It sounds like you're trying to scare me."

"Has anyone been following you?"

She paused, thinking, and he could tell she was going deep. "No . . ."

"Have you seen the same stranger's face at more than one place?"

"Not that I can remember."

"Think."

"I am. No . . ."

"My advice is, start paying attention."

She looked at Netherwood: "Is he serious?"

Coventry continued: "Start memorizing faces, look for people who might be watching you. Especially people who look like they're covering up, people with sunglasses or baseball caps, or people who look away too fast when you turn in their direction."

Netherwood said, "I think he is."

"If you think someone's following you, and this is important, lead him into an area where there's a security camera, some place like a hotel lobby or the cash register in a store, something like that. Then call me right away so we can get the tape."

"I can't even believe we're talking about this."

"If he calls you, get whatever information you can and let me or Detective Netherwood know right away, but don't play with him. And if he does turn out to be someone looking for a lawyer, refer him to Jack Cable, that's C A B L E, he's in the Legal Directory. He's a real lawyer, so don't worry."

She cocked her head: "I'm assuming that this Mr. Cable doesn't exactly read the privilege rules the same way I do."

Coventry shrugged.

"Maybe not."

THEY SPENT THE NEXT HOUR ASKING HER pointed questions, with Shalifa Netherwood now taking the lead, peeling back her past, looking for a common denominator that might connect her to Saturday night. She cooperated fully, because she actually was scared now, Coventry thought. He could see it in her eyes and hear it in her voice.

She told them that she grew up in Chagrin Falls, Ohio, at that time a slow-moving, country town south of Cleveland, given to rolling hills and maple trees and nothing really very bad, unless you counted gossip or chicken pox. Her father, now retired, was a judge, her mother a physician, she had two older brothers, one younger sister, all very successful but otherwise Leave it to Beaver. After high school she attended Case Western Reserve University, with a major in biology and minor in chemistry. She then stayed on at Case to get her law degree, took a three-year clerkship with a federal judge in Cleveland, and moved to Denver four years ago to accept an associate position with Holland, Roberts & Northway, LLC. She'd be up for partnership vote in four years or so and spent her life working her ass off.

In other words, no obvious connection to either D'endra Vaughn or anyone strange.

WHEN THEY FINALLY LEFT, and the elevator opened on their floor, there was no one inside, just a big old empty space.

"Just the way you like it," Netherwood said, stepping in.

He grunted. No way it would last.

As the big metal box took them down, floor by floor without stopping, Netherwood looked amused and said: "That woman is hot for you, Coventry, you dog."

He chuckled. "Cut the bullshit, that's Katona's turf."

"I'm serious, I can tell by the way she was looking at me. She was trying to figure out if we were doing it."

He raised an eyebrow.

"Were we?"

She laughed, a little too loud, if the truth be told. "In your dreams, maybe."

IT TOOK THE TWO DETECTIVES FOREVER TO LEAVE. And when they finally did, Kelly Parks immediately walked over to the winding oak staircase and climbed it to the top floor of the firm where the rainmakers lived.

She felt dirty and scared.

She felt dirty for lying to Coventry.

He had a certain edge to him, something she couldn't quite put her finger on, but something totally different from the law-yers and quasi-men who paraded in and out of her life. There was something about him pulling her in for a closer look. He had a toned body that had no doubt been downright hard once upon a time, an incredible face, thick brown hair given to flopping down, the kind you'd more likely find on a sailboat than in a boardroom, and eyes that pulled you in and made you stare at them until you figured out that one was blue and one was green. She liked his size, also, which she guessed to be in the neighborhood of six-two.

She felt scared because she didn't know what was going on, but did know it was serious.

She had to talk to senior partner Michael Northway, Esq., right away, this very minute. Whatever was going on was somehow connected to the little stunt they pulled last May.

That much was clear.

Chapter Two

Day One
Monday Morning

THE THING THAT IMPRESSED KELLY PARKS the most about Holland, Roberts & Northway, LLC, when they flew her out from Cleveland to interview four years ago, wasn't the grandeur of the offices, or the ivy-league credentials of the attorneys, or the sheer size of the firm, or the list of clients that read like a Who's Who of the big and relevant. Most established firms had that tapestry in one weave or another. The thing that made the deepest, most lasting impression was that Michael Northway himself picked her up at the airport. Now here's a man whose legal commentary you could catch with increasing regularity on CNN, personally driving to the airport, parking the car, making the trek inside, and then waiting for her with the masses, like she was somebody and he didn't have a single other thing in the world to do.

She reached the top floor of the firm.

There the staircase entered the Jungle, a one-of-a-kind space designed by Alan Willbanks out of New York, built for no other reason than to impress the hell out of clients. Brown cobblestone paths wandered through dense jungle foliage and water features. At the top of the stairs she walked around the Piranha display, then to the left past six suites, where the path eventually ended at the desk of Lori Chambers, Michael Northway's executive assistant.

"Lori, hi," she said. "Tell me Michael's in or I'm going to scream."

Lori, a Marilyn Monroe type, the third in fact of that particular genre to sit at that desk, looked sympathetic. "He is, but barely. I'm dragging him out of there at nine-fifteen for the airport. And even that's pressing it."

Kelly looked at her watch: seven after, meaning an eight-minute window. "Where's he going?"

"The D.C. office."

"How long?"

"Until Friday."

"Damn it. Okay, I'm going to have to interrupt him," she said, heading for the door that, at the moment, was closed.

INSIDE, SHE FOUND MICHAEL NORTHWAY sitting behind his desk, feet propped up, talking on the phone with someone he appeared to enjoy very much judging from the look on his face. She sensed a woman. He waved her in and looked glad to see her. She closed the door, took a chair, crossed her legs, pulled her skirt up just a touch and waited.

The wall behind him was covered with photographs, mostly Michael with people of recognition—politicians, athletes, actors, businessmen—and not just standing together for some quick snapshot at some public relations function but really doing things; deep sea fishing, sailing off Bermuda, climbing fourteeners in the San Juan mountains, biking in Aspen . . .

One picture in particular always captivated her—namely Michael sitting on the bench of the United States District Court for the District of Colorado, wearing a black robe with a thoughtful, pensive expression. That picture above all else defined him. Who else could have left the firm to take an appointment as a federal judge, only to then resign the position of power and lifetime tenure three years later to return to private practice? As far as she knew he'd been the only person in history to do that, at least that quick and that young. "All the fights have other people in them," he said. "You're just the referee. Where's the fun in that?"

He's an attractive man, with an ability to turn on a waterfall of charisma at will, who now spends most of his waking hours trading favors, doing them and getting them at levels that most people don't even know exist. Technically he's the manager of the law firm's Employment Law Department, a group of more than sixty lawyers. Un-technically he's the firm's principal rainmaker, not to mention a bare-knuckles, much-feared trial lawyer.

The minute he hung up she spoke. "Michael, two people from homicide showed up at my office this morning, out of the blue. Do you remember D'endra Vaughn?"

His face wrinkled as if recalling a name he'd rather not. "Of course."

"Well, she's dead," she said. With that, she told him everything she knew so far, including the fact that someone telephoned her on Sunday using D'endra Vaughn's cell phone, which Lieutenant Coventry interpreted as a possible warning that she was next. She studied his expression as she told the story and couldn't help but notice the furrow slowly growing between his eyes.

"The only thing in my life that connects me to D'endra Vaughn is last May," she said. "Whatever it is that's going on is somehow tied to that."

SHE WAS REFERRING TO THE EVENT that took place almost a year ago. Senior partner Michael Northway walked into her lowly little associate office one day, closed the door, fumbled around, and said: "Kelly, I need your help. The firm needs it, to be precise."

She knew from the tone of his voice that he had something serious on his mind. She took off her reading glasses, set them on the desk and looked at him. "How so?"

He hesitated, as if caught in indecision. "This is going to seem a little out of the ordinary. I'm going to propose something, but before I do, I want you to know up-front that you don't have to do it. I want to be absolutely one hundred percent clear about that. Do you understand?"

"You sound like you want me to kill someone."

"Hardly, but it is something serious. And I guess, technically speaking, maybe a little illegal."

"*Michael . . .*"

"Think of it as client development," he said, "if you really want to get to the heart of it. Client development at its most basic, primitive, ugly level. All I ask is that if you feel this is beyond you, this conversation never happened. I mean you mention it to no one, ever." He paused, then added: "I need that assurance before I can continue."

"Are you serious?"

"Your name came up because we felt you could be trusted."

"We?"

"Some people here in the firm," he said. "I can't tell you any more than that right now. So, have I totally freaked you out? I can leave, just say the word . . ."

She didn't hesitate. "There's no way in hell you're going to get out of here alive without telling me what in the world you're up to."

"You're sure? There's absolutely no repercussions if you . . ."

"God, Michael. You're like a vibrator on slow speed."

He laughed and seemed to picture it. "Okay, but remember, after I outline this, you can say no. Agreed?"

"Fine."

"All right," he said. "Let me give you a little background first. This is a firm that's always helped people. Most of the time, ninety-nine percent of the time, that simply means providing first-class legal services or trading a little politics or making a special phone call. But sometimes, once in a great while, it means something more than that. On rare occasions, and only for very special friends of the firm, it means getting something done for them." He looked at her as if waiting for a reaction.

"Talk about vague . . ."

"Okay," he said. "On unique occasions, when it comes to our attention that a client has a bona fide need, there's a small group of people here in the firm that gets together to discuss it. I happen to be one of the people in that group. I also serve as the spokesperson of that group for meetings like the one you and I are having right now."

"So who all's in this group?"

"That's not relevant right now. And to be honest, never will be. That's why we only have one visible spokesman."

"Can you at least tell me how many . . ."

"Even that . . . no . . . it varies." He looked at her, sympathetic: "I know this is unfair, but it has to work this way. You look hesitant."

"Not hesitant, surprised. I had no idea that anything like this was going on."

"Few do," he confirmed. "Even most of the partners around here don't know, which is why, no matter what else happens, you have to keep this quiet."

She nodded.

She would do that.

"But getting back to the point, we recently came across a situation that required the group's attention. I can't give you all the details, but here's the gist of it. Someone very relevant to the firm is interested in helping a young woman by the name of Alicia Elmblade."

"Alicia Elmblade?"

"Right," he said.

"Why?"

"Why does he want to help her?"

"Yes."

"That's a good question. But it's a piece of information that he hasn't volunteered," Northway said. "We do know, however, that it's very important to him to help her and he's let us know that in no uncertain terms. That makes it important to us."

"Is she a mistress or something?"

"I don't know." A pause: "To be honest, she could be. She's a stripper."

"A stripper?"

He nodded.

Kelly cocked her head. "Don't tell me. He's married and she's pregnant."

"No," Northway said. "It's not that. It's something else."

"Meaning . . ."

"Meaning she wants to disappear off the face of the earth," he said. "She wants something to happen to make it look like she's dead. She wants to fake her own death."

"Why?" Kelly questioned.

"Another good question."

"Jesus, Michael," Kelly said. "This sounds strange. Are the cops after her or something? How do you know you're not participating in a scheme to hide a fugitive?"

"No," he said, chuckling. "It's nothing like that."

"How do you know?"

"I just do," he said. "Trust me on that."

"This is so convoluted. I mean, we're *lawyers,* aren't we?"

He looked at her and she could feel him sizing her up.

She exhaled, weighed and balanced it for a split-second, then looked in his eyes: "Okay, the client wants to help this woman, who in turn wants to disappear."

"Right, disappear in such a way that no one would ever try to find her, because she's dead. We've already come up with a plan. Let me tell you how you fit in, if you agree to help."

Chapter Three

One Year Earlier

THREE DAYS AFTER THAT CONVERSATION with Michael Northway, on a creepy moonless night in May almost a year ago now, Kelly Parks sat alone in the dark behind the steering wheel of her 3-Series BMW, parked on the shoulder of a beat-up country road a half mile down from an equally beat-up place called Rick's Gas Station.

Waiting.

Excited but apprehensive.

Excited that Michael Northway and other still unknown but obviously high-ranking partners trusted her enough to do this.

Apprehensive about breaking the law.

What they were about to do, although innocent enough looking at first blush, was actually serious business. She'd spent a couple of unsettling hours in the library looking up the statutes and the case law. Once it was done, if caught, they could be prosecuted under a number of felony offenses including perjury, obstruction of justice and conspiracy. Hell, they were already guilty of conspiracy. And there's no shortage of prosecutors around who would love nothing more than to notch their belt with the high and mighty.

Suddenly lights appeared behind her—a car approached. It slowed, pulled up next to her and stopped. A touch of dust kicked up.

It loomed there as a large black shadow, darker than the night but not by much, and she recognized it as a van. Inside Michael Northway sat behind the wheel, his face tight and faintly illuminated from underneath by the dashboard lights, motioning for her to roll her window down. She inhaled, turned the key to auxiliary power and brought down the glass. The sound of the van's engine abruptly burst through the open window, punctuated by a fan belt given to slipping and squealing.

He stayed behind the wheel and leaned toward her as far as he could. "They haven't come by yet, have they?" His voice was tense, anxious, so tight in fact that she caught the feeling herself.

"No."

He exhaled, and the burrow between his eyes visibly eased back.

"Where have you been?" she questioned. "You're late."

"Traffic. Are you ready?"

She hesitated. "Yes."

"You don't sound sure. You need to be sure. We can't afford . . ."

She cut him off. "I'm sure. Your getting here late didn't help anything, that's all."

He looked at her hard, glanced at his watch, then at the rearview mirror. "They should be here any minute. I'll give them a five-minute head start, time to gas up and get positioned. When I leave, give me thirty seconds before you take off. Then bring your speed up to twenty-five and hold it there . . ."

"I know."

"I know you know. I'm just being sure."

"Thirty seconds, twenty-five miles an hour. Relax."

"Watch my taillights. If you get too close, back off. Timing is everything." He looked at her and she looked back at him, realizing that this was it. "Okay, point of no return. Anything else?"

She thought about it.

Was there anything else?

If so, it wasn't popping up in neon.

They talked it over at lunch, twice. She drove the area yesterday and knew the layout. She played it out repeatedly in her mind, running through *What Ifs* one after the other. The cell phone signal was strong, no problems there. But something was out of place. What? The van? The weirdness of seeing Michael out here in the dark?

"Where'd you get the van?" she questioned.

"Borrowed it."

After a moment: "If we get caught . . ."

He cut her off. "We won't."

SUDDENLY THERE WAS A LIGHT ON HIS FACE, a flicker of illumination present and then gone, and she realized that headlights from behind them were reflecting in his rearview mirror and into his eyes. She twisted and saw them, snaking up the road, punching out fleeting images of trees and brush and asphalt as they approached. They looked eerie and for a brief moment she wondered if she was really going to go through with this, but knew that she had already come too far to go back.

He turned his eyes from the rearview mirror and looked at her. "Looks like we're up."

She nodded. "See you in hell."

He smiled. "Dramatic. I like that."

Northway pulled up in front of her, on the shoulder, and waited with the engine running, looking in the driver's side rearview mirror at the approaching car. From behind, the headlights grew brighter. The inside of her car started to light up. She turned on her parking lights as a safety precaution and the dashboard sprang to life. She could hear the whine of the approaching car's tires now.

It pulled up next to her and stopped. There were three figures inside, all women, she could tell that from the hair and profiles, two in the front and one in the back. She could see well enough to tell that she didn't know any of them. The sound of a radio dropped off, she could hear them talking to one another, but couldn't make out the words. Then she saw Michael with his arm out the window, waving them forward, and they must have seen it too because they pulled up next to him and stopped. She heard a brief exchange of words, laughter, then more talk. Then they took off. Whoever was in the passenger seat waved an arm out the window. The whole thing reminded her a little of high school, when they'd pull over somewhere and decide whether to head to Dairy Queen or down by the river.

She looked at her watch.

Ten fifteen.

Be home by midnight, she thought.

There was nothing to do now but wait. Wait for five minutes, then Michael'd take off; wait for another thirty seconds, then she'd take off. Wait and hope that another car didn't come along and screw things up.

SHE SHIFTED IN HER SEAT and tried to clear her head. Tomorrow morning would be busy. Russell Travis, the horniest man on the face of the earth, wanted to meet her for an early breakfast at the Brown Palace, ostensibly to discuss his case. He put in the infrastructure for an upscale residential subdivision and then enticed five builders to construct spec houses, at their cost, with an understanding that anyone who bought a lot in the future in the subdivision would have to use one of the five 'approved' builders to construct their house. Now, some jerk wanted to buy a lot and use an outside builder. Travis wouldn't sell the lot to him. So the want-to-be buyer sued, claiming that the approved-builder system was an illegal tying arrangement, an antitrust violation, in that someone couldn't buy a lot without being tied to a group of five particular builders. Travis wanted to discuss defense strategy. Emmit Jackson, one of the firm's law clerks, was researching the law for her. He was supposed to e-mail her a memo by nine tonight, but it hadn't showed up by a quarter to when she left the house. Worst-case scenario, she'd fill the breakfast with smiles and let Travis spend some time with a younger woman. Maybe wear the black skirt and a white sleeveless blouse if he was lucky.

SUDDENLY MICHAEL STARTED OFF, with a short honk and a rigid thumbs up. She fired up the engine, it started just the way it was supposed to, bless those Germans, then looked at her watch. It didn't have a second hand. The realization unnerved her. So basic, yet missed. What else had she overlooked? No time. *One thousand one, one thousand two, one thousand three . . . one thousand thirty.*

Pulling out, according to plan, she brought the car up to twenty-five miles an hour and held it there. The half-mile to Rick's Gas Station took no time at all. The place was a two-pump, paint-peeling shack with a neon sign in the window that said *Bait* and another one that said *Coors Light*. No video cameras, which is why they chose it. The women's car, now recognizable as an old green four-door sedan, sat on one side of the pump, the side closest to the station. Northway's van sat on the other side. At first she didn't see any movement and wondered if something had gone wrong.

Then everything happened at once.

Michael appeared from around the back of the van, dragging a limp body that was unmistakably a woman's. For some reason, he didn't look like himself, really strange, some kind of trick of the night. Two women came out of the station, walking towards their car. One of them looked in Michael's direction and started to yell.

Hey, what the hell . . .

Game time.

Kelly stopped the car and dialed 911. A voice answered, a calm woman's voice, asking her short questions that sounded like they came off a cue card. Now Northway's van was pulling out, fast, but not powerful enough to squeal the tires.

The cops showed up almost immediately, within three or four minutes, max. Way too fast. Damn it. What if they actually caught him? Three police cars, pulling in from the same direction she'd come from, slid to a stop. Red and blue lights bounced through the air and suddenly everything became very real.

She bit her lower lip and clenched the steering wheel.

One of the cops was out of his car now and running over to her. He had a hand on his gun, as if ready to draw.

"What happened?"

"A man . . . he took a woman."

"What is he driving?"

"A van."

"What color?"

"I don't know . . . dark . . ."

"Did you get a license plate number?"

"No."

"Okay. Which way?"

She pointed. "That way."

"How long ago?"

"Just a few minutes."

He ran back to the car, shouting "Stay where you are," over his shoulder.

Get to the freaking freeway, Michael. Goddamn it, anyway. Interstate 25 was a mile up the road . . .

Two of the cop cars squealed off and the smell of rubber filled the air. The third car stayed behind. There were two cops inside. One of them talked into a radio, very excited.

The other two women stood by their car. A man had joined them, someone with baggy jeans and a flannel shirt, undoubtedly the person who worked at the gas station. The women were attractive, somehow she could tell that even from here. The flannel shirt looked like he might be coming on to them, something about his body language, the way he stood a little too close.

THE COPS GOT OUT OF THE CAR. One went over to the

group and one came over to her.

"Good evening, ma'am," he said. "Are you the one that called 911?" She thought, the one *who* called 911, not the one *that*. He was short, surprisingly short for a cop, maybe five-four, with a baby face. He couldn't have been on the force for more than a few years.

Even she could kick his ass if she had to.

"Yes," she said.

He held a spiral notebook and opened it up. "I'd like to get a statement, if you don't mind. Why don't you come over to my car? I've got the heater on."

Sitting there in the front seat, by the shotgun, she told him what she saw. She was just starting to pull into the station to get some gas when she saw a man drag a woman's limp body around the back of a van. He slid open the passenger-side door, threw her in and took off. It all happened in a matter of seconds. She called 911.

"Describe this guy," the cop said.

"Well, I didn't get a real good look," she said, "because he was sort of hunched over, dragging her under the arms. He was Asian, that much I did see."

"Asian?"

"Yes," she said. "Whether he was Korean or Japanese or Chinese, that I can't tell you. But something like that."

"You're sure about that?"

"Positive," she said. "I mean, I couldn't pick him out of a lineup, but I saw his general features pretty good."

"Was his face flat, or more rounded?"

She shrugged. "I don't know."

He nodded vaguely, and said: "So, this Asian guy, what are we talking about size-wise? Small, I assume."

She nodded. "Yes. I didn't exactly run up to him with a tape measure . . ."

He smiled, as if picturing it.

". . . but he was definitely on the smaller side. He had baggy clothes, but they were hanging on him like he was skinny. And he didn't appear to be overly strong. It looked like he was having a pretty hard time with the woman, especially when he tried to get her through the door."

"Okay."

"Black hair."

The cop grilled her for another five minutes, and then seemed ready to wrap up. "Oh, one more thing. You see those two ladies over there, talking to the other officer?"

"Yes?"

"Have you talked to either of them?"

She shook her head negative. "No. I called 911 from my car and you guys showed up almost right away. That was pretty impressive, by the way. The other officer that came over to me, before he took off, told me to stay where I was, so I just stayed here."

He nodded. "Good."

"Why good?"

"It just helps us when the witnesses haven't talked with one another. We get the stories fresh without contamination. Do you know any of those other people, by the way?"

She looked at them, then back at him. "No. I've never seen any of them before in my life."

"Okay. Wait here, if you would."

She watched him walk over to the group. He came back about five minutes later, opened the door and slid behind the wheel.

"Cold out," he said, holding his hands up to the vent.

"Summer's coming."

"Not fast enough. The wind is starting to kick up, too." Michael had gotten away. That much was clear, otherwise he would have said something or she would have heard it over the radio.

"The two women saw the same thing as you," the cop volunteered. "Story is, there were three of them. They stopped for gas. Two of them went inside to pay. The other one, the one that got taken, stayed behind to clean the windshield. Her name is Alicia Elmblade. When they came out of the station an Asian guy was dragging her into a van. Weird."

"What about the guy from the station? Did he see anything?"

"No. He had the Rockies game on."

She tried to look disappointed. "Too bad."

"Yeah, too bad. The other two women are D'endra Vaughn and Jeannie Dannenberg. The guy is Rick Marlow, Jr. It's his dad's place. You don't know any of them, huh?"

"No. I was just stopping for gas."

THAT WAS LAST MAY. RIGHT NOW, TODAY, Michael Northway shifted behind his desk and looked at his watch. D'endra Vaughn was dead. Someone had used her cell phone to call Kelly Parks yesterday. Lori would be on his case any minute to get him off to the airport. "So you didn't tell these homicide detectives anything?" he asked.

Kelly Parks shook her head negative. "Of course not," she confirmed. "Nothing. I acted like I'd never heard the name D'endra Vaughn."

He nodded. "Good. That was the right thing to do."

She chucked, as if contemplating the conversation. "What would I say? I don't really know who killed D'endra Vaughn, but would you like to hear this really neat story about how we both happened to be at the same gas station last year and gave the same lies to the police?"

He laughed. "I'm in the same boat as you, remember that."

"Yeah. Two men in a tub."

"Rub-a-dub-dub."

She grew serious, uncrossed her legs and leaned forward: "Michael, I need to know who this mystery client is, the one who put you up to this charade."

He immediately shook his head. "Not possible."

"But . . ."

"Kelly, it's not . . ."

"Damn it, it's my ass on the line."

". . . an option."

She could tell by the look on his face that it wasn't going to happen, at least not right this moment. "I keep turning this over in my head," she said, "and there's only one thing that I can think of that even makes an iota of sense. This client, is there any reason he would want us all gone? I mean everyone who was involved in that charade? Do we suddenly pose some kind of a threat to him or something?"

He considered it, taking his time, and finally said: "No, and even if he did, why would he be playing games with the cell phone? No. Not him. He's not behind this."

"Then who?"

He shrugged. "I don't know."

Suddenly Lori's voice came from the intercom, sweet and syrupy, Marilyn-like. "Michael? It's time for the airport."

"Okay, two seconds."

He waited until he intercom hum died, then looked back at her. "Let me think about it. I'm going to make a few calls. In the meantime, stay calm."

She exhaled. "Right, no problem."

Coventry's pictures of D'endra Vaughn jumped into her brain.

Not just killed.

Mutilated.

Chapter Four

Day Two
Tuesday Noon

DAVID HALLENBECK MANEUVERED his 27-year-old God-like frame down the 16th Street Mall in the heart of downtown Denver, feeling better than good, on the hunt. This was most definitely one of his favorite parts. Circling, closing in, watching. Total foreplay. No stress, no precision, no complications. Take it all home later, close your eyes in the dark and pump your dick to it.

Around him the street scurried.

Step on an anthill and you'll get the same effect. The lunchtime crowd was just starting to spill out, grabbing food and nicotine and gossip. Spitting and scratching and strutting. Shuttle busses ran up and down the street, in and out of the shadows of the city's tallest buildings. A hot dog peddler standing under a tattered umbrella slung buns and meat and change with greasy hands, trying to move a line four deep. Twenty yards down from him three cops sat on brown horses, wearing shades and being nice to kids. Who were they trying to fool with the shades? We weren't supposed to figure out they were there to hide their eyes when they looked down mommy's blouse?

Dumb-ass cops.

There were tons of pretty little things all around, parading up and down the street like they meant something, all decked out in their little nylons and dresses and black leather pumps. He could pick any one of them at random, hunt them down and snap them like a stick figure. The pure and simple thought that they continued to live only because he allowed them to held a little tingle. It made the corner of his mouth turn up ever so slightly; especially when he saw one he might actually choose.

But right now he was interested in only one person, one very special person.

Megan Bennett.

He was fairly certain at this point that he'd end up spending some quality time with her, but his mind wasn't totally made up. She'd been an orphan. Good old daddy shot mommy in the head one drunken night and then stuck the barrel in his own stupid mouth. That happened when she was two. Hallenbeck just found out about it yesterday. It shouldn't matter, but for some reason he kept coming back to it.

He looked skyward as he walked, seeing more brick and mortar than he remembered. The old cow town was growing up. Damn, what a gorgeous day. What was it about the spring? He wore faded jeans and a simple long-sleeve, solid-blue, cotton shirt that was thinning at the elbows, nothing that would stand out or be remembered. That was the rule, one of many. Always be invisible, even when you have a treetop-lover frame and go-rilla muscles. In his left hand he carried a sack lunch in a plain brown bag.

HE TOOK OFF HIS BASEBALL CAP and ran a hand over his scalp, wiping the sweat off, and then dried his hand on his pants.   For over a year now his hairline had been in a battle with his forehead and the forehead was slowly kicking ass, getting bigger and bigger every day.   Another one of life's precious little ways of saying thanks for being here.

The hair thing was just the latest variation on the theme. There had been the acne, landing almost heels and toes with those god-awful, black-rimmed eyeglasses that trailer-trash mom found on a rack at some stupid-ass drugstore for fifteen bucks. Ninth grade, the first of his Clark Kent years.   It was in the middle of that year that he took his second life—Michelle Spencer—with her perfect little blond hair and her perfect little face and her perfect little friends, everything about her so god-damned perfect.   All he really wanted to do was be invisible, bury himself in his books, eventually get a college scholarship and come out the other side of puberty as unscathed as possible. But she was too perfect for that, with her little whispers and giggles.

He hadn't set out to kill her, down by the river, and that's the honest-to-God truth.   He only wanted to make a point, about what could happen to pretty little bitches if they weren't careful.   She shouldn't have screamed, he even told her that up-front.   It's not like he didn't warn her.   She crossed a log and somehow fell in the river and drowned, that's what the cops eventually figured.   They couldn't imagine anything even a shade darker, with their puny little brains and small-town thoughts.   Everyone they interviewed confirmed that the girl couldn't swim, even her parents.   Huge teary-eyed funeral, end of case.

Amazing, really.

No more *googly eyes* from Michelle Spencer after that.

HE STAYED ON THE EAST SIDE OF THE STREET, in the sun. It felt good, perfect actually. It had been a long gray winter in Cleveland. He walked slowly, taking his time, getting caught at a red light at Fremont. People washed up around him, then washed away when the light changed, like a tide. The outdoor sidewalk seating at the Paramount Café, a ways further up, was already filled when he walked past, jammed with business types doing their so-called power lunches.

They thought they had power.

They had shit.

Not a one of them had the focus or self-control, not to mention the gonads, to even know what power was. About the best they had was *normal*. Look back throughout history, go back as far as you want, and try to find one truly great man who was normal. You won't find one. Normal is for sheep, for losers, for people who think that getting a promotion or a new house or having a baby is something really special.

Kill me please.

SOON AFTER HE PASSED the Rock Bottom Brewery he spotted her, Megan Bennett, right on schedule, sitting on the ledge of a tree planter next to the sidewalk, eating with her ankles crossed, a Subway bag on her lap. The ledge was lined with a half-dozen people with the same idea, mostly guys, watching the parade of noontime skirts slink by. She wasn't particularly pretty, in fact, leaning the opposite way if anything, and the glasses didn't help. But there was something about her. Her body was strong and solid. She'd taken good care of herself. He could respect that, but there was something more. She actually seemed attainable on a personal level, and someone within reach had always been sexier to him than a hundred centerfolds.

When the old bag next to her got up and left, he hustled over, slowed down at the last minute and eased in. "Hope I'm not crowding you here," he said, absently reaching into the sack and pulling out a sandwich. He watched as she turned his way, saw her look into his face and then at his hat, sizing him up, not showing much of a reaction one way or the other. He wasn't bad looking now, better than average, actually. The acne left no scaring and he sprung for corrective eye surgery two years ago. He had a solid, prominent nose that gave him character, like a Roman warrior. More than a few women had come to his bed voluntarily, although he really didn't pretend to have any extraordinary bragging rights in that regard.

"No, not at all," she said, looking back at her food.

He took a bite, chewed, then closed his eyes and pointed his face to the sun. When he opened them she was packing up and getting ready to leave.

"I'm a profiler," he said, suddenly needing to keep her there.

She looked at him, slightly interested. "As in the FBI?"

"That's right. Special Agent Ron Stokes. Point to somebody, anyone you want, I'll give you a quick snapshot."

She looked around, at least a hundred people in close proximity, then pointed: "There, that woman over there with the kid."

He looked at the target.

"Okay, let's see . . . based on her age I'd guess that her most impressionable music years were in the late '60s and early '70s. The carryover hippie look tells me she probably has a lot of favorite songs from the Eagles, Elton John, James Taylor, the Supremes, and the Beatles, of course, a few by the Stones, but probably not many, she doesn't look quite radical enough. The kid is about what . . . ten? So she had him later in life, which probably means during a second marriage. She's a good person, you can tell because the kid touches her a lot, which means he likes her. Her back door has a crack in the glass . . ."

Megan Bennett looked mystified.

Hers did too.

"How would you know that?" she questioned.

He chuckled. "I don't, I just wanted to see if you were paying attention. But, actually, it could be true. See how energetic the kid is? I was the same way when I was his age. Some kids have a tendency to be a little rough on things." A pause, then: "Have you got any kids?"

She shook her head negative, then mustered a smile: "Wow, the FBI. Have you worked on anything big, I mean something I'd know about from the papers?"

"Let's see, maybe I have . . ."

LATER THAT NIGHT, AFTER DARK, he slipped his car into an open space on 10th Street, between Corona and Downing, a block-and-a-half west of Megan Bennett's house. He killed the engine, slipped out, and quietly closed the door. He left it unlocked, like always, in case he needed to get back in quickly. Then he walked in the direction away from her house, a baseball cap pulled down over his face. The neighborhood seemed at least fifty years old, crammed with small two-story houses. Some were run-down and looked like crack houses, while others were meticulously maintained; probably by older people who never managed to break out. All had postage-stamp front yards. The streets were jam packed with cars, mostly junkers, but something halfway nice every once in a while.

Megan Bennett and her two roommates rented a detached house on Lafayette Street, two blocks west of Cheesman Park. Ordinarily roommates would be a problem, but in this case he had no intentions of spending the quality time with Megan at her house. He had another place already set up for that, a perfect place. As far as snatching her went, he could do that just about anywhere. Hell, as friendly as she'd been today, he could probably just arrange for her to meet him there. The thought played with him but only for a second.

With the sun gone now for more than three hours, a sharp chill gripped the night. He wore his shadow clothes; a dark blue sweatshirt, jeans and gray running shoes. He wasn't going to take her tonight. He just wanted to be around her and maybe firm up a few details in his mind. The need wasn't there quite yet, although he could feel it building, like a balloon slowly filling with air.

Pop, pretty soon.

HE'D COME A LONG WAY since his first kill. That was at age eight, out sledding with Chris Schneider on a hard-packed slope with about two inches of fresh powder, on a cold, slate-gray, winter day. They made about ten runs on those old wooden, two-runner sleds. He was at the bottom of the hill, waiting. Chris was flying down, a big shit-eating grin on his face, lying on his belly, face forward. Just before Chris got to the bottom, something flashed in Hallenbeck's brain, and he pushed his sled out so Chris would either have to bail off or T-bone it. The dumb shit didn't bail, he had time, but tried to swerve around instead. Wrong move. The front of Chris' sled nosed under the front of the other one, and brought it up, straight into his forehead. His skull shattered instantly with the pop of a cracking walnut. He coasted to a stop, still on the sled. And then the blood came, the reddest stuff you'd ever seen in your life.

Afterwards there was a lot of motion, desperate useless motion that did no one any good as far as he could tell. Most of that motion landed on him one way or another. Everyone in town knew his name, even the big kids.

HE CIRCLED AROUND THE BLOCK and back towards Megan Bennett's house, enjoying the night. Tomorrow was supposed to be warm and sunny, a repeat of today.

It certainly was good to be alive.

Eventually he came to her street. Her house was completely dark. At eleven-thirty on a Tuesday night, that's pretty much what he expected. All three of the women who lived there worked.

Then he suddenly saw something out of place, movement on the side of her house, underneath a window. He stopped, waited for a second, and then ducked between two cars where he could watch. The shapes weren't much more than shadows but he could tell that there were two of them. Either they weren't talking at all or were talking so low that he couldn't hear. One of them worked at the window with some kind of a tool, a crowbar or a long screwdriver or something.

The little shits were breaking in.

To rape her or rob her.

Probably both.

Screw that!

Now they had the window open and were pushing it up ever so slowly. When it was all they way up, they stopped and looked around. Then, seeing no one, one of them cupped his hands together to give the other one a boost up.

He charged at a dead run, chemicals colliding in his brain and the fine-tuned gorilla muscles rippling under his clothes. As he came closer, he saw there were three of them, not two, and couldn't care less. He screamed like an ancient warrior and realized that some kind of recessed gene had just kicked in.

Chapter Five

Day Two
Tuesday Evening

TUESDAY EVENING, AFTER DARK, Kelly Parks drove down Colfax with one eye in the rearview mirror, trying to determine if some crazed maniac was following her. She zigzagged through a number of side streets until she felt safe and then parked the BMW just off Colfax on Lowell, feeling like anything but a lawyer.

She locked the doors and then circled back on foot to a place called the Mountain View Apartments, wearing a hooded navy blue sweatshirt over jeans. A chilly wind blew through the dark and fingered its way into her clothes.

The apartment complex looked like a last-chance dive that hadn't had a code inspection in twenty years. In the parking lot, she walked past a couple of dark figures sitting in an older model Chevy with the engine off and the windows cracked. She only noticed them because of the glow of a cigarette. She could tell they were looking at her, sizing her up as she walked past, by the way the orange spot stopped moving. She half expected a door to open. Then she heard one of them laugh, a woman's laugh. She caught the faintest scent of pot, triggering a flash of the old high school days, riding around in the back of a car, crazy laughing, an unskilled hand reaching under her blouse . . .

The building had two stories, with exterior wooden stairs at each end and a walkway that ran the length of the second story, like an old hotel. Apartment H, Jeannie Dannenberg's place, was on the second level at the far back, at the top of the stairs. There was light inside behind the shade.

Good.

She stopped at the bottom of the stairs and looked around, seeing no one. Even the car with the cigarette was blocked from view by something that looked like an old Ryder truck. A faint smell of urine hung in the air, and she pictured some drunk two or three nights ago pissing all over the ground right where she stood.

She headed up, ever so slowly, one step at a time, so quietly that she couldn't even hear herself breathe. She stood outside Jeannie Dannenberg's door for a moment but didn't knock, then eased over to the window, found a one-inch slit at the edge of the shade and peeked in. Two women sat on an orange couch, watching a small TV topped with rabbit ears. She hadn't anticipated friends over, or a roommate.

Shit.

What to do?

She needed to talk to the Dannenberg woman alone.

They were nursing beers, staring at the screen, with their legs propped up on a coffee table. A half-empty bag of Frito Lays sat on an old wooden end-table. The carpet was worn and the linoleum scratched. A black microwave sat on the counter, a white fridge further to the left, the old kind with the freezer on top.

SUDDENLY SHE FELT A VIBRATION, turned, and saw the shape of a man at the last second. He grabbed her arm above the elbow with a vice grip and spun her around. She smelled whisky and smoky clothes. His face hid behind long greasy hair. He jerked her over to the door, smacked it hard with an open palm, and tightened his grip. From inside the apartment the blinds moved and then fell back limp. The door opened a crack, clanging at the end of a chain.

"Do you know her?" The man snapped her over, so her face was by the door, then grabbed her hair and held her still.

A pause. "No."

"Well she's looking in your window."

"Well screw that." A chain rattled and the door opened. "Bring the bitch in."

The man pushed her inside and slammed the door behind him, warning her to give him a reason to knock her goddamn head off. The two women stood in front of her, both bigger than her, with lots of muscles.

"Looking for something that isn't yours, baby?"

"No, I . . ."

"Shut up!"

The man slapped her across the face. A flash of intense heat burned her skin.

"We've been waiting for your ass to show back up."

Blood ran from her nose, into her mouth and down her chin.

"Put her on the floor," one of the women said.

Suddenly her feet went out from under her and her back hit the carpet with a spine-jolting thump. Before she could twist away the man straddled her chest, grabbed her wrists and pinned them over her head.

"Don't say a goddamn word," one of the women warned.

The man moved up farther, his crouch almost on her face, and sunk his weight down hard. She heard fumbling noises and realized one of the women was rifling through her purse.

"Her name's Kelly Parks," one of the women said. Then: "She's a lawyer, look at this."

"This is screwed," the man said, burrowing his weight down and tightening his grip on her wrists.

She could hardly breathe, but managed to say, "D'endra Vaughn . . ."

A question: "What? What about D'endra?"

She couldn't breathe, heard "Ease off her, Jack," then felt the air rush back in her lungs. "What about D'endra, damn it . . . don't you . . ."

"She's dead."

"Let her up, Jack."

THE MAN STOOD UP, RELUCTANTLY, continuing to loom over her. Sweet, sweet air rushed back into her lungs. She breathed deep, concentrating on it, not moving an inch, not giving anyone an excuse.

She muscled her way into a standing position and then, before she could stop herself, swung a fist at the man, going for his hooked nose but catching him on the side of the head instead.

"You goddamn . . ."

Wham!

He pinned her back on the floor, his hands gripping her wrists so tight that her fingers tingled. A pain like needles ran up her spine.

A panicked voice, "Don't hurt her, Jack!"

Jumbled words came through the commotion, which she finally heard as: "Are you going to behave yourself? I said . . ."

"Screw you," she said, but there was no fight in it. In a few moments her body relaxed and the man moved his weight off her chest, then finally let go of her wrists and stood up. She moved her arms down, turned her head away and lay there.

One of the women spoke: "D'endra's dead, is that what you said?"

"God, something's broke . . ."

"Shit, you're okay." Then, "Here, get up." She found herself pulled up and onto the couch. "Are you okay?" Cigarette smoke suddenly filled the air. "Jesus, Rachel, grab something, she's bleeding all over the goddamn cushions." Water ran; then the Rachel woman applied a cool cloth to her nose, wiping the blood off her lips and chin.

She grabbed it, "Get off me." She looked down; her sweat-shirt was spotted with blood. But the fight was all over, she knew that, and nothing else mattered for the moment.

"The bitch ruined my pants!" the man complained, wiping blood off his leg. One of the women pulled two twenties out of Kelly's purse. "Here, she's sorry." Then: "I think we have it under control now."

"You positive . . . ?"

"Yeah, thanks."

He wasn't quite certain whether to leave. "I'll stop by later, be sure you're all right . . ."

"Fine."

Then he was gone.

"What happened to D'endra?" one of the women asked.

Parks recognized her as Jeannie Dannenberg, looking different now, but definitely her. She had a strong, toned body; thick black hair, almost down to her waist; liquid brown eyes; probably about twenty-two or twenty-three.

"I'll talk to you in private," she said.

"Screw private. You talk to *me*," Jeannie Dannenberg said, "you talk to *Rachel*."

She stared at her. "That's not negotiable. My ass is already hanging out."

Jeannie looked at Rachel, then back at her, and said: "What's the difference? I'm going to tell her whatever I want anyway."

A pain shot up her back. She worked at it by twisting from side to side. She thought, *The difference is, if I say something and she hears it from you, it's hearsay, it never gets to a jury. If she hears it from me, it's an admission, she gets to sit on the witness stand and play like a human tape recorder.* But that was too complicated: "Alone or nothing."

"This is bullshit."

She could tell that the woman still didn't recognize her. "I'm getting tired, here. Do you want to know what happened to D'endra or not?"

Dannenberg looked at Rachel, who held up her hands as if in surrender. "Whatever. The air in here stinks, anyway." She grabbed her purse, headed to the door, then turned around and pointed at her: "You I don't like."

Then the door slammed.

THE TWO WOMEN STARED AT EACH OTHER. Then Dannenberg laughed, got up, and headed for the bedroom, turning to say, "You really know how to make an entrance, girlfriend." In a moment she returned with a plastic bag and some papers, threw them on the table and began rolling a joint. Then she lit it up and took a deep drag, closed here eyes, held it in for as long as she could and blew it out. She said, "Not the best, but doable," and passed it over to Kelly Parks. She wore cutoff jeans and a white T-shirt, no bra, with breasts that looked too perfect to be fake and too perfect to be real.

Kelly Parks took the joint, surprised that she did and, holding it between her index finger and thumb, sucked the smoke in quick and deep. Her lungs rejected it immediately, sending her into a fit of coughing that brought tears to her eyes. Then she breathed deep three times and took another hit, this time not as long or intense, and managed to hold it in. When she finally blew it out Jeannie Dannenberg smiled with approval, and said, "Like riding a bike."

Kelly felt everything soften. "Yeah, except I never rode that many bikes."

Dannenberg grabbed two cans of beer from the fridge, handed one to her, popped the top as she sat back down and asked two very good questions: "So who are you? And what happened to D'endra?" A cigarette danged in her left hand; if you closed your eyes, you'd swear you were in a bar.

Kelly tipped the bottle and took a long swig, ice cold, the best beer she ever tasted. She looked at the can, Bud Light. Then she twisted her torso, working the pain out of her back.

"I was the woman in the other car at the gas station, the night that Alicia Elmblade was supposedly abducted. I was the one who called 911."

Dannenberg looked like she was traveling back in time, then said: "That was you?"

"Yes."

"Well screw me."

She felt heavy. "Screw both of us. D'endra Vaughn is dead and somehow it's because of that night. And whoever killed her is after me . . ."

"What?"

"And if me, then *you*. That's why I'm here. To warn you."

Dannenberg dangled the cigarette near the ashtray, flicked it without looking and threw ash on the table. "Well talk, woman."

Parks saw her keys and wallet sitting on the end table, grabbed them, and stuck them back in her purse, before she forgot.

She organized her thoughts, then said: "This is all hearsay, from the cops, I never met D'endra myself." With that, she told her what she knew about how D'endra Vaughn had been violently murdered Saturday evening, strung up by her wrists on her back porch, gagged, beaten and cut to death.

"Look," she said. "Here's the weird part, and why I'm here. Whoever killed D'endra took her cell phone. On Sunday afternoon, after D'endra's definitely dead, he uses it to call me at the law firm. I'm not there when he calls and he doesn't leave a message. But the connection shows up in D'endra's cell phone records. The detective in charge, a guy named Bryson Coventry, a lieutenant actually, finds out about it and pays me a visit. He thinks that the call is a message from the killer that I'm next. I'm thinking if I'm on this guy's list, then you probably are too, and you have a right to know about it."

"Jesus." She took a deep drag and blew it out her nose. "Poor D'endra."

Parks' eyes narrowed. "My only connection in the world to D'endra Vaughn is from the night at the gas station. Whatever's going on goes right back to that."

DANNENBERG STRETCHED HER LEGS out on the coffee table. Kelly couldn't help but notice they were just about perfect, firm and smooth. "I'm starting to get a buzz," Dannenberg said. Then: "The asshole."

Neither spoke.

Kelly finally said: "Were you two close, or what? I mean you and D'endra . . ."

Dannenberg rolled the aluminum can in her fingers. "We were once. We kind of drifted after she turned into a teacher."

"Mmm . . ."

"Poor D'endra." She paused, as if recollecting, then said: "She had a charisma, that girl. People just took to her. She was one of those women that guys talk to for the first time and in five minutes they want to buy her a car. She had this hypnotic quality." She got a look in her eye. "But she was wild, too. I remember one night, when Alley was dancing . . ."

"Alley?"

"Alicia Elmblade."

"Oh."

". . . right, when Alley was stripping down at Cheeks, me and D'endra go down to see her. We start slamming shots, I mean, we're getting ripped, we're sitting at the bar and guys are buying us drinks and shit. Alley gets up on stage to do a set, and out of the blue D'endra climbs up with her. She starts peeling off her street clothes, all the way down to her panties. The guys are going nuts, I mean, she's on her back giving crack shots, the whole thing." She tasted the beer and smiled: "She had the body for it, too. I'll hand her that. The girl took good care of herself, did aerobics, the whole bit."

Parks got up, walked over to the window, pulled down a slat in the blind down and looked out. Everything looked the same as before.

Nothing had changed.

Everything looked dark and empty.

No creepy guys hanging around that she could see.

"What I'm thinking," she said, "is that if we put our heads together, maybe we can figure out what's going on. About all I know about the night in question is that your friend was in some kind of trouble and wanted to have her abduction faked so she could disappear. Then . . ."

"Whoa!"

Kelly was confused. "What?"

"No, no, no."

"No what?"

"Alley wasn't in any kind of trouble."

"She wasn't?"

"Hell no. Who told you that?"

Michael Northway, she thought, wondering if she should disclose his name or not, then said: "Michael Northway. He's the one who got me involved in this whole thing in the first place. He's the one who drove the van."

Dannenberg lit another cigarette and sucked in. "I never knew his name," she said, blowing out smoke with the words. "Who is he, exactly?"

"He's a lawyer in my firm."

"A lawyer, huh?" Then, after a drink of beer, Dannenberg said: "Here's the deal. Alley was living here with me and stripping at Cheeks. One night she comes home, I'm sleeping of course, and she starts jumping up and down on the bed, all excited, waking me up and shit. Some guy had come into the club and offered her a hundred thousand dollars if she'd agree to fake her abduction and then disappear from Denver."

"Who?"

"I have no idea," Dannenberg said. "Alley wouldn't say. But the man was serious, he had the whole thing planned out and she was convinced he had the money."

"It had to have been Michael Northway."

Dannenberg looked vacant. "Makes sense."

"He has that kind of money."

She nodded.

"So then what happened?"

"Okay," Dannenberg continued. "The man wanted a witness or two to be with her when it happened, you know, someone to be there when the abduction took place, to tell the police that they saw an Asian man take her. We were supposed to say Asian, just to keep any heat off him in case the police actually caught up with him or something."

That was the same explanation Michael Northway had given her.

Dannenberg continued: "Alley told him about me and D'endra as the possible witnesses. We were kind of a Three Musketeers back then. The guy was going to pay us ten thousand each to participate."

"Did you get paid?"

"In cash, sweetheart, every last penny. So did D'endra."

"Well, that's good, at least."

Dannenberg shrugged. "It didn't last long."

"So, did you know that I was going to be there too?"

"Yeah," Dannenberg said. "Not you specifically, but Alley told us there'd be a third witness, to give the whole thing even more credibility. She told us that the third witness, you, would tell the cops the same thing as us, namely that she just saw an Asian man abduct someone."

"So where did Alicia go, after that night?"

"L.A. as far as I know," Dannenberg said. "That was her plan, anyway."

"What? You're not sure?"

"I'd say L.A."

"What do you mean, you'd *say* L.A.? You don't know?"

"No."

That was weird. "Are you telling me that you never heard from her after that night?"

"No, not really."

Kelly Parks felt a chill. "Don't you find that strange?"

Dannenberg considered it, seemed to tense for a second, then relaxed. "Not really. She told us ahead of time that the guy was absolutely serious that she had to vanish as if she was actually dead. She said for a hundred thousand dollars he deserved to get what he paid for. It was her intent to actually start a brand new life with a different name and everything. He had it all set up for her in LA. A new name, a driver's license, everything."

"What name?"

Dannenberg shrugged.

Kelly Parks got a feeling that she couldn't shake. "Still, I think if I was her, I'd sneak in at least one little call, just between friends."

"You sound like she really is dead."

Kelly Parks stared at her. "No. I'm sure she's okay."

Chapter Six

Day Two
Tuesday Night

AT ONE POINT IN HIS LIFE, the oversized country-western bar would have been perfect. The smoke and beer and drunk women reminded him of the getting-laid days. But now, to-night at least, Bryson Coventry found the band too loud, the bodies too many, the air too thick and the hour too late. There had to be at least a thousand sweaty people in here circling around. He elbowed his way to the bar, flagged down the bar-tender with his badge, and got pointed to a fat man standing at the end, chatting it up with a couple of guys in the second or third stage of disrepair.

He worked his way over through the bodies. "Are you the manager?" he questioned, flashing his badge for effect and get-ting in close enough to be heard over the noise.

The fleshy eyes of the fat man narrowed and Coventry felt him running through the liquor laws, trying to find the most likely fracture.

"Yes, Jack Lawson."

He shook his hand, feeling sausage fingers and too much palm. "Relax, Jack Lawson," he said, "I'm not here to bust you.

There's a guy over there sitting at the bar. You see him?" He pointed: "White shirt, next to the blond talking to that other guy?"

"The one with the long hair?"

"Yeah, the rock star," Coventry said. "He's peeling the bottle."

"Got him. That means sexual frustration."

"What does?"

"Peeling the bottle."

"I thought chewing ice meant that."

"That too."

"Figures," Coventry said. "I do them both. His name's Aaron Whitecliff. You could do me a big favor by going over there. Tell him a detective by the name of Coventry is wandering around in here flashing a picture of him. Tell him I look real mean and serious, like maybe I have a warrant for his arrest, or want to crack in his head, which I do so you won't be lying. Go ahead and describe me. Say whatever you want, just be sure his knees shake and he heads for the door."

The fat man smiled, visibly relieved that the problem belonged to someone else. "That could be arranged."

WAITING OUTSIDE IN HIS CAR, with Whitecliff's red Explorer in line-of-sight, Coventry made a quick call. "Bochmann, Coventry. I'm down here at the *Grizzly Flower* . . . give me a break, I don't have my hip boots on . . . listen, the manager, a guy by the name of Lawson, is doing a little favor for me . . . overlook something next time you're in here . . . yeah, something on that scale, not too grand . . . be sure to mention my name, let him know I didn't blow him off . . ."

Two minutes later Aaron Whitecliff walked out of the bar, looked around, walked over to a red Explorer and slowly pulled out into the night. Coventry let him get to 53rd Street then turned on the lights and pulled him over. Whitecliff already had the window powered down when he walked up to the door.

"License and registration," Coventry said, giving the words a rough, no-nonsense edge.

Whitecliff had a flabbergast look. "*Coventry*? What's going on?"

"To begin, you ran that stop sign," Coventry said. "But now I think we have a bigger problem. Have you been drinking?"

"Coventry, I did not kill my own girlfriend."

"Yeah," Coventry said. "You're in mourning, I can tell. You smell like a brewery. That's serious."

"This is harassment," Whitecliff said. "I've already spent more than two hours with you guys . . . I've cooperated . . ."

"Let me tell you how a DUI works, in case you've never had the pleasure," Coventry said. "I call a special unit on the radio and we sit here and squirm in our seats until they arrive. When they get here, they set up a video camera and you're the star actor in something called a roadside sobriety test. When you fail that, which you will, things start to get really fun. You can take a breathalyzer test and then be arrested, or you can decline, and we arrest you anyway. Either way, you're now the proud owner of free room and board. We book you in, take your clothes, do a full cavity search, give you some lovely orange coveralls and then take you to a place with concrete and steel to meet some new and exciting friends. You're going to love it."

"What *is it* you want?" Whitecliff questioned, the words thick with frustration.

"What is it I want?" he echoed, as if considering every possible answer in the world. "I want world peace, I want a giant, big-ass sailboat, but most of all, to be honest with you, I just want to go home and go to bed, which is something you'll understand better in ten years. But I can't, because I'm standing out here in the middle of the night jerking-off with you."

Aaron Whitecliff frowned. He was five-foot-eleven with shoulder-length blond hair, a former high school track star and all around good guy, just ask anyone. "Detective Coventry," he said, "I've . . ."

"Lieutenant," Coventry corrected him.

"Lieutenant Coventry, I've cooperated fully. You've asked me a thousand questions. I've given you a thousand honest and straightforward answers. You know where I was the night D'endra got killed, every minute of it. I don't know what it is that you want."

"Stay where you are," Coventry said, all patience gone, now walking back to his car and letting Whitecliff track him in his rearview mirror. He picked up the dispatch radio, talked into it, then sat there with his arm strung over the back of the seat and his head cocked, putting on a show.

HE DIDN'T MOVE FOR A FEW MINUTES, looked at his watch, saw it was five minutes to ten, noted he was flirting with danger, then thought *Screw it* and picked up the cell phone to call Kate Katona.

"Kate, Coventry."

She sounded grumpy. "Hey."

"You're in a lovely mood," he said.

"I'm in bed," she said, "as in, some of us actually sleep.

Where are you, anyway?"

"Squeezing D'endra Vanghn's boyfriend," Coventry said. "I wanted to touch base real quick, to see if you had anything new on him that I should know about."

"Aaron Whitecliff? Nothing definite one way or the other yet," Katona noted. "That strip-club that he claims to have gone to after he left D'endra's, I spent some time there this afternoon. Nobody remembers seeing Whitecliff on Saturday, or any night for that matter, based on his picture, at least."

"What about surveillance cameras?" Coventry questioned.

"The manager, a guy named Morrison or Mortenson or something, it's in my notes, said he'd give us copies of the tapes from that night, provided we agree not to use them outside the investigation."

"Meaning?"

"Meaning," Katona said, "he's a tad concerned that if they got in the wrong hands, they might show the girls getting a little too friendly at times, which might not look so dandy to the liquor board."

Coventry nodded. "Sounds reasonable."

"Otherwise," she said, "he's going to have to run it by his lawyers."

"Screw the lawyers," Coventry said. "I'll swing by there on my way home and give him my personal word that nothing's going to come of it." Then: "Unless the D.A.'s already got his nose in it."

Katona laughed. "I saw it as our call."

"Right," Coventry said. "Okay, got to go. Whitecliff's holding something back and he's either going to tell me what it is or wish he had."

HE SAT THERE FOR ANOTHER FIVE MINUTES, then a police car pulled up behind him and turned the bubbles on. A second layer of red and blue light bounced around with a jagged eerie motion. Coventry got out of his car, walked back to the police car and leaned in the window. Pickard, a veteran with an unsubstantiated bribe allegation in his file, sat behind the wheel. Next to him was a new guy, his face still an eager one, with no visible signs of bureaucratic scar tissue yet.

"Pickard," Coventry acknowledged, ducking down to get a look at the new face. "Who's your co-conspirator?"

The passenger responded for himself, extending a hand. "Adam Foster, sir. I've been hoping to meet you. It was the Patterson case that got me interested in joining the force."

"Mister freaking whoop-de-do," Pickard said, referring to Coventry.

"That was pretty amazing," the new guy said.

Coventry's eyes darted, a flash behind them for a nanosecond, rapid images of hours and hours at his desk, the hunch, working his way through the dark, the blood pumping through his veins, the sudden movement behind him . . .

"That was a team effort," he said.

"Mister freaking modest," Pickard said. Then to the passenger: "Don't try this at home, boys and girls." Back to Coventry: "So what are we doing here, exactly?"

Coventry filled them in, then walked over to Whitecliff's car and leaned on it, wearing his most severe face. "Okay, the DUI guys are here. Once they begin, I won't have any power to stop them," he said grimly. Then he waited.

Nothing.

So he started to walk back, screw him.

"Wait," Whitecliff said.

Coventry was almost in the mood to let it pass, to let the son-of-a-bitch take a little trip downtown, but found himself walking back and putting his hands on the door. "What?"

"There's only one thing I can think of," Whitecliff said. "When I first met D'endra, this was maybe a year ago, she kept a lot of cash in the house. She used it to pay for all kinds of stuff: groceries, car repairs, everything. Then it ran out and she started using checks and plastic like everyone else."

"How much cash?"

Whitecliff narrowed his eyes. "I don't know. A lot."

"One thousand? A hundred thousand?"

"How should I know? Ten or twenty . . . a lot."

Coventry nodded. "Where'd she get it?"

Whitecliff shook his head in apparent bewilderment. "It was before my time and she never said. But I got the feeling that she didn't deposit it in a bank because she didn't want a record of it."

"So something illegal?"

Whitecliff shrugged. "Something secret, at least, even from me."

"Drug money?"

"No, she was never into that."

"You sure?"

Whitecliff nodded. "Yeah."

"What else you got?"

"That's it," he said.

Coventry paused, giving him time to reconsider, then finally said, "All right." He looked in the direction of the police car. "I'm going to tell these guys back here that I don't smell beer anymore. But I can't let you drive, it's different than it was fifteen years ago." He paused, then added: "Everything could have been a lot easier if you'd have come out with this in the first place."

"I didn't think of it until now."

"Funny how the mind words," Coventry said. "Step out. Let me see you lock your keys in the car before I leave."

THIRTY SECONDS LATER he was on the phone to Shalifa Netherwood. "Shalifa, I know I'm a major pain in the ass calling you this late, but tomorrow I need to know who was in D'endra Vaughn's life a year or so ago. Get what you can on them, occupations, addresses, all the usual, and run full criminal background checks. It turns out that she ended up with some mystery money in her pocket sometime around then and my gut tells me that's connected to why she's dead now."

A pause. "Who is this?"

He smiled. "See you in the morning. Love you."

"Don't you ever sleep?"

NO SOONER DID HE HANG UP than Barb Winters, one of the night dispatchers, a woman with new breast implants and a new wardrobe, and a few new friends, called him. "Coventry. We've got two dead bodies on Lafayette. Richardson is supposed to be on call but phoned in sick. Should I call Katona or do you want it?"

"What's wrong with Richardson?"

"Food poisoning," Winters said. "That Chinese place on Court Street."

"Wongs?"

"Yep."

"No way," he said. "I've eaten there for ten years."

"Did you eat there today?"

"No."

"Okay then. Two dead bodies on Lafayette. You got 'em, or what?"

Chapter Seven

Day Two
Tuesday Night

FROM THE NORTH EDGE OF THE CITY Coventry took I-25 south to the 6th Avenue freeway and then headed east, trying to decide which was more important, heading straight to the crime scene to be sure it was properly secured or stopping for coffee. Two minutes later he screeched into the 7-Eleven on Lincoln Street, a white florescent oasis in an otherwise murky night. A kid at the cash register looked up from *Deals on Wheels* when he walked in.

"Coffee," he said, picturing a quarter pot of burned brown goop.

The kid looked startled and pointed towards the rear of the store. "In the back. I just made a fresh pot."

"No way. My life doesn't work like that."

He wished he had one of his six or seven thermoses with him, but they were all safe and sound back home, so he bought yet another new one, dumped in five French Vanilla creamers and then filled it to the top with regular. Wasted money, the thermos, but the thought of running dry after just one cup wasn't an option. A double homicide held a distinct possibility that he'd still be working at daybreak.

From there he went straight to the crime scene, which he recognized, pulling up, as a house with a reputation. A medium-weight drug pusher by the name of Leonard Smith was running crack out of it not more than two months ago, a fact totally unknown to anyone in the department until he managed to wander in front of an RTD bus one night at the unjust age of nineteen. The landlord, a retired police office, took back possession and, after seeing the basement, made a proper but rather embarrassing phone call to the Narcotics Bureau. "The new tenants will be better," he promised.

The yellow tape was already up and three or four uniformed officers were stationed in front of the house, a good sign. The Crime Lab had apparently just arrived and was in the process of setting up halogen light-stands on the south side of the house. He checked in with the scribe, put on his gloves and headed in that direction. The auxiliary lights suddenly went on and illuminated two bodies on the ground, both black men, both with faces covered in blood. The violence was palpable.

A HUGE FIGURE WANDERED OVER and said, "Coventry, have you got that five bucks you owe me or am I going to have to think unpleasant thoughts about your health." It was Sammie Jackson, referring to the collection he was taking up to get a sixtieth birthday present for the chief.

He started pulling his wallet out. "You have change for a hundred?"

"Man . . . don't even start that shit with me." Jackson was a black man standing six-seven, part of the Gang Bureau, as if anyone ever started shit with him.

Coventry handed him a five. "Now don't forget that I gave that to you. So what do we have here? A gang fight?"

Jackson laughed, a deep rumbling baritone of a laugh. "Hardly. The dead brothers are both gangsters, all right—Crips actually—but they got killed by a white guy, one white guy." Then added: "If you can imagine."

Coventry paused, shifted to his left foot, and thought, *Here we go.* "What do you mean, *if you can imagine?*"

"I mean, if you can imagine."

"So what are you saying, that white guys can't fight?"

"No, no," Jackson said, "White guys fight just fine." Then added: "In fact, in my humble opinion, every bit as good as they dance."

Coventry chuckled. "Oh, so now white guys can't dance, either?"

"No, no," Jackson said, "White guys can dance real good." Then added: "In fact, as good as they play basketball."

Coventry grinned, "So what you're saying, if I have this right, is that a white guy in a fight is a lot like a black guy on a polo field."

Jackson laughed, and slapped Coventry on the back. "Yeah, there you go, now you're starting to get the picture."

COVENTRY TURNED HIS ATTENTION back to the bodies, wanting to burn the scene into his mind before things got crazy. A baseball cap lay on the ground and a Crime Lab Detective by the name of Liberman was in the process of putting a photo marker by it. About a foot away lay a long screwdriver. The side window had been jimmied open, no doubt with the screwdriver, you could see the gouges in the wood. A garden-variety break-in. Maybe the white guy was part of it, and it turned ugly for some reason—wait, no, not with Crips. Maybe he was just some poor slob passing by, finding himself in hero mode and now wrapped up in a double homicide. Or maybe he was someone with a score to settle and took an unexpected opportunity. Both of the dead men were a good size and in their primes, probably no older than twenty-two or twenty-three. They weren't the kind to go down easy.

He looked around for weapons but didn't find any. There didn't appear to be any blood on the screwdriver or stab wounds on the bodies.

Someone had beaten them to death with his bare hands.

A white guy.

One white guy.

IT WAS A GOOD FORTY-FIVE MINUTES before he finally got a chance to sit down with the person who had been home when the killings occurred. She turned out to be Megan Bennett, a young woman bravely struggling to appear unaffected.

Coventry liked her immediately.

She was one of those people who come across as genuinely good and wholesome. She wore glasses, which became her, and had changed into street clothes, a pair of sweatpants and a thick sweater. The house was starting to get cold from the constant opening and closing of the front door.

After a few words in the downstairs kitchen, they went up to her second-floor bedroom, partly for a quiet place to talk but mostly because that's where the window was that she watched the fight from. Coventry wanted to see the scene from her vantage point. The window, it turned out, was directly over the fight.

He suddenly remembered that the inside of the house wasn't part of the crime scene and that it was fair game to drink coffee in here. He excused himself, ran outside, and returned about thirty seconds later with his Styrofoam cup and thermos.

"Just start at the beginning and run through it in as much detail as you can remember. I've got coffee, if you'd like some," he said, indicating.

"You don't mind?" she questioned with hesitation, as if she didn't want to intrude.

"God, no," he said. "You can get a cup or . . ."

"I'll just take a little of yours," she said. "If that's okay."

He handed her the Styrofoam cup and she took a sip, then another, and handed it back. "I just want to kill the chill," she said with a smile.

He nodded. "I have plenty. So what happened?"

"Okay," she said, obviously ready to explain. "I'm home alone this week because both of my roommates are in Breckenridge. I went to bed around a quarter to ten, my usual time when I have to work the next day. Then sometime after I fell asleep, I heard this scream outside, like an Indian war cry or something."

He pictured it. "A war cry?"

"Like someone running towards the house, attacking."

"Attacking, huh?"

She nodded. "Yeah, something like that."

"I never heard anyone do a war cry."

"Me either. It scared the crap out of me."

Coventry chuckled. "I'd imagine. What next?"

"I went over to the window and looked out and could see a fight going on," she said. "So I grabbed my glasses off the nightstand and looked back out. There were four men fighting. After a moment I could tell that it was three against one, three black men and one white man. But the white man was winning. Two of the black men went down, it seemed like within seconds of each other. I opened the window and screamed that I was going to call the cops. Then the other black man ran towards the back yard. The white man looked up at me, for just a second, and then went after him, but he was moving kind of slow, and I could tell he was hurt. I watched for a second more then went to the phone and called 911. When I got back, no one was there, except the two men still on the ground."

Coventry picked up the thermos, refilled the cup, took a slurp and handed it to her. "Could you identify the white man, if you saw him?"

"Oh, no," she said. "He looked up, I could tell he was white, but it was dark. I never got a look at his features. Sorry."

"That's okay."

"I wish I did."

"No, really, that's okay."

"I could tell that he was big, though."

Coventry's eyes narrowed. "How big?"

"I don't know."

"Bigger than me?"

"I think so, but it's hard to tell with you up here and him down there."

He had an idea. "I'll tell you what. I don't want to mess up the scene right now or turn off the lights. But tomorrow night, if you're available, I'd like to bring some guys over and let you see them from your window. Maybe you can pick a guy close to the size of the guy you saw."

"Sure, if you want."

Jim Michael Hansen

"Good. Actually, a detective by the name of Richardson will coordinate that. So, what was the white guy wearing?"

"I don't know." She scrunched her face. "Dark clothes, I guess."

"Was he fat, thin, regular?"

"He wasn't fat. The way he moved, he was all over the place. He impressed me as being strong."

Coventry couldn't help but grin. "There are two dead men out there that would probably agree with you."

She smiled. "I think you're right."

THE BEDROOM WAS SPARTAN, economically speaking, and he could tell she was just barely making ends meet. The closet door was open and he could see five or six good dress suits, about one for each workday, but no more. The mattress was lumpy and the dressers were cheap painted pine. His curiosity got the better of him, and he asked: "So what do you do for a living?"

"Me? I'm an industrial hygienist with RK Safety Consult-ants. We help employers develop programs to comply with OSHA regulations, things like asbestos, noise control, air moni-toring, ergonomics, stuff like that." He looked around and she added: "The pay really isn't that bad. But I've got some stu-dent loans I'm trying to get behind me."

"Oh yeah? Where'd you go to school?"

"Ohio State University, for my undergraduate degree. Then got a masters at CSU."

"Hey, my Alma Mater. I heard they totally remodeled the library, after the flood."

She nodded. "I never saw it beforehand, but it's really nice

81

now. They have a couple of hundred computer stations on the first floor. You can pop in, check your e-mail, get on the web, print things out, whatever you want."

He shook his head. "Nothing like that in my day."

"It's nice."

"We had abacuses," he added.

THEY TALKED FOR ANOTHER FIFTEEN MINUTES. Coventry brought her around full circle a couple of times until the story stopped getting bigger. When it looked like they were just about to wrap up, she asked him a question: "So what happened, in your opinion?"

He looked away for a moment, then back at her: "This is preliminary, but a drug dealer used to live in this house. My guess is that the guys breaking in were after drugs or money or both. The white guy's a mystery. My suspicion is that he just happened to be passing by and for some reason he interceded."

"Like a good Samaritan, or something?"

He smiled. "Maybe."

She ran her fingers through her hair and then grew serious. "Are you going to run a toxicology test or whatever on the dead men, to find out if they were on drugs?"

He nodded. "Yes, that's standard."

"Do you run a criminal background check too?"

"Yes. Why?"

She paused. "I'd like to know what you get."

"Why's that?"

"I'm just curious to know how close I came to . . . well . . . I mean it's pretty obvious they were going to end up in my bedroom sooner or later." She looked a little embarrassed:

"Morbid, huh?"

He looked at her. "Yeah, a little. But you've earned it. I'll let you know what we find out." He reached for his wallet: "Look, in the meantime, I'm going to give you my card and put my home number on the back. You can call me anytime, day or night."

Suddenly his cell phone rang.

Who the hell could that be at this hour of the night?

Chapter Eight

Day Three
Wednesday Morning

THE MORNING AFTER THE FIASCO at Megan Bennett's house, David Hallenbeck woke up with a tight, achy face and a sharp pain in his lower back. There was dried blood on the pillow. He crawled out of bed, took a long heaven-sent piss and then studied his face in the bathroom mirror. The cuts had all stopped bleeding but his nose was swollen and cocked slightly to the left. He touched it to get a feel for the pain, then braced himself and pushed it over to the right, until it was just about straight. When he looked back in the mirror tears steamed out of his eyes.

Goddamn wimp, he said.

He called room service to have some band-aids, antiseptic, gauze, scissors and a newspaper sent up. Five minutes later a bellboy in a monkey suit showed up with everything, damned impressive. The Adams Mark Hotel was good that way, but for the money they charged they ought to be. Not that he cared about the money; he wasn't paying. He tipped the monkey a five and then set to work doing what he could to fix the mess. If he had his choice, he'd just stay in the room all day and let him-

84

self heal, maybe work the laptop a little. But Yorty would be expecting a phone call later and, after all, Yorty was footing the bill.

He found the incident of last night reported in a short story about halfway through the paper. So, both of the assholes died. Too bad, but it was their own sorry-ass fault.

AT TEN-THIRTY, APPROPRIATELY DRESSED in fresh Dockers, a crisp white cotton shirt, soft black leather shoes and a lightweight wool-blend blazer from Brooks Brothers, he left his hotel room and took the fire stairs down to the parking garage. There he got into a black Toyota Camry—a rental from Avis with five thousand miles on the odometer and more door-dings than wheels—and set a map of Denver on the passenger seat. Donald Vine, the man he was going to meet, lived in Cherry Hills Village.

So far he didn't know much about Vine, other than he had a 1959 Porsche Speedster for sale. But all these guys were the same: in their fifties or sixties, living in big houses with frigid wives—the bad news—but rich enough to keep a rental somewhere in the city under a different name—the good news. Pulling into Vine's driveway a half hour later, it looked like he pretty much fit the bill.

The house itself, from the outside, was a contemporary study with an abstract water-feature in the front yard. Getting out of his car and heading towards the entry, he estimated the place to be worth somewhere just under the two million dollar mark, assuming the Denver market wasn't too different from Cleveland. It was a respectable dwelling but definitely not the biggest one on the street.

A well-dressed, medium-sized man in his fifties opened the door. He had the indoor look of a bean counter. "You here about the Porsche?"

"That's me."

"I'm Donald Vine," the man said, extending his hand in a reflex movement, as if greeting someone on the board. "What happened to your face?"

Hallenbeck shook the man's hand, felt the weakness of someone physically down the food chain, and followed him inside. "I got mugged."

"You're kidding, really?" Vine looked shocked, as if muggings didn't actually happen. "Did he get anything?"

He smiled and couldn't resist the urge. "Yeah, more than they bargained for."

Vine seemed to be in genuine awe. "*They*? I'm impressed."

"Yeah, well . . ."

"You are a big boy, though, aren't you?"

THEY ENDED UP IN THE SO-CALLED GARAGE: a large dry-walled room with oak trim; fifties-style, black-and-white tile flooring; and a wall of oversized UV resistant windows. "I built this area just for my babies," Vine offered. He wore black wool slacks and a gray Polo shirt, as if unable to dress down even in his own home.

"Impressive."

There were seven cars in the space, with room for an equal number more if you wanted to jam them in. He recognized them all immediately: two Ferrari Testerossas, late eighties vintage, plain vanilla but marketable; a Viper, fast but relatively worthless; a '55 Corvette convertible, a really gorgeous car that he definitely needed to look at closer; a '57 Chevy, in beautiful condition; a burgundy Prowler that looked like it had no miles on it; and, of course, the Speedster, Guard's Red, thank God.

"So, just the Speedster's for sale?" he questioned.

"Technically, but hey."

The way Vine said that, Hallenbeck could tell he needed cash.

They walked over to the Speedster, one of the world's all time most beautiful vehicles, best known as the car that killed James Dean. Porsche hadn't built that many to start with and the ones that were left were definitely classics. You'd see one on the road every now and then but those were kit cars. This particular one was an original, a 356 Super 90, powered by a 90 horsepower flat-four engine and capable of 110 mph.

"Everything's original," Vine said. "The paint, the interior, everything."

"A survivor, huh?"

He felt under the front fender, looking for signs of body damage, found nothing, proceeded to the rear and, under the driver's side rear panel, felt a jagged edge. "Do you have a flashlight?"

Vine looked hesitant. "Yeah, what is it?"

"Have you had some body work done back here?"

"No, of course not."

Vine left for a minute and returned with a flashlight. Hallenbeck got down on his back under the car and Vine joined him. "See this rough edge? That's not supposed to be like that. This back quarter panel's been replaced at some point."

"Couldn't be."

They got back up.

"You didn't know about that?" he questioned, with a tone

like he'd be really pissed if Vine was being less than honest.

"No, honest to God."

"Okay," he said. "In the future, be more careful when you buy these things. Did you ever get a full documentation of the history?"

"Yes, I think so . . ."

Hallenbeck shook his head. "That's the problem, when cars are passed on like this with a blank title. You're never sure, unless you got someone like me doing the research for you. This one's been damaged, at least to some degree, at some point."

The shock on Vine's his face was tangible: "Screw me."

"That obviously affects the value," he said in his most sober voice. Vine said nothing. "That panel might be completely aftermarket."

He continued the inspection. "Well, you still have the original manufacturer's plate in the door jam," he said. "At least that part wasn't involved in the accident." Always give them something positive, it increases your credibility. He looked around some more underneath with a flashlight. "The numbers are all matching up, that's good. At least it's a numbers car." He found the books and maintenance records in the glove box and thumbed through them.

The paint did look like the original lacquer, but it was faded a little too much and had road rash on the nose. The passenger seat had a water spot in the leather that would never come out. The back taillight had a crack but that could be replaced. The outside mirror was aftermarket.

"As far as everything being original," he said, "that used to be the way people looked at cars like this. Now, unless it's an absolute pristine survivor, they want it original, but restored to

Concours standards. This particular unit is a long way off the mark. Good paint alone will run twenty grand. The interior needs to be gutted; you're looking at another fifteen or twenty there, to get it right. The whole car needs to be torn down to the frame, sanded and painted. We don't know what condition the engine is in without doing a diagnostic. And we still have the major problem of the accident."

Vine looked distraught, beautifully, wonderfully distraught. They stood in silence for a couple of seconds, then Vine said: "So what do you propose?"

Hallenbeck looked as if he was perplexed. "Honestly, I don't think my client's going to be interested in this particular unit, he doesn't like to mess with fixing them up too much. Let me call him though, you never know."

"Do you need a phone?"

"No," he said. "I have a cell, if you could just give me a moment."

Vine went back in the house, leaving him alone in the garage.

HE DIALED JAY YORTY'S CELL, his red one, and got connected immediately. Yorty is a 28-year-old Miami brat who spends all his energy on the club scene, being visible, snorting coke and getting laid. His money comes from a combination of old family trust funds, plus well-timed real estate investments. For the past few years he'd been busy buying and selling classic cars, having a lot of fun and making some good money at it. Hallenbeck was his eyes and ears, his personal broker, the man who flew around the country, kept him away from the bad eggs and made the good ones come home. Hallenbeck had a dozen more clients just like Yorty, which was more than he needed.

"Jay, it's David."

Yorty seemed anxious to hear from him. "Where the hell have you been?"

"Working hard on your behalf, as always. Listen up, here's the deal." He described the vehicle, walking around it as he talked. Near the end, he added: "She's a beauty. There was some bodywork done on the rear panel but it was minor and won't affect the value. The panel itself is still original. The important thing is, it's a numbers car. The rest is just sweat and money."

"Damn," Yorty said with obvious excitement. "So what do you recommend, price-wise?"

He thought about it. "Okay, he bought it twelve years ago." Then he gave him the price, which he knew would give Yorty a big old boner.

"What, he told you that?"

"No," he chuckled. "He wasn't smart enough to pull the bill of sale out of the records."

"Jesus. He stole it."

"Which is good for us," he said, then continued: "Right now, as it sits, its worth twice what he paid, all day long. But I beat it up pretty bad and he's real jumpy about the fact it was damaged, which it was, but no big deal. If you could get it for, say, his original investment plus a hundred thousand, you'd be way ahead. You could leave it like it is, or get it up to Concours for another sixty or so. Either way, you'd have some serious equity and a damn fine vehicle."

"Do you think he'd go that low?"

"He needs the money," he said. "If you came up with immediate cash, I mean the full purchase price in his hands tomorrow, that might get him to do something stupid. He can justify the price because he's still making a small fortune on it."

IT TURNED OUT THAT VINE AGREED with the proposed purchase price, with a ten grand bump. Forty-five minutes later Hallenbeck had a duly executed agreement in hand.

Walking back to the Camry under a clear cerulean sky, he felt the warm rush of the closing and smiled. The transaction meant a twenty-five thousand dollar commission for him, and Yorty paid like clockwork. That would bring his total earnings to one-fifty, year-to-date.

Not bad considering it was only April.

Equally important, Yorty would love the car and be slobbering all over himself for another deal.

WHEN HE LEFT VINE'S, HE TOOK BELLEVIEW WEST to Santa Fe Drive and then headed south, parallel to the Rocky Mountain foothills. He let his thoughts turn to Megan Bennett. The road was now only one lane in each direction and taking him into the country, farther and farther away from Denver. Crowed residential communities gave way to less crowed ones, which gave way to farms and horses.

The sky looked bigger now.

Black-and-white Magpies were everywhere.

He came to a side road and turned right, towards the mountains, floating up and down through rolling hills with the window open and a perfect April day overhead. Five miles later the asphalt dead-ended at a dirt road. He turned left, even deeper into the country. To his right, about a mile off, giant Cottonwoods snaked through the land, sucking up to a small river. Two miles later he came to a private dirt road. Hanging on a split-rail fence was a sign—For Sale—with a phone number that you could barely read anymore.

He stopped, pulled it off, and threw it as far as he could out into the brush, just as a precaution.

LAST WEEK HE CHECKED THE PROPERTY first, found it to be unoccupied, then called the number on the sign and met an elderly man by the name of Ben Bickerson there a couple of hours later. His daughter, Cheryl Miller, actually owned the house, but she moved to Oregon two years ago, and was currently on vacation in Australia. Bickerson, who lived on the next farm over, was supposed to be selling it for her, but wasn't trying too hard, just in case daughter-dear decided to come back. Hallenbeck made him an offer to rent the place for one month for one thousand dollars.

"What for?" Bickerson questioned.

"Have you ever heard the phrase, Publish or Perish?"

Bickerson was an old-time farmer with a scarred nose that suggested he'd had a chunk of sun cancer cut out of it. "Can't say as I have."

"It's used at colleges," Hallenbeck explained. "When you're a professor, you either have to keep publishing articles to show how smart you are, or you go get a job pumping gas somewhere. So what I do every year is find a quiet place to hole up, without any distractions, and stay there until I get my writing done."

"So, what, you're a professor then?"

"Guilty, I teach at D.U. Professor Frank Janks."

"D.U.?"

"University of Denver."

Bickerson cocked his head. "So you're a smart fellow."

"Not really," Hallenbeck said as humbly as he could. "All I ask is that I don't get any distractions while I'm here. If you're inclined to rent it, I have cash with me . . ."

That was that. In hindsight, he probably could have gotten it for five hundred, but who cares?

HE TURNED DOWN THE DIRT ROAD, covered with weeds. It snaked through rabbit brush for more than a half mile and ended at an old farmhouse with a barn next to it. Rusted hulks of automobiles and dead farm machinery cluttered the grounds. He recognized the outline of a 1962 Olds, perched up on cinder blocks. He drove past the house, parked by the barn and got out. The sunlight immediately warmed his face and threw a strong shadow under him. It felt so damned good.

He was a million miles from nowhere.

Smack dab in the middle of Megan Bennett country.

The air was absolutely still without even the faintest hint of a breeze. He couldn't remember a quieter place.

The tall bulky doors of the barn were closed. He muscled one open and stepped inside. The odor of rotten hay and wood impregnated the air. It was cemetery quiet and almost impossible to see. A few streaks of sunlight intruded from the roof, illuminating an airborne dust that glimmered against the dark background.

He picked his way into the structure one step at a time. The black silhouette of a tractor squatted at the far end of the building, and even in the dark, to his untrained eyes, he could tell it was ancient. Empty horse stalls occupied the wall to the right. A makeshift wooden ladder lay on the ground, broken and decayed.

He smiled and found a place to sit down. There was work to do, but it could wait a few moments. He closed his eyes, unzipped his pants and allowed the fantasy of Megan Bennett to float up to the top.

Soon baby.

Very, very soon.

Chapter Nine

Day Three
Wednesday Night

———————

KELLY PARKS LEANED AGAINST THE BRASS RAILING on her
loft terrace, six floors above LoDo, and turned her face into the
cool of the night. It felt good. The voice of Billy Holliday
came from a CD player in the living room and wandered
through the air like smoke, out the open sliding doors and into
the night, painful and lamenting, with tales of broken hearts and
love gone wrong. Down below, at street level, people flowed in
and out of sports bars and restaurants, laughing, and sometimes
talking so clear and loud that she could actually make out strings
of words. Usually they made her feel happy, which is one of
the reasons she stretched to buy the place. But tonight the motion and activity seemed just that, so much motion and activity.

D'endra Vaughn's death wouldn't leave her alone.

She had no watch on her wrist right now but guessed it was
almost nine-thirty. She had a deposition scheduled for eight in
the morning and ordinarily would be heading to bed. Tomorrow, she'd get a whole day sitting in the same room as opposing
counsel Mitch Phillips, a whiny little lawyer-man who liked to
paper the file with correspondence so full of lies and half-truths

that she seriously wondered about his mental health. She was defending, so it'd be relatively easy, apart from having to breathe the same air as that jerk. She could get to bed as late as eleven, if she wanted, and still be more than rested enough.

What to do?

Lightning crackled in the distance.

Rain was coming.

The air smelled of it.

She wandered back inside. The place made her feel comfortable, it always did, with minimal furniture, all contemporary, expensive and earth toned, accented by splashes of color from an occasional throw pillow, a hot pink lamp, a bright yellow coffee maker.

She was safe.

Why leave?

She found the phone on the counter of the kitchen island, hesitated, put it back down, picked it back up, dialed Jeannie Dannenberg, got an answer and found herself asking if they could meet.

Dannenberg sounded high. "Sure, but not here. Rachel's in the bedroom with a guy, smoking and shit."

THEY ARRANGED TO MEET AT THE RAINBOW BAR, a two-block walk up the street for Dannenberg, who didn't own a car. Kelly took Colfax Avenue all the way, got there in fifteen minutes, found four vehicles in the parking lot, all junkers, and parked the BMW in the last slot in the back, five empty spaces down. A habit of hers; she'd rather walk than get door-dings hammered out.

The place was one of those Mom-and-Pop neighborhood

dives. She'd driven by a million of them but never been in more than one or two. They'd both been the same—cheap beer and drunken mumblings about how crummy life was.

When she walked inside, Jeannie Dannenberg was already there, sitting at the bar with a half-empty bottle of Bud Light in front of her, smoking a cigarette and talking to the bartender who was leaning on the counter like he'd been settled in for a while. Kelly saw him look at her as soon as she came through the door, as if he'd been expecting her, and expecting her to be someone worth looking at. Three other men perched on barstools also turned their heads, older guys, harmless, neighborhood drunks. Even in cotton khaki pants and a casual blouse she felt overdressed. The place may have been only one bar but it smelled like ten. She couldn't imagine what the floor looked like by the light of day.

Dannenberg must have read something on her face, because she smacked the bartender on the arm and said, "Ray, stop gawking at the lady. You've seen women before." Then to Kelly: "Don't worry, he doesn't kill that many people."

The man smiled. "Not that many, but you're on the list. You know that, I hope." To Kelly: "What can I get for you, pretty lady?"

"Bud Light and a glass of ice, thanks."

"Glass of ice?"

She nodded. "Right."

"Ice water?"

"No, just a glass of ice."

"You don't want water in the glass or nothing?"

"No, just ice. For the beer. I like it cold."

He shook his head. "Never heard of such a thing. *Glass of ice . . .*"

Dannenberg looked at him: "Raymond, some day when I'm feeling generous I'm going to sit down and explain to you why you can't get laid." To Kelly, "Come on, let's get a booth." Back to the bartender: "Girl talk."

He smiled. "Booths cost extra."

"Screw you."

"And hey, I get laid plenty."

They took the end booth, an orange vinyl unit held together with duct tape, and a stained wooden table that more than one person had felt the need to carve something important on. Beers in hand, and now able to talk in private, Kelly poured the beverage into the ice, watched it foam up, took a drink and got right to the point: "We need to find out if Alicia Elmblade is alive or not. Personally, I have my doubts. She would have called you sooner or later if she was."

Dannenberg smelled like weed and had a glaze over her eyes that looked like it wasn't about to go away anytime soon. She questioned, "Why?"

Kelly rolled the bottle in her fingers. "Because, if she's dead, we participated in an actual murder instead of a fake one. Which means that the man who got us involved, namely Michael Northway, is either in on it somehow, or got duped just like us. Either way, this thing goes to a whole new level."

"Look at that," Dannenberg said.

Kelly looked outside. Rain was starting to pummel down with an incredible force, bouncing off the asphalt and pounding on the windows.

An ominous figure scurried past outside, hunched against the weather, wearing a dark windbreaker and baseball cap. He looked huge and powerful. Instead of continuing down the street he headed around the corner of the building. She expected the door to open at any second but it didn't.

Strange.

"He seemed nice, from what Alicia said about him," Dannenberg said.

Kelly looked back at her. "Who?"

"This Michael Northway guy."

"Why? What'd Alicia say?"

"I don't know, that he was always just real polite, didn't treat her like a piece of meat, that kind of thing."

"But you never personally talked to him?"

Dannenberg shook her head. "I *saw* him in the van that night but, no, I never talked to him or anything."

Kelly contemplated it. "So, the ten thousand dollars, he didn't personally give that to you?"

"No, Alicia got that from him and passed it on."

"Okay."

"Earlier that day."

"Okay." Kelly looked around, a habit of hers lately. "I have to admit, I really can't find an upside for him to knowingly get involved in a situation where someone would actually be murdered. But he did lie to me about why she wanted to disappear."

Dannenberg contemplated the statement, took a hit on the cigarette, blew smoke out her nose, and said: "Run that one by me again." She held up the beer, and added: "By me and my Bud."

Kelly leaned in. "Okay, to get me to participate in the charade, he told me that there was this client of the firm that wanted to help Alicia Elmblade, and that she wanted to fake her own death, because she was scared of something. But you told me she wasn't scared of anything, she only did it for the money."

"A hundred grand."

"Precisely."

"Okay. I remember now."

"So he lied to me," Kelly added. "That seems bad, but I don't know for sure that it is. I've known him for a long time and have more respect for him than you can imagine. This is the first and only thing that's been out of character for him, and there may well be a good explanation."

"So why don't you just ask him straight-out what the hell's going on? Just say, hey, mister big-shot, what the hell's going on?"

Kelly felt the bartender's eyes on her. She looked in that direction but saw that he was pulling glasses out of a sink and drying them with a tattered towel, paying no attention to her and Jeannie whatsoever.

She looked back at Dannenberg.

"That's not an option," she said. "If he is somehow messed up in this, the last thing I need is for him to know that I know that he lied to me, that'll just clam him up. The only thing that we have going for us right now is that he doesn't know that we know that he lied to me. He doesn't know that you and I are talking, and we need to keep it that way."

Dannenberg smiled. "We could have Jack pay him a visit. He could get some answers. He hates lawyers anyway. Damn near killed his ex's divorce lawyer, actually served a year in Canyon City . . ."

Kelly shook her head. "No. What we need to do is find out if Alicia Elmblade is still alive, on our own, quietly. If it turns out that she is, we can talk to her, and maybe she'll have an idea why someone might have killed D'endra or be after us."

"And if we can't find her, then what?"

Good question.

"Then we need to regroup. Here's something I've been thinking about. It's just a theory, so don't get too excited. But suppose someone actually wanted to kill Alicia Elmblade from the start. Somehow, someway, he gets Michael Northway to set up this charade. Alicia participates and disappears and three witnesses say they saw an Asian man take her. One of those witnesses is a lawyer in a prominent law firm, me."

Dannenberg nodded.

"Later," Kelly continued, "maybe even that very night, he really does kill her. And he has the perfect alibi, because he's a white guy. Not only that, he was someplace public with plenty of witnesses at the time she was abducted at the gas station. Plus, he knows that I can't change my story even if I wanted to, because I'd end up loosing my license and probably even land up in jail. What we did is a felony offense, in case you're interested."

Dannenberg shrugged, like she didn't particularly care, then noted: "He'd have to be awful smart. I mean, that's a lot of planning." Then asked, "Why would anyone want to kill Alicia?"

"You tell me."

Dannenberg drew a blank, drained her bottle, held it up and waved it at the bartender. "Hey, Raymond, if you're not too busy playing with yourself." She looked at Kelly's bottle, saw that it was almost empty, and said, "Two." Then to Kelly: "Everyone liked her. And she wasn't messed up in anything serious. I would have known."

KELLY REMEMBERED THE DARK FIGURE OUTSIDE, the man who hadn't come in. She walked to the other end of the bar and looked out. There he was, walking out of the parking lot. He had massive shoulders and a strong looking physique, not the hunched over depressed look of someone who'd kill time in a dive like this. Now he headed down the street. She watched him until he disappeared in the storm.

Weird.

What the hell was he doing back there in the parking lot?

Screwing with her car so she couldn't drive?

"It's called rain," the bartender told her.

She chuckled.

"Do you have any surveillance cameras outside?"

"You're kidding. Those cost money. Why?"

"No reason."

BACK AT THE TABLE, DANNENBERG SAID: "So what do we do, to find out if Alicia is alive or not?"

Kelly focused: "I've already worked the Internet to exhaustion, which has been a giant dead-end. So we need to get a grassroots search going. We talk to her old friends and find out if any of them have heard from her or know where she might be. And find out if she has any family and whether they've heard from her."

"I know a lot of the people she hung with."

"That's what I was hoping." She took a swallow. "The first thing we have to do is get you a car." She reached into her purse, pulled out an envelope and pushed it across the table. "There's five hundred dollars in here, for gas and stuff. Go to the Budget on Colfax in the morning, I'll have a car rented by then for you to pick up. You have a driver's license, right?"

"Sort of . . ."

"Sort of?"

"It's not really real, but looks real. Jack got it for me after the DUI."

Kelly shook her head. "Well, whatever. You're going to need a driver's license to pick up the car. See if it'll work. If it doesn't give me a call."

"Yeah, sure." She looked outside, nodded in that direction, and added: "It's getting worse."

KELLY LOOKED OUTSIDE. The man in the windbreaker was across the street now, looking in their direction as he passed.

She bit her lower lip.

Then looked at Dannenberg.

"I want you to sleep at my place tonight," she said.

Dannenberg laughed. "Listen, you're cute and all, but girls really aren't my thing."

Kelly ignored it and pulled her car keys out of her purse. "Come on. We'll be safe there. See if you can get Raymond to walk us out to the car."

"Hey, Raymond. Feel like getting drenched?"

"Not really."

"Well too bad, because you are."

Chapter Ten

Day Three
Wednesday Night

DAVID HALLENBECK CAME TO A STOP at the 7-Eleven gas pump and killed the engine. The night was dark and water fell out of it, lots and lots of rain, from one of those pent-up spring storms. He pushed the emergency brake down, threw a lightweight jacket over his head and stepped out. The storm immediately pounded him, bouncing off his jacket and smashing onto his pants. He selected Pay Inside, removed the nozzle, stuck it in the gas tank, and flipped the lever up. Nothing happened. He stood there for a moment, then mashed the green start button with his thumb. A second later the pump hummed and then the hose bulged and shifted like a startled snake. He ducked back into the car, slammed the door and waited.

It was almost midnight.

He felt like a balloon on the verge of busting.

The gas shut off with a loud clank and the humming stopped. He got out, put the handle back, screwed in the gas cap, and trotted towards the store with the jacket over his head, kicking up puddles of water with his feet. Inside, an old fart with white hair told him the bill was $26.93, which he already knew. He paid with a twenty and a ten, pocketed the change, and headed back to the car. No credit cards, no traces. On the other side of the street sat a Total. He drove over to it, parked at the left corner of the store in front of the pay phone, and killed the engine. The phone was slightly protected by the overhang of the store, but not by much. The security cameras were over by the pumps and shouldn't be a problem. He got out, threw the jacket over his head, which he kept pointed away from the cameras, scurried over to the phone and dialed Megan Bennett's number.

She answered on the forth ring.

"Hello?" She'd been asleep.

"Megan Bennett?"

"Yes?"

"Listen carefully and do exactly what I say," he said. "This is FBI Special Agent Ron Stokes. We met on the 16th Street Mall on Monday. Do you remember me?"

"Yes . . ."

"Good. That meeting wasn't an accident. I'm in Denver because I'm following a man by the name of Sam Arnold, who we think is linked to the OSU murders that we talked about the other day. We believe that he's after you. We think he's getting ready to make a move tonight and we need to get you out of there and get a decoy set up in your place. What I want you to do is throw some clothes on and meet me out front. I'm going to be there in three minutes to pick you up. Do you understand?"

"Yes." She sounded panicked.

"Is anyone else in the house with you?"

"No, they're in Breckenridge."

"Okay. I'm going to pull up in front of your house and

flash the bright lights. I'm driving a black Toyota Camry. Come out your front door and run straight to the car and get in the passenger side. Do you understand?"

"Yes."

"Good. I'll be there in three minutes. And don't worry, you're safe."

Hallenbeck wiped his prints off the receiver with his jacket, ran back to the car and got in. He was drenched, absolutely soaked.

This is it.

THERE WERE TWO CARS PARKED IN FRONT of Megan Bennett's house, big silhouettes, barely visible. The rain beat down like a madman. He pulled up next to the car closest to her driveway and flashed the lights. A pause for a half-beat; nothing. He stared at the front door. Nothing.

Damn it!

Was she having second thoughts?

Calling 911?

Then suddenly the front door opened, she ran out, slamming the door behind her, now racing towards him. A second later the passenger door opened, the sound of the rain intensified, then she was in, a spray of water following her.

He immediately took off down the street.

"You're okay now," he said, with as much a sigh of relief as he could muster. "Everything's going to be fine."

"God, I'm shaking," she said. Her voice was full of nervous relief.

He looked at her. She was beautiful; absolutely gorgeous. "You have a lot of questions and I'm going to answer every one of them, but right now just let me concentrate on the driving, I want to be sure no one's following us."

"Where are we going?"

"To a safe-house. It's out in the country. In about two minutes a swat team and a body-double are going to be moving into your place to set up."

"Jesus."

He quickly glanced at her, then back to the road. "I'm sorry we have to do it this way, but catching him in the act is our only option."

The storm pounded against the windshield and flew into the headlights. She occasionally looked over at him, then back out. After a time, he said: "Here's what's going on. We recently came across information that led us to believe that this Sam Arnold was involved in the Beth Williamson murder at OSU. We think he's still targeting people from the psychology class you were in. When he came to Denver three days ago we followed him here. That first night, he parked his car on your street and sat there for about an hour. We ran the list of people from the psychology class and found out that you live there."

"Why me?"

"Who knows? But there's no doubt at this point what he's up to," he said. "Tonight, just a little while ago, we lost him." He paused: "When that happened we couldn't take any chances and had to get you out of there, even if it meant blowing our cover. Which, hopefully, it didn't because if he figures out that we're on to him, he's gone."

He felt her staring at him. "What happened to your face?"

He nodded, as if expecting the question. "We had a complication. When those three men tried to break into your house, I was on stakeout that night. I went over, I had to, things got out of control and I had to defend myself."

"So that was you?"

He nodded. "Unfortunately."

"You saved my life. Thank you, thank you so much." She scooted over and hugged him. After a moment she added: "They were high on crack. The detective called me later and told me. I know for a fact that they would have raped me."

He expected her to move back over to her side, but instead she stayed where she was. It felt so strange, good strange though. "That complicated things," he went on. "We weren't working with Denver at the time, on the surveillance, and they started investigating it before we got the inter-departmental notification in motion."

They were silent for a few minutes, then she asked: "So what happens, if you don't catch him tonight?"

"We'll get him," Hallenbeck assured her. "You're safe, so don't even think about it."

He could feel her breathing, deep, and she said: "I'm probably crowding you here . . ."

He patted her knee. "You're just fine."

AFTER WHAT SEEMED LIKE A LONG TIME the traffic thinned and the city lights lost their individuality and clumped together in little groups like far away galaxies. The Camry had taken them off the freeway and into the country now. At one point on what appeared to be a long lonely road, Hallenbeck made a right-hand turn.

The asphalt rose and fell and twisted, not unlike the last hundred yards of a roller coaster. Hallenbeck stared straight ahead, concentrating on what he could see of the nightscape through the wipers. He tried to think of a joke, something to lighten the mood, but nothing came to mind except a few bona fide duds. It was so weird having her this close. He'd played the whole thing over in his mind a million times, and it had never been like this.

"Are you okay?" Megan questioned.

He looked her way. She wore white cotton shorts that took on a pale green glow from the dashboard lights. "Fine. Another fifteen minutes or so. Do you want some music? I can . . ."

"No, I like the sound of the rain."

He nodded.

She added: "It reminds me of camping trips, when I was a little girl."

A dormant memory for Hallenbeck. "I used to do a lot of hunting in the San Juans, down by Durango, up around Rock Lake, Moon Lake, way off the beaten path," Hallenbeck offered. "The most spectacular country you ever saw, but the rain could drive you crazy."

"I love the rain."

"Sometimes you wouldn't see the sky for three days straight. You end up in a tent playing Hearts and drinking Everclear."

"I'd trade for that, right now."

She shifted back to her side of the car. A side road approached from the right. Hallenbeck turned off, drove a hundred yards, killed the lights, waited a good minute, saw no other cars following, and then came back up to speed.

The road crested and then slipped into a deep valley.

The pressure was building in his loins, so much so that he had to fight to keep it out of his voice. He'd forgotten about that part. Out of the corner of his eye he studied her legs, those strong, perfectly sculptured legs. "We're almost there," he said. "We've got hot chocolate to microwave, if you want."

WHEN THEY FINALLY GOT TO THE TURNOFF, they found a slalom course of mud where there should have been a dirt road. Hallenbeck studied the puddles, picking his way through as best he could while keeping his speed up. The Camry was way out of its element and could get stuck if he didn't keep the momentum going. At the end of the road he stopped. The farmhouse sat dark and sullen, without a single light on. He blew a sigh of relief and killed the engine and the headlights. The sound of the rain immediately intensified, pounding on the metal over their heads.

"This is it," he said. Then: "Sorry, no umbrellas."

She sat there, staring at the house. "I thought there'd be other people," she said.

"There will be," he said. "Right now they're all busy at your house."

She was barely visible next to him, but he could feel her looking his way. "So what's standard procedure? Do you check it out first, or what?"

"Of course," he said. "You wait here." He opened the door and said on his way out, "I'll get a towel or something for your head."

"Thanks."

Outside the rain was cold, damn cold. It pounded on his already-wet clothes and pushed the chill straight into his bones. The front door was a barely perceptible shape and he fumbled with the key . . . at least it was on it's own key ring . . . there . . . got you . . . you little shit.

He shoved the door open, stepped inside, and removed the key. Almost immediately he heard water at his feet, draining off his clothes. He walked through the house, turning on lights as he went, letting Megan Bennett see that he was checking all the rooms like a good little agent.

He shivered.

In the upstairs bathroom he grabbed a towel for the woman's head. Then headed down the creaky wooden stairs.

He'd keep her in the house tonight, tie her up on the bed and do a little exploring. Spend two or three hours of quality time with her. There was no reason to move straight into the grand finale.

Suddenly a noise.

Coming from outside.

HE STOPPED DEAD ON THE LAST STAIR and focused on the sound. An engine. He bounded out the front door just in time to see the back end of the Camry swinging around in the mud.

The bitch was leaving!

A crowd of thoughts jammed into his head, all at the same time, the things that might have tipped her off.

She expected other people at the house.

He never showed her a badge.

A safe-house would never be this far out.

He killed two men.

She saw him staring at her legs.

The place was too creepy.

He was too creepy.

All these thoughts jammed in his brain in no more than a second, all while he ran as fast as he could towards the car.

He had to catch her.

Catch her!

So damned stupid to let her stay in the car!

So damned stupid to leave the keys in there!

She was panicked. He could tell by the way she hammered the accelerator, spinning the tires, out of control, jerking the car all over the place.

He ran.

He ran like the madman that she'd turned him into.

Mud splashed into his face and eyes. He fought the burn and pushed it out. His pants got heavy, weighed down by the water and mud, and he pushed forward even harder to keep his speed up. He was gaining on her . . . if he could just get along side . . . get to the door handle . . . get a hand inside . . . wrap his fingers in her filthy hair . . .

If she got away he was screwed!

No car.

Out here in the middle of nowhere.

Fingerprints everywhere.

Bitch!

Come here you bitch!

He concentrated on bringing his knees up even higher, like a sprinter, igniting an even deeper burn in his quads. Screw the pain. He was even with the back bumper now. Faster, faster asshole. Now he was right next to her. He reached for the door handle. Then suddenly she looked right at him. He could read the panic on her face. It was there in her eyes when she screamed and jerked the steering wheel at him.

Chapter Eleven

Day Four
Thursday Morning

BRYSON COVENTRY, AS USUAL, was the first person to show up for work in the morning, getting there while it was still dark outside, before all the pandemonium kicked in. He flicked on the fluorescents, kick-started the coffee machine, and then headed for his desk, weaving through the gray space dividers, past the mismatched metal filing cabinets and around the desks suffocated with paper. His space was over by the windows, overlooking Cherokee Street and a rat's nest of old two-story houses that had been converted into bail bond dens, painted in cartoon colors. His predecessor, the prior person in charge of the Homicide Unit, kept an office down the hall; a real office with four walls and a door that you had to knock on to get in. So had the person before that. Three years ago, when Coventry was promoted into the position, he sat in that room for two miserable days before reclaiming his desk back out on the floor.

"Closer to the coffee machine," he told everyone. But when they actually paced it off it was one step farther.

This month's edition of *Old Car Trader* sat on his desk, dog-eared to the 1967 Corvettes. He didn't much care for the new

Vettes, but the old ones, the midyears from 1963 to 1967, were works of art. The 1953s to 1962s were nice, too, but he really couldn't picture himself driving a single-axle car with drum brakes. And he would drive it, if he ever got one. No trailer queens for him. Yes, the midyears were the ones to have. And of those, the 1967 was the keeper. Dual break solenoids, parking brake in the center counsel instead of up near the dash, and the last good Vette made before the Sharks came out in 1968. A major step backwards, that, if you ask him. But the 1967s were pricey, even the small blocks.

HE SPOTTED PAUL KUBIAK'S FORENSIC REPORT in the D'endra Vaughn case sitting next to the *Old Car Trader*, a pleasant surprise, and started thumbing through it while the coffee machine gurgled.

A considerable amount of trace evidence had been collected from the scene. A large number of hairs had been collected from hairbrushes, the bathrooms, the shower drain traps, the carpeting, clothing, the victim's car and other locations. Items that may have come in contact with a person's mouth had been collected. A large number of fingerprints had been lifted. The bedding, of course, had been bagged. It contained blood, urine, saliva and semen. Three footprints had been lifted from one area in the backyard where the ground sunk down and held the moisture. Because of that, Kubiak had coordinated with the scribe, obtained the names of everyone who had been at the crime scene, including the medical responders, and taken imprints of their shoes, so as to be able to rule them out.

Now the ball was in Coventry's court.

What items, if any, did he want DNA tested at this time?

Did he want the testing expedited?

Obviously much of the DNA evidence would point to the boyfriend, Aaron Whitecliff. But they already had his statement that he was there the night the woman was killed. Plus, he reported having sex with her.

Before he could make a decision his morning got sucked into a series of meetings and a pile of must-have-by-yesterday paperwork.

SHALIFA NETHERWOOD SHOWED UP shortly after noon, looking harried. She waved at him, stopped for coffee, fell into a chair at his desk and crossed her legs. She took a noisy slurp from the white Styrofoam cup and wrinkled her face. "This stuff sucks," she said. "We need to get some Starbucks in here."

Coventry cocked his head. "D'endra Vaughn. What do we have so far in common between her and the lawyer, Kelly Parks? Anything?" He threw his legs up on the end of the desk, facing away from her so she wouldn't have to look at the bottom of his shoes.

She shook her head negative and made a sour face.

"So far," she reported, "there's no overlap at all, that I can tell, other than the obvious, they're both attractive women and they're both white. Other than that, though, they have totally different friends; that was the thing I looked at the hardest. They also went to different colleges, never worked for the same employer or even in the same building, they have different hairdressers, they live in different neighborhoods, they have different interests . . . what else? . . . oh, yeah, they do have the same bank but different branches, they go on different types of vacations, they were raised in different states, they have *very* different money—a lot like you and me—that's about it. Different, different, different."

"Different parents?"

She made a face: "Bad, even for you."

Coventry narrowed his eyes. *Both attractive women.* If the man they were looking for was nothing more than a garden-variety hunter, the link may be nothing more than that. They both turned him on.

"How's our lawyer-friend been, cooperative?"

Netherwood smiled. "Kelly Parks? She asks a lot of questions about you."

He kept his face blank, with some effort. "And?"

"And I lie, on your behalf." She leaned forward. "Are you going to make a move on her, or what?"

He grunted. "Here we go . . ."

"She'd be good for you, Bryson. She's down to earth, mature, and emotionally stable. You could do worse."

"Don't say it . . ."

"Got to, *and have.* And I'll bet you one of those stupid old Corvettes that you're always drooling over that she's good in bed, too. She has a tattoo on her ass, you know what that means."

"Really?" He raised an eyebrow. "What of?"

"A butterfly."

"You saw it?"

"No," she said. "I just asked her if she had any since the D'endra woman did."

"Don't tell me, different tattoo shops."

"Different countries, even. The lawyer got hers down in Mexico. She has quite a story to go with it, smashed on Tequila, spring break, second year of law school. The way she tells it is hilarious. She said she couldn't sit down for two days. I like her, Bryson. You ought to go for it. She's got a wild side. You wouldn't be bored."

He picked up a pencil and wove it through his fingers. "A butterfly, huh?"

"Smack dab on her lily white ass."

"Interesting."

"Let me know how big," Shalifa said.

"You don't quit, do you?"

"Get those wings flapping," she added.

He laughed, picturing it.

Then, more serious: "I'll take anything you can get me at this point—a place where he may have run into both of them, a restaurant, a store, a park, I don't care how vague, just something I can put my hands around and squeeze."

She didn't seem enthused: "I'd like to, Bryson, but I've about run out of rocks to look under."

He could read the look on her face. "Well, keep thinking," he said. "Let's talk about the mystery money that Whitecliff says she had. Where we at on that?"

She took a noisy slurp of coffee and seemed to brighten. "I've been able to rule out an inheritance."

Coventry was intrigued. "So it really is mystery money."

Netherwood nodded. "Apparently so. I'm getting a pretty good list of her friends and I've taken about seven phone interviews so far, but haven't seen anything yet that gets me wet."

He winced. "Two words. H and R."

"What, *gets me wet?*" she questioned.

He nodded.

"Okay, let me rephrase it," she said. "I haven't seen anything yet that would give you a hard-on."

He shook his head and chuckled, then said: "I keep thinking, if she came into money that she wanted to keep quiet, where would she get it? Maybe she blackmailed someone, and then later he finds out who she is and takes her out. Or maybe she was involved in some kind of Bonnie and Clyde deal and later Clyde decides that he really can't afford a loose Bonnie running around. Something like that."

She chuckled: "Bonnie would be turning over in her grave if she knew you were comparing her to a school teacher. I mean, give the woman a little respect."

He chuckled, then grabbed his coffee cup: "Refill?"

"I'll walk over with you."

He poured for both of them and had another thought. "I'm not totally convinced that this Aaron Whitecliff isn't worth squeezing some more, too. I have a gut feeling that he didn't tell us about the mystery money before because he's involved in it. Do you believe that he's banging her for a year but never knew where the money came from?"

"It seems thin."

"Paper," Coventry said.

"You said, *banging her.*"

He looked at her, as if confused. "And?"

"And you can say *banging her*, but I can't say *gets me wet?*"

"They're different."

"They are?"

"Dramatically."

"You're sure?"

"Yes."

"You want me to check with HR, just to be positive? Maybe Beverly would be kind enough to give us a professional opinion."

He smiled. "Oh, I'm sure she would."

SERGEANT KATE KATONA WALKED into the room and Coventry waved her over. She was a catcher of things since her tomboy days, with short wash-and-blow hair, a pleasant face, and an easy smile for just about everyone. She never flaunted her chest but Coventry didn't know a man in the department who wouldn't lay down a twenty for a peek.

She walked over to the coffee machine, poured a cup, added creamer and no-calorie sugar, took a careful sip and then pulled up a chair and joined them.

"*Chicago's* coming to the Buell," Katona told them.

Coventry was shocked. He'd watched the DVD about a hundred times but always thought he'd have to go to New York to see it live. "Really?"

"Yeah, really, and to remind you, you really said you'd take me if it ever did."

Ouch, expensive.

"You're thinking of someone else, someone nice."

"And me too," Shalifa reminded him.

Coventry waved his hands in surrender. "I'll get the tickets."

Shalifa looked at Katona. "Get ready for the last row, far right, by the kitchen and the elevator." Then added: "With a post obstruction."

Katona laughed, then got serious: "Did you hear about Megan Bennett?"

Coventry recognized the change in her voice and focused. Megan Bennett was the woman who had the fight outside her house, with the two dead Crips.

"No, what?"

"She's missing."

"Since when?" he questioned.

"Since sometime last night, apparently."

Chapter Twelve

Day Four
Thursday Noon

———————

WHEN BRYSON COVENTRY WALKED into the interview room, a young woman was sitting at the wooden desk with a look on her face, the kind you see in a dentist's office. On the table in front of her sat an unopened Diet Pepsi. She had raven black hair and pale alabaster skin, almost a gothic look, minus the black lipstick and face piercing. She was Jasmine Temple, one of Megan Bennett's two roommates.

Detective Richardson had been assigned as the primary detective in charge of the two killings that had taken place at Megan Bennett's house, so he took the lead in the interview and got her talking while Coventry sat back and watched. Richardson had a boyish face that belied the mind behind the eyes.

"Jackie and me drove back from Breckenridge this morning," she explained. "I dropped her off at her boyfriend's over by Wash Park and then went home. Megan was missing."

The long and short of the roommate's story was that Megan Bennett's six o'clock radio alarm had never been turned off, she wasn't home, she hadn't shown up for work, she didn't leave a note, there was no sign of forced entry, and her car was still parked outside on the street. Her tennis shoes were gone and so was her purse.

"Maybe someone called her on an emergency basis during the night and picked her up," Richardson speculated. "Whose name is the phone in?"

"Mine."

He nodded.

"Good. We're going to want you to sign a letter to the phone company authorizing them to release your phone records from last night to us. We'll fax it over to them."

"You need my permission for that?"

"Unfortunately, yes. That or paper."

They talked for another twenty minutes. At the end Coventry felt the need to say something positive: "Ninety-nine percent of the people who seem like they're missing or are reported as missing actually aren't. They're somewhere and they show up, usually with an explanation that you wouldn't have thought of in a thousand years. That's why we usually wait seventy-two hours before we take a missing person's report."

She looked at him. "But you're not waiting this time."

Coventry frowned. "No."

"So your pep talk is pretty much bullshit."

He shrugged, "Pretty much."

WHEN SHE LEFT, COVENTRY AND RICHARDSON had the same thought: the white man who killed the two Crips had returned to eliminate a witness. "Some of the blood that ended up on the ground the other night has to belong to this white guy," Coventry said. "Let's get going with the DNA testing."

"You wanted it expedited, then?" Richardson questioned.

"Expedited to death."

SEVERAL HOURS LATER THE FAX MACHINE GURGLED. The sound made Coventry realize that the room was quiet, and everyone else had gone home. He wandered over to it. The fax was from the phone company, bless their hearts. Someone had called Megan Bennett's number at 11:47 last night. The call came from a pay phone located at a Total, not more than three blocks away from her house. It lasted only one minute.

He picked up his jacket and headed down the hall, past the elevators, to the stairs. Maybe the store had something on videotape.

Chapter Thirteen

Day Four
Thursday Noon

NORMALLY, KELLY PARKS LOVED downtown Denver at lunchtime. There was energy in the air and you could push the workday aside for a precious few minutes, stretch your legs and take a deep breath of life. But she didn't feel like that today. Today she felt more like she was in a shower and someone or something had just stepped in behind her.

She stood outside Ruffy's on Court Place, waiting, five minutes early. People paraded back and forth. Most of the men looked in her direction as they passed. A convertible drove by and a few bars of "Satisfaction" filled the air and then dropped off.

The day was warm but the sky was clouding up. She wouldn't be surprised if it stormed again this afternoon.

Bryson Coventry.

She hadn't seen or talked to him since that one and only meeting on Monday. She half-expected that he would have made up some excuse to call her by now but he hadn't. Maybe he already had someone in his life—maybe that detective, Shalifa Netherwood. She had Coventry's business card in her wallet. Maybe she should make up some excuse and call him—give the man an opportunity to ask her out.

SYDNEY SOMERVILLE SHOWED UP AT 11:30, exactly on time, looking like a model who had intentionally dressed down into khakis and a simple blouse, with her hair pulled back into a ponytail. Every time Kelly saw her she was astonished at how much she looked like Marilyn Monroe, except lighter and firmer.

They hugged and Sydney's oversized chest pressed into hers.

"Sydney, you look great!"

"You too. God, it's been so long!"

"I know."

"I'm going to need all the gossip," Sydney warned.

"Me? You're the one suddenly all over the place."

Ruffy's, a landmark restaurant-slash-bar, always filled up and formed a waiting line by a quarter to twelve. Kelly loved it, probably because it was so simple and unpretentious. It still had the old hardwood floors, nicked and scuffed like you couldn't believe, and the chairs and booths were all red vinyl, a fashion statement from somewhere back in the dinosaur days. When you walk in there's a bar on the right that runs the entire length of the place, with seating for at least fifty. Lots of the men like to eat right there where they can watch the news and check out the barmaids.

Some nondescript waiter with a white apron and a lot of smiles ushered them to a booth and then disappeared.

"So, are you still with what's-his-name, Brad?" Kelly questioned, sliding in.

"Blake," Sydney corrected her. "No, he's history." She

leaned forward and lowered her voice: "Now I'm dating Mr. Vibrator," she said.

Kelly laughed.

"Buy stock in Eveready," she added. "I'm serious."

They ordered chicken salads and passed names back and forth while the noise of the place washed over them. Sydney Somerville worked at the law firm as Michael Northway's personal assistant for four years, before leaving six months ago to *do that modeling thing*, as she called it. If anyone knew what Michael Northway was up to, or had been up to, it would be Sydney.

"We have a situation at the firm, which is why I needed to talk to you," Kelly explained. "This is all on the hush-hush, by the way."

Sydney put on a mischievous face. "Oooh, juicy."

Kelly wasn't exactly sure how to broach the subject, or just how much to disclose. "Have you ever heard anything about a secret group in the firm? A group that Michael Northway's in?"

Sydney looked confused. "A secret group? What do you mean?"

Kelly leaned in. "A group, I get the sense it's a small one, that takes special care of important clients, something over and beyond legal services."

Sydney shook her head negative. "I never heard of such a thing. Who else is in it, besides Michael?"

"I don't know," Kelly told her. "He wouldn't say."

"Huh."

"Supposedly," Kelly continued, "most of the partners don't even know about it."

"But you do?"

Kelly nodded. "Michael solicited me to do something."

"Meaning what, exactly?"

Too many details wouldn't be a good idea at this point. Sydney was a good friend and good person, but not the world's best secret-keeper. "I really can't get into details." Then: "Does Rick's Gas Station mean anything to you?"

Sydney looked genuinely confused. "No, nothing. Should it? Rick's Gas Station?"

"No."

"Jesus, Kelly, what's going on?" Kelly could see the frustration on her friend's face and wanted to spill out the story but couldn't risk having anything get back to Michael Northway at this point, especially details that only she knew.

She played with her fork. "Let's just say I've got a situation that I'm trying to get my arms around. I know that's vague, but it has to be at this point. Bear with me, please. While you were with the firm, was there anything weird or unusual going on that involved Michael Northway?"

Sydney looked like she was reaching back and had found something. "No," she said, hesitantly.

"You sure? You look like you're not sure."

Kelly could feel her deciding. Then Sydney seemed to weaken. "There is this one thing," she said.

The waitress appeared from out of nowhere, placed two salads on the table and wanted to know if everything was all right.

Yes, peachy keen.

"Actually, I don't know if it's something or not," Sydney went on. "Maybe there's an explanation for it, but something did happen one day that I found to be out of the ordinary, to say the least."

"How so?"

SYDNEY FINISHED CHEWING A MOUTHFUL of salad and said: "One day, Michael's out of the office. He's going to be gone a couple of hours. Maxine Randolph was working on something for him, helping him get ready for something or other. She calls me, desperate for a file that she thinks is in Michael's office. So I go in to look. Usually he keeps his desk pretty clean, but this particular day it was all jumbled up. So I'm digging around and come across this unlabeled expansion folder, buried under a pile of other files, and open it up."

Sydney paused.

"And?"

"And, well, inside there are pictures of a dead woman. Ten or twelve of them, of this dead woman, some from farther away, some from close up, from different angles, almost the kind of pictures you'd expect the police to take at a crime scene. And they were graphic. I mean, this poor woman was cut and stabbed and I mean a lot. There was blood all over her face and her clothes. She was such a mess that you just couldn't believe it. I remember one picture in particular, which was a close-up of a knife sticking out of her stomach."

Kelly could almost see it and felt her breath stop. "Jesus."

Sydney nodded. "Tell me about it. I mean this was really sick stuff. But there were other things in the file, too, besides the pictures. There were photocopies of the kinds of things that you'd find in someone's wallet, like a driver's license, credit cards, stuff like that. It was like someone had taken her wallet over to a copy machine and just made a duplicate of everything."

"That's weird."

"That's what I thought," Sydney said. "So I naturally try to relate all of this to something that Michael's working on, a criminal case or a wrongful death or a CNN commentary or something, but I'm not coming up with any matches. And, like I said, the file was unlabeled, which I found really strange, since Michael's such an obsessive-compulsive organizer. There were some newspaper clippings in there, too," Sydney added. "Articles about the murder."

"So she was definitely dead?"

"Oh, yes, definitely. You could just tell that by the pictures."

"And the pictures? What are we talking about? Three-by-fives, or what?"

Sydney shook her head. "No. They looked more like digital pictures that had been printed out. They were almost full page size."

"So what was the woman's name?"

"I don't know," Sydney said. "I mean, I looked at the copies of the stuff from her wallet, close enough to tell what it was, but didn't stop to actually read anything."

"Okay."

"Now I wish I had."

"Yeah."

"Oh, that's what I was going to tell you. Here's the weird-est part of all. In the file, there was a regular letter sized envelope, too. I look inside and there's hair. I'm guessing from the dead woman. Now that really freaked me out."

"Hair?"

"Hair, a lock of hair, not a lot, maybe fifteen or twenty strands, but actual hair."

"Damn. So what did Michael have to say about all of this?"

"Nothing," Sydney said. "I just put everything back the way I found it and waited for him to bring it up. He never did. I kept watching for signs of where it might fit into something he was working on, but never did see a connection to anything. And that was the only time I ever saw it. I made a point of keeping my eyes open when I was in his office after that, but never saw it again."

"Is there any reason to suspect that a client gave him that file?"

Sydney contemplated it. "It's certainly possible. Lots of people walk into his office and the door gets closed. That file could have come from anywhere."

"Would you recognize this dead woman, if you saw a picture of her?"

"Maybe, but I kind of doubt it," she said. "I mean her face was covered in blood and had hair matted on it and everything. Plus, the way I talk about it, it probably sounds like I was looking around for a long time, but in reality the whole thing probably lasted less than thirty seconds."

"When exactly did you come across this file?"

Sydney scrunched her face, obviously going deep, then said: "I'm guessing sometime around a year ago, maybe April or May of last year, give or take."

Kelly made a mental note that the incident at Rick's Gas Station was in May.

"Does the name Alicia Elmblade mean anything to you?"

Sydney shook her head negative. "No. Who's Alicia Elmblade? Is she the dead woman?"

"I don't know," she said. "Maybe. I'm going to try to get a photograph of someone for you to look at, and see if you can tell me whether it's the dead woman you saw in the file. Will you be home tonight?"

"Yes." Then: "You look freaked out."

"I'm coming over tonight."

A HALF-HOUR LATER, KELLY PARKS WALKED down the 16th Street Mall, heading back to work, knowing that she definitely had to find out if the dead woman in Northway's file was Alicia Elmblade.

If she could get into Northway's computer, she might be able to find something, maybe even the digital photos themselves. But that would be just about impossible. First she'd have to somehow get his password, then get some serious quiet time in his office. Plus, would he really be stupid enough to leave an electronic trail if he was actually involved in a murder?

No. Forget that for now.

It would also be interesting to know if someone took a lock of the dead teacher's hair, the D'endra Vaughn woman, since her death was obviously connected to Alicia Elmblade somehow. If both women had a lock of hair taken, that would point to a common killer.

That would be worth knowing.

Bryson Coventry would know about D'endra Vaughn's hair. In fact, he was the only one she could think of to tap for that information, except maybe Shalifa Netherwood.

She spotted an empty bench as she approached California Street, headed in that direction and sat down. She pulled Coventry's card out of her wallet and called him on his cell phone. He answered almost immediately:

"Lieutenant Coventry," she said. "This is Kelly Parks, the lawyer."

"Kelly," he said. "Right. What's going on?" He sounded like he was glad she called. That was good. She pictured his face and almost felt him there with her.

"Nothing, really. I just thought I'd touch base, see if there was anything else I could do to help you or Detective Netherwood."

He paused and she could tell he was thinking about it. "There was something I wanted to ask you," he said. "But it's not floating to the surface. Maybe I'll think of it in a second. How've you been? Anyone following you around or anything?"

Was the man outside the bar worth mentioning?

Or would he just think she had an overactive imagination?

"You know, I'm not sure," she finally said. "But Tuesday night, I was in this place, a bar, and there was a guy walking around outside in the rain. For some reason it creeped me out."

"What'd he look like?"

"I have no idea."

"Mmm. Was he big, small, young, old, black, white?"

"He was big, that much I could tell. And muscular, you could tell by the way he moved."

"A big guy, huh?"

"Yes."

"And muscular?"

"I'm guessing so."

"Interesting."

"How so?"

He paused and said, "Nothing in particular," but she could tell that something had struck a cord with him.

"Oh," she said, as if surprising herself with an afterthought. "Maybe you could help me with something. I was talking to another lawyer in the firm about D'endra Vaughn, he used to do some criminal law work, and he asked me if a lock of her hair had been cut off.   I know you showed me the pictures, but I couldn't remember looking at her hair that close one way or the other.   It's just been bugging me ever since he asked."

"No, no hair missing," Coventry said.

"So that's something that you look for, then?"

"Not always, necessarily. But in this case, there was enough strangeness involved to suggest that we might be dealing with a souvenir collector, so we paid pretty close attention to the possibility of things like missing hair, missing fingernails, missing jewelry and the like."

"Well," she said, "that answers that."

THAT NIGHT, AFTER WORK, SHE DROVE over to Jeannie Dannenberg's apartment to pick up the one and only photograph that Dannenberg had with Alicia Elmblade in it.   While she was there, Jeannie—who was obviously feeling no pain—took the opportunity to report that she'd been able to track down quite a few of Alicia Elmblade's old friends, thanks to the use of the rental.   Not a single one of them has heard from Alicia since last May.

Kelly drove the photograph of Alicia Elmblade straight over to Sydney's house in Cherry Creek and showed it to her.

"Is this the woman you saw in Michael Northway's file?"

Sydney studied it hard and shrugged.

"I don't know."

"Could it be the same woman?"

"It could be, but it could not be, too," Sydney corrected her. "This woman does strike me as being about the right age and the general level of attractiveness.   Other than that, though, it's impossible to tell.   Remember, I only saw that file for a few seconds and that was a year ago."

Kelly Parks felt her frustration level push towards the limit. "Look harder. Is this the woman in the pictures or not? Just give me your best guess."

"My best guess?"

"Yes."

"Okay, that's her."

"It is?"

"I don't know. That's my best guess."

"Okay."

"That's what you asked for, my best guess."

"I know."

"If you want my best guess, that's her. If you want me to say if it actually is her or not, then I don't know."

Chapter Fourteen

Day Four
Thursday Morning

***

DAVID HALLENBECK REALIZED there was a good amount of light in the room and that he had slept into the day.   The thought immediately troubled him on some deep level but he didn't know why.   He opened his eyes enough to look at his watch without letting enough brightness in to hurt.   Eight-thirty in the morning, way past six.   He closed his eyes, rolled onto his back, and felt every muscle in his body burn.

Then the events of last night jumped into his brain.

He remembered Megan Bennett turning the car into him, her loosing control of the vehicle, sliding sideways off the road in the mud and then slamming to a stop.   Then she was out of the car, running into the night.   She was damn fast.   He remembered the burning in his lungs and the fear that his oxygen would run out before he could catch her.   He remembered being scared to death that she'd get far enough ahead to lose him in the darkness, and that he'd somehow have to get the hell out of there and back to the city.   Then he was on her and, *wham*, he had her on the ground.

He remembered pounding her with closed fists.

Teaching her a lesson for screwing with him.

Working her over, knowing he should stop, that he was killing her, but not being even close to controlling the rage. Then she went limp and stayed limp and he wasn't sure if he killed her or not. He threw her over his shoulder and carried her lifeless, mud-soaked body for an eternity, with every step bringing a new pain to his universe. Then she regained consciousness, not fully, but enough to walk on her own, and he gripped her arm like a madman and dragged her all the way back to the house. There was no way in hell he was going to let her make a break for it again.

When they got inside the house, he stripped her naked and threw her in the shower, then got in with her. She didn't even react. He washed the mud out of her hair and ears and they stayed there until the hot water ran out. Then he toweled her off, put her in a long-sleeve button down shirt and tied her to the bed with her arms over her head.

Then he mounted her.

Savagely.

Not caring.

Giving her what she deserved.

That was last night.

Now it was morning.

HE SUDDENLY SAT BOLT UPRIGHT and looked at the bed next to his. There she was, just like he left her, flat on her back with her arms tied to the head rails.

By the light of day she looked terrible.

What had he done?

Her face was so bashed up that it looked like a solid surface of black and blue with hardly any normal places left. Her lower lip was puffed up at least twice its normal size. Her right eye was swollen so bad that he doubted that she'd be able to open it for days. There was dried blood in her hair. She must have still been bleeding after he washed her.

He swung his feet over the side of the bed and sat there, staring at what he'd done. His legs began to warm and he realized that sunlight was streaking through the window, landing on him. He had no clothes on.

Bitch.

Serves you right.

Screwing with me like that.

He remembered the car, still out in the field somewhere. He hadn't had the strength last night to deal with it. Now he needed to get it back to the house, especially if it could be seen from the road, which he wasn't sure of one way or the other. That was the first order of business. The last thing he needed right now was for someone to see it and start poking around.

Damn it.

All he wanted to do was sleep.

This day was going to be absolutely screwed.

He was half-tempted to smack her again, right there as she slept, for getting him in this predicament.

He stood up, sore from head to toe, especially his lower back, and walked over to her. The ropes securing her wrists to the headboard were in good shape. No way she could escape from them. That was good. Her shirt her had ridden up during the night and was now above her belly button, leaving her exposed from there down.

The sight gave him an erection.

He sat down next to her on the bed and started undoing the

buttons.

She opened her eyes when he climbed on top.

"Don't say a word," he said. "Just enjoy it."

Chapter Fifteen

Day Four
Thursday Evening

THIS TYPE OF INVESTIGATION was way beneath Bryson Coventry. Any first-year detective would be able to handle it just fine. But it was late on a Thursday night and if Megan Bennett had in fact been abducted last night he needed answers now, which pretty well meant that he had to get them himself.

Pulling in from the street, the florescent lights shining from inside the Total seemed extra bright, emphasizing that the sun was down and the coolness of the thin night air had taken over. The pay phone was located outside on the far left corner of the store. He maneuvered his truck past the pumps and parked directly in front of it.

This was the phone that someone had used to call Megan Bennett from just before midnight last night.

There was no sense trying to fingerprint it. There'd been a ton of rain, plus it had already been exposed to the public for over eighteen hours.

Someone in a Jeep Wrangler pulled in next to him, on the passenger side. He looked like a high school kid. Coventry hated it when Wranglers parked next to his truck because their doors opened so wide and sat so high. One careless move and he'd end up with a door-ding. He walked around to the front of his vehicle and stood there staring at the driver, not in a threatening way, just a watchful one. He must have made an impression because the kid was real careful to hold onto the door as he got out. No contact with Coventry's truck.

Okay.

A door-ding avoided.

Coventry looked around for the surveillance cameras, spotting two, one on each side of the pumps. Only one had any potential for picking up the phone area and the way it pointed the chances seemed slim, unless it was really wide-angled.

A 7-Eleven stood directly across the street. Later, he may as well check over there too, in case they had a camera angled in this direction.

He could almost feel the temperature drop even farther as he looked around. He stuffed his hands in his front pants pockets and hurried inside. "You're Going to Lose That Girl" spilled out of speakers somewhere off in the corners. Hearing it, he wondered why it never got much airtime; it had to be one of the best Beatles songs ever.

He hadn't planned on getting a cup of coffee, but once inside it seemed like the right thing to do. Then he remembered he had a big aluminum mug in the truck, went out, got it, hurried back in, poured in five vanilla creamers, filled it to the top with decaf and immediately took a sip.

Good stuff.

Nice and hot.

A young lady, no older than nineteen or twenty, with tattoos running up her neck and blue streaks in her hair, took his money at the counter. He explained who he was and told her that he wanted to check the surveillance tapes from last night.

"I'm not supposed to let anyone do that," she told him. "That kind of stuff's all supposed to go through corporate." A pause, then: "But, hey, what'd corporate ever do for me, right?" She rang open the bottom drawer of the cash register, pulled out a key and handed it to him. "It's the room in the back, by the johns."

Coventry smiled, pulled a card out of his wallet, wrote "We owe her one," scribbled his initials, and handed it to her. "If you ever get stopped for speeding or something, give them this. No guarantees it'll work but you can always try."

"Hey, thanks, man." Then, as he was walking away: "Hey, do you ever do phone sex?"

He grinned.

"'Cause I could call you tonight, if you want," she added. "I get off at 11:30. It's fun."

"Thanks, but that's probably not a real good idea."

THE ROOM WITH THE VCRS for the surveillance cameras turned out to be the stocking room, which was jammed to the ceiling with inventory. Coventry kept the door open so the walls wouldn't close in, and popped in unlabeled tapes until he found the one he needed. Beautifully, the recording was imprinted at the bottom with a date and time. The call to Megan Bennett had been placed at 11:47 last night. He fast-forwarded yesterday's tape to 11:45, then switched over to the play mode and sat back to watch.

Bad news.

The surveillance camera didn't view the payphone area. Everything at the station last night was pretty dead. There were no cars at the pumps. The rain beat down like a madman. Second after second went by and all he had to watch was the rain.

Then the bottom half of a car suddenly appeared in the screen as it drove past the pumps. It disappeared almost immediately as it headed into the area where the phone was located. He could only see the side view of the car from about the door handle down. No license plate, no driver's face. He didn't recognize the manufacturer or make of the vehicle, but that's the kind of thing the lab should be able to determine without too much trouble. A few seconds later a second car pulled up, into the pump area, and stopped. The license plate was in direct view. He paused the tape, pulled one of his cards out of his wallet, and jotted the number down.

Then he hit play again.

A middle-aged white man wearing a Bronco's jacket got out of the second car and walked into the store, probably to prepay.

A minute of so later, the first car left. Again, though, all the videotape showed was the bottom half of the car for a second or so.

He shifted the tape to fast-forward and watched it for another few minutes. Nothing else happened, other than the man at the pump finished and eventually drove away. There was no reason to believe that he had ever squarely looked in the direction of the pay phone, although obviously it would be worth the time to track him down and find out.

Whoever made the phone call hadn't gone into the store so there was no eyewitness there to talk to. He hadn't purchased any gas so there was no credit card number to trace.

The lab would be able to determine what kind of car he was driving, though. That wasn't a lot but it was more than he had an hour ago.

He popped the tape out of the VCR, walked out of the room and locked it behind him, damn glad to get out of there.

It was almost as bad as an elevator.

Except it couldn't fall and kill you.

The young lady at the register smiled when he came back to give her the key. She handed him a napkin and he took it, not knowing what it was.

"That's my number," she said. He looked at it and saw a handwritten phone number and the name Janessa. "In case you change your mind about the you-know-what."

He handed it back.

"Thanks, but I can't," he said. "I'm taking one tape. I'll have to keep it, as the original, but I'll have the lab make you a copy and drop it off sometime tomorrow."

She smiled. "Why don't you just drop it off yourself?"

He grinned. "Thanks for everything. You stay young, all right?"

HE REMEMBERED THE 7-ELEVEN ACROSS THE STREET. Was it still worth checking out? He looked at his watch, nearly nine o'clock. What the hell, it would only take a minute.

He left his truck where it was and walked across the street, sipping coffee on the way. An older gentleman worked the cash register and the sight reminded Coventry to keep contributing to his retirement plan. He explained who he was and said, "I'm investigating something that happened across the street at the Total at about midnight last night. I was wondering if by any chance your surveillance cameras pick up any of that area."

The gentleman shook his head negative. "No. Sorry, they

don't."

Coventry nodded. "Okay, I didn't think so, but thought I'd check anyway."

"They're basically to get license plate numbers, for drive-offs," he added. "So we keep them pointed at the pumps."

"I understand."

"You'd be surprised how many people don't pay."

Coventry nodded.

The man lowered his voice: "I did it myself a few times, back in my younger days."

Coventry grinned. "Me too." Which was true.

"You almost have to, if you don't have the money," the gentleman said. Then: "Just don't tell anyone."

"Likewise."

"They really frown on that kind of thing around here."

When he got back to his truck, he remembered the Wrangler, now gone, and walked over to the passenger side just to be sure he hadn't been dinged.

Unbelievable.

There it was.

A son-of-a-bitching dent right there in the middle of his door.

Damn it.

It'd cost him sixty bucks to get that taken out.

Plus the inconvenience.

HE GOT BACK IN THE TRUCK, called the station, and gave them the license plate number of the second car that had been there last night. It was registered to someone named Ralph Long. Dispatch was kind enough to look up his phone number. Coventry got him on the line, explained who he was and said: "You bought some gas last night at a Total, just before midnight. While you were there, someone was over at the pay phone on the left side of the building. Did you by any chance see that person or remember anything about that?"

A pause.

"A lieutenant?"

"Right. Lieutenant Bryson Coventry, Denver Homicide."

"What's higher, lieutenant or sergeant?"

"Lieutenant."

"So the sergeants are under you?"

"That's right."

"And they have detectives under them?"

"That's right."

"So you're way at the top?"

"In some ways, yes, but it's really just one big team."

"Interesting," he said. "Okay. Sorry for the side trip, I just wondered who I was talking to. Anyway, last night, I did happen to see someone over at the pay phone when I pulled up."

"You did?"

"Well, briefly," the man reported. "I saw him out there in the rain, and thought to myself that it was really weird, because, number one, everyone has a cell phone nowadays and, number two, if you don't have a cell phone and need to make a call, there's a lot of places around where you can find a phone inside. Why would someone be standing out in the pouring rain?"

Coventry was excited. "So how good did you see him?"

The man must have felt his enthusiasm, because he warned, "Don't get too worked up. I never did see his face, because, number one, I only looked at him for a second and, number two, he was holding a jacket over his head, because of the rain."

"So you never saw his face at all?"

"No, never. When I came back out of the store he was already gone."

"What about his size, could you tell how big he was?"

"Oh, yeah," the man said. "Now *that* I did see. This guy was huge. He must have been six-four at least. He was definitely a big boy."

"Yeah?"

"Tall, but filled out, too. He looked strong."

"You could tell that? Even in the rain?"

A pause: "Yes, I guess somehow I could."

Coventry talked him into coming down to the department tomorrow to give a formal statement to Detective Richardson, for the file.

THEN HE CRANKED UP THE ENGINE, pulled out of the Total and was on the 6th Avenue freeway within five minutes, heading west towards home. It had been a long day, sixteen hours to be exact, and suddenly he was exhausted. Traffic was minimal, as it should be on a Thursday night. A few miles out of downtown, near Sheridan, the speed limit increased from fifty-five to sixty-five, and he brought the Tundra up to sixty-eight and set the cruise control. Someone in a late model sedan closed in on him from behind, switched over to the fast lane, passed him, and then cut back over right in front of him, not more than a car-length ahead.

They were the only two vehicles on the road.

There was no reason for him to cut back in that fast.

It reminded Coventry that he already knew how he was going to die. Some idiot wielding two tons of steel was going to take him out.   Of that he was certain.   There were way too many dumb-asses out there armed with cars.   He brought the truck out of cruise, let it coast until the sedan got a safe distance ahead, and then reset it.   He exited at Union/Simms, headed south to Cedar then snaked up into the Green Mountain foot-hills, to home.

Ten minutes later his head was on the pillow and he found himself reflecting on the telephone call from Kelly Parks this afternoon. It had been nagging at him all day. She called him to find out if a lock of D'endra Vaughn's hair had been cut off. She tried to make it seem like an afterthought, but it wasn't. Now why did she want to know that?   Clearly she knew *some-thing* she wasn't sharing.

But what?

And how hard should he be trying to find out?

Chapter Sixteen

KELLY PARKS SAT AT HER DESK with a cyber-smear file in front of her. Two disgruntled ex-employees of Unicom were smearing her client, Charles Weber—the CEO and President of Unicom—up and down the Internet. Mr. Weber wanted them strung up by their thumbs or, at the very least, enjoined. She tried to rein him in early on since there weren't enough money damages for the suit to make economic sense, but he was insistent on gagging those two jerks and willing to pay big company bucks to get it done. So she was working the case and that's why it was sitting there.

But that's not where her mind was.

Today was Friday and Michael Northway would be back in the office this morning. This would be the first chance she had to talk to him since that brief conversation on Monday before he ran off to the airport.

She'd learned a lot since then.

For one, Michael had lied to her about the abduction of Alicia Elmblade. For two, he had a file in his office memorializing the murder of a woman.

What to do?

She could tell Bryson Coventry everything she knew and just let him run with it. But that phone call, once made, would be irrevocable. No one would be able to put the Genie back in the bottle.

Serious damage could be done to the firm.

Their offices would almost certainly be the subject of a criminal investigation, the media would find out and leverage its way in, and then serve the whole thing up on a juicy primetime platter. Clients would jump ship and lots of good, hardworking people would lose their jobs.

Michael Northway would be disbarred.

She would too, not that that mattered.

And if it turned out that Michael wasn't in fact criminally involved, or that Alicia Elmblade was actually alive, all the damage would have been for nothing.

That was the disturbing fact.

The fact that told her to keep her mouth shut.

Plus, what kind of woman would she be if she squealed on the one person who had taken her under his wing since day one?

So she would hold back, at least for the moment, and pray there was some legitimate explanation for everything.

Okay.

The plan for right now is to keep quiet, play dumb and listen. That might change after she met with Michael later today, but it was the plan for now.

SHE JUMPED WHEN THE PHONE RANG. It was Michael Northway.

She looked at the clock. Ten-fifteen.

"Kelly," he said. "Michael here. We need to meet today, but my schedule's busting at the seams. I feel like a banana that someone threw into the gorilla cage. I have an oral argument scheduled for eleven-thirty at the Colorado Court of Appeals. Any chance you could meet me there afterwards, about noon, and we could walk back to the firm together?"

"No problem. See you there at twelve."

"I really hate to put you out like this, but . . ."

"Michael," she said, cutting him off. "*Not a problem.* Read my lips."

"That's why I love you."

"See you at noon."

SHE ACTUALLY SHOWED UP AT ELEVEN-THIRTY, just as the court called the case to the docket. Michael apparently represented the Appellee, so the other side took the podium first. The panel judges were wide-awake and actually appeared to be interested. They asked quite a few pointed questions and had obviously done their homework and even read some of the case law. She studied Michael as the other side argued. He wasn't taking notes and, on closer examination, didn't even have a notepad in front of him. In fact, there wasn't anything on the table in front of him, except a water pitcher and three or four drinking glasses turned upside down. Michael's briefcase sat on the floor next to his chair but he hadn't opened it.

He'd told her before: *It's very simple. The secret to being a good lawyer is the ability to listen. The secret to being a good listener is sit there and shut your big fat trap every once in a while.*

She couldn't help but smile.

He sat there quietly with his hands folded in his lap, not reacting one way or the other to anything the other side said, being the perfect gentleman.

When the Appellant's attorney eventually sat down, Michael stood up, approached the podium with nothing in hand, and said: "The Court has asked twelve very good questions. Let me tell you the straightforward answers to each one of them."

Which he then proceeded to do.

AFTER THE ARGUMENTS, when they were out of the building and walking back to the firm, he said: "God I'd hate to have their job. No power at all. The trial judge is the one with the power."

The weather was just about perfect, sunny and seventy.

"So how have you been?" he asked her. "Anything strange happening since Monday?" He appeared genuinely interested in her welfare.

"No. I'm okay."

He nodded, apparently satisfied. "I've actually been working on this matter quite a bit this week. I talked to the client a number of times, the one we were doing the favor for. He has a theory, but nothing concrete."

"What theory is that?"

"It goes something like this," Michael said. "Alicia Elmblade witnessed a murder or crime or something, which is the reason she wanted to disappear in the first place, although she never actually said that in so many words. Somehow, whoever it was that was after her in the first place, learned that her abduction was a fake. Now he's out to teach everyone a lesson."

"Including you?"

Michael shook his head negative. "He probably wouldn't know my name. But you and the other two witnesses, your names are in the police report, which isn't all that hard to get."

She considered it.

Michael must have seen hesitation on her face because he said, "He also has a permutation of that theory, which goes like this. Someone was after Alicia Elmblade in the beginning, which is why she wanted to vanish. He somehow finds out her abduction is a fake and finds out that D'endra Vaughn is involved in it. He suspects that she knows where Alicia Elmblade is and tries to get it out of her, except she dies in the process."

Kelly considered it.

Plausible as well, even a little more so.

"So what did happen to Alicia Elmblade?" she questioned.

Michael smiled. "The client set her up in California with a brand new identity, a driver's license, a social security card, some pretty sophisticated stuff, when you stop to think about it."

"Under what name?"

Michael shook his head and sighed. "You're better off not having that information, just in case someone really is trying to find her. For your sake as well as hers."

Kelly tried to hide her disappointment. "Okay."

"Oh," Michael added, "get this. The client told me he even gave this Alicia Elmblade woman a hundred thousand dollars, to help her get situated. I knew he was going to give her something, but had no idea it was so much. He also gave her two friends ten thousand each just to encourage their continued silence." Michael shook his head as if in wonder. "He must have liked this Elmblade woman an awful lot."

"I'd say."

"I almost feel sorry for the poor guy."

"Why is that?"

"Well," he said. "He goes to all this trouble and then two months later she stops calling him."

"Really?"

"Yep," Michael confirmed. "She moves out of the apartment he set her up in and drops off the face of the earth."

"Wow. Strange." Then, before she could stop herself, she said: "Maybe, in actuality, he killed her."

Michael looked at her as if she was crazy, and laughed. "Not likely," he said. "But I'll tell you one thing, once a sap always a sap. You know what he's doing right now, even as we speak? He's working with one of the best private investigator firms in Los Angeles to find her, just so he can warn her about what's going on back here in Denver."

Kelly found herself going back to the hundred thousand dollars. She couldn't help but think that maybe Michael Northway and Jeannie Dannenberg were *both* telling the truth, in their own ways.

"So he actually gave her a hundred thousand dollars?"

Michael nodded and grinned. "Nuts, isn't it? But trust me. For this guy, that's pocket change."

"Umm."

"Saturday night fun money," he added.

HE LOOKED LIKE HE REMEMBERED SOMETHING, then reached into his inner suit pocket and pulled out a black device about the size of a cell phone. "Got a present for you," he said, handing it to her.

She looked at it. It was a black box with a large button on it and a small red light, and the imprint of a company name, Anderson Security Services.

"It's a GPS security alarm," Michael said. "If you're in trouble, you press this button. It sends a signal back to the security company and feeds them your exact location using GPS. They then call the police."

"GPS?"

"Global Positioning System," he explained. "Based on latitude and longitude, supposedly accurate to within twenty feet. And the signal is registered to you, so when you press it, the security company can tell the police who they should be looking for."

"Interesting."

"Compliments of the client," he added. "He also wants to get you a bodyguard."

Kelly shook her head no. "We already talked about that," she said.

"I told him you'd say no. But remember that the offer remains open if you change your mind."

"I won't."

"Oh," he said. "He also wants to get you a gun, if you want one."

She shook her head. "Absolutely not."

"I told him you'd say that."

"I've never touched a gun in my life," she emphasized.

They were on 17th Street now, walking in the heart of downtown, almost at the firm's building.

"So, what now?" she questioned.

Michael considered it. "Now we just be careful, keep our eyes open and let the client continue his investigation. The one thing we can't do is get the police involved. There's nothing we can do or say to help them, anyway. And if they ever do find out about Rick's Gas Station, a lot of damage is going to result." He paused and looked at her: "You understand that, I assume."

"Of course I do."

He must have seen something in her face, because he added: "And stop thinking bad thoughts about the client. I can guarantee you that he's not involved in any wrongdoing."

She felt herself nod.

"And neither am I, for that matter," he added. "So stop worrying. This whole thing's going to settle out and everything's going to get back to normal. Trust me."

"Trust a lawyer?"

"No, trust a friend."

Chapter Seventeen

Day Five
Friday Morning

———————

BRYSON COVENTRY'S ALARM CLOCK pulled him out of sleep with all the subtleness of a freight train. It sat safely on the other side of the bedroom, on the dresser, where he couldn't smash it with his fist—an old college trick.

It was only four in the morning.

Why'd he set it so early?

Then he remembered.

Megan Bennett.

He washed his face, popped in his contacts, and then checked to see if anyone left any messages on his home phone, office phone or cell phone. Fifteen different people had been told to call him immediately if Megan Bennett showed up.

No messages meant that she was still missing.

Not good.

Today would be critical.

He ruffled his hair with his fingers, threw on some gray sweats and jogged out into the chill of the night. He lived in a split-level house near the top of Green Mountain, third house from the end, backing to open space. That meant that flat streets were scarce, which meant that if you wanted to run around here you'd either be going up or down. He didn't particularly like either.

He started off too fast, as usual, but then eased into a sustainable pace as he began to wake up. The rest of the world still slept. Cats prowled and the occasional backyard dog, which would have completely ignored him by light of day, let out a good stiff warning bark just in case he was thinking about doing something stupid. Every once in a while he caught a whiff of pine scent, which reminded him of camping trips when he was a kid.

He ran through the darkness, clicking off the streetlights, letting his legs stretch and his lungs burn, thinking about how to find Megan Bennett.

One hour later he was showered and shaved and sitting at his desk downtown, the only living being in the room, with a cup of very hot, incredibly good coffee in front of him. He was wide-awake. The lack of sleep last night might start to weigh on him sometime this afternoon, but right now the caffeine was moving him forward just fine.

Megan Bennett.

Most missing persons turn out to be statistics if they don't turn up in the first thirty-six hours or so.

The oversized industrial clock on the wall said 5:45 in the morning and continued to twitch the seconds off even as he looked at it. Megan Bennett had been missing about thirty hours at this point.

The hour of truth was coming.

He grabbed a fresh notepad and uncapped a blue pen. Then he jotted down the things that needed to be done today on the case, in no particular order of priority.

PAUL KUBIAK, WHO COVENTRY CALLED AT HOME last night and asked to come in early this morning, showed up at the requested time, six-thirty. He had a half-eaten donut in one hand and a white bag in the other, presumably with more of the same.

He looked grumpy. "You owe me one," he warned.

"I owe you ten," Coventry agreed. "Thanks for coming."

Kubiak extended the bag. "Donut?"

Coventry paused, seriously considering it. "They low-cal?"

"Absolutely," Kubiak said, patting his big old truck-driver's gut. "That's how I keep this baby looking so fine."

Coventry grinned, pulled one out, white cake with chocolate frosting, and took a bite. Delicious. "So you can do this?"

"Shouldn't be a problem," Kubiak said. "You got the tape?"

"Yep."

"Then let's have a look."

Kubiak cued up the videotape that Coventry obtained from the Total last night, the one that showed the car pulling up to the pay phone that someone had used to call Megan Bennett from the night she disappeared. He downloaded it into a computer and then manipulated it with some type of software. What started out as a vague moving vehicle in the rain now showed up as a fairly clear stationary picture of a car on a 20" flat-panel screen.

"Looks like a Toyota," Kubiak offered, printing out a copy for reference.

Coventry nodded, not really knowing one way or the other. "They all look the same to me," he said, which was true.

Kubiak looked as if that was an understatement "That's because they are," he said. "Everyone out there building cars nowadays uses the same little cookie-cutter formula. There's no guts in the boardroom anymore, no Carol Shelbys, that's the problem."

Coventry nodded.

"You know what a donkey is?" Kubiak questioned.

"No, what?"

"It's a horse built by a committee."

Coventry smiled and repeated it to himself. It was worth saving.

"There are too many committees building cars, nowadays," Kubiak went on. "It's not like it was in the fifties and sixties when cars were actually different. When something came down the road back then, you could tell from a block away whether it was a Vette or a Mustang or a Goat or a Bird. I remember in eighth grade, I could tell you the name of every car on the street."

Coventry didn't totally agree. After all, no one would mistake a Hummer for a Mini Cooper, but he understood Kubiak's point. "Those days are gone," he offered.

Kubiak nodded, returned to the computer's main screen and clicked open another software program, something derivative of the insurance group's Auto Theft Book.

"Okay," he said. "Here we go."

He pulled up a checklist and marked a few of the search items—Car, Four Doors, Passenger Side—and punched enter. The screen filled up with about thirty vehicle photos, all profiled from the passenger side, page 1 of 23.

Within five minutes Kubiak matched a car to the one from the Total videotape.

"Toyota Camry," he said. He pulled up earlier models of the

same vehicle until he found a change in the body style. "Could be this year's model, last year's or the year before that," he concluded. "They used the same body style for all three years."

Coventry was impressed. "That's one slick program," he said.

"You like that, huh?" Kubiak questioned, obviously pleased with himself.

He nodded. "Very nice."

"It sure beats the old hit-and-miss books we used to use," Kubiak said.

Then he pulled up a screen that showed the color schemes that were available for Toyota Camry for the last three years. "Okay, we're getting a black and a dark blue exterior color available for all three years," he said. "The car we're looking for could be either one, it's too hard to tell with this black-and-white video."

"That's good enough," Coventry said. Then an additional thought popped into his head. "Is there any way to tell if we're looking for a rental?"

Kubiak took a bite of donut, chewed with his mouth open, examined the reference print and shook his head negative. "Not from this," he reported. "If we had a view of the glass, we'd probably be able to tell, since most rentals have some kind of decal on the window that tells you who to call if you lock the keys inside. It could be a rental, but there's no way to tell from what we have."

Coventry nodded.

"Okay. Good enough."

He looked at his watch, almost seven. Kate Katona should be in soon. "Thanks Paul, I owe you one."

"Just find the woman."

COVENTRY REALIZED THAT HE HADN'T REFILLED his coffee cup once since Kubiak arrived a half hour ago. He walked back down the stairs to homicide, poured a fresh cup and slurped it at his desk. Kate Katona showed up a few minutes later, before he could think of anything new to jot down, and he brought her up to speed.

They both agreed that Megan Bennett had to be the department's priority item today.

"What I'd like to do," Coventry said, "is start generating a list of male drivers, six feet and taller, who own a black or dark blue Camry, no more than three years old."

"Drivers not more than three years old? That seems improbable."

"No, the *car* isn't more than three years old."

She smiled. "I knew what you meant, but someone has to mess with you."

He shook his head.

Then she got serious and he watched her as she thought about it. "What we'll need to do is get a list of Camry owners first, which is easy. But then we'll have to pull their drivers licenses and get their heights. That'll take a little time."

He nodded.

"Perfect, because that's exactly what we have—little time."

That complete, Coventry was ready to move on to the next subject. "I'm thinking that we also want a press conference, to get a picture of Megan Bennett and a Toyota Camry on the news, starting with the noon news today if we can move that fast."

Katona agreed. "You going to be the talking head?"

He didn't mind the cameras, in fact he liked them. Also, it might make an impression on Kelly Parks if she saw him on TV.

Kelly Parks.

Why was she so much in his thoughts lately?

"I wouldn't care," he said, "because I know exactly what I want to say. But if it starts getting political, and everyone starts jockeying for position, I'm not going to have time to deal with it. I'll tell you what. Can you talk to the Public Information Officer and the Chief and get it in motion?"

"Will do."

"If it falls into my lap without too much trouble, I'll be happy to do it," Coventry said. "If it gets dramatic and starts generating a bunch of closed door meetings, just pull my name out of it."

"Will do."

She looked at him weird.

"What?" he questioned.

She looked down at his coffee cup and he followed her eyes to it. It sat there, empty as could be, and he just realized it had been like that for more than fifteen minutes.

He shook his head.

"I'm cutting back," he said. "Didn't you get the memo?"

"You can't do that."

"Why not?"

"Because whole economies will get out of sync," she said. "People in distant places are depending on you."

He smiled. "I never thought about that."

"They have children to feed," she added.

LATER THAT MORNING HE STOPPED IN unannounced at RK

Safety Consultants, where Megan Bennett worked. The offices were located on a second-floor walkup, above a bar and grill in LoDo. Only one of her coworkers was there, a man in his late twenties by the name of Andrew Andrews. He was bald on top and shaved the sides to match. He had an easygoing, friendly manner, and seemed to have just a touch of a gay edge to him. Not that Coventry cared; live and let live as far as he was concerned.

The office was filled with a variety of meters and pumps, plugged into outlets to keep charged. The space also had a wall of reference books, computers, printers, and five or six desks covered with papers. There was a dartboard on the north wall, two darts sticking in the wall, and a hockey stick leaning up in the back corner. It was clearly a place for work and not for impressing clients.

"We've all been interviewed over the phone, by someone called . . . Shalifa . . . I think," Andrews told Coventry.

"Detective Netherwood," he said. "I'm aware of that and in fact have read her reports word for word. We appreciate your cooperation. What I'd like to do at this point is look through Megan's desk, and her computer, just to see if there's anything that might be of help."

The young man nodded towards the last desk in the back. "That's hers," he said.

Coventry walked over to it and looked around while the young man booted up Megan's computer. Everything on the desktop and in her drawers appeared to be work-related. Nothing struck him as important to her disappearance.

"No pictures of guys," he said, looking at the young man. "Was she seeing anyone that you know of?"

Andrews shook his head negative. "She met some guy on

the 16th Street Mall last week that she got a little excited about, but they never exchanged numbers or anything. She's had some bad experiences with guys," he explained. "It seems to take her some time to warm up. And by the time she does, the guy's moving down the road. I keep telling her that guys don't like waiting around for it."

Coventry understood perfectly. "I used to have a three-date rule," he confessed. "If they hadn't put out by the third date, poof, I was gone." Then: "Of course, I don't do that anymore, I'm a lot more mature now."

The young man looked interested. "So now how many dates does it take now before the big poof?"

For some reason he thought of Kelly Parks, her slightly crooked smile, so damn nice. Was she the next woman he'd make a serious play for? Yes, she was. He just realized that this second. The thought almost startled him, as if it had been thrust on him by some outside force, and he really hadn't had much say in the matter one way or the other.

"I don't know," he said. "I'm still managing to do fairly well early on."

The young man laughed. "So as far as the three-date rule being gone, what you're saying is that it's gone *in theory*."

"No, it's gone *for real*," Coventry replied. "I just haven't had the opportunity to prove it yet."

"Someone get me a shovel, please."

On Megan Bennett's computer, they pulled up her directory and read the file names. Only one appeared to be of any interest, titled *Personal*, but all the sub-files dealt with taxes, recipes and other equally unhelpful stuff. Then they logged onto the Internet and read her e-mails. There was nothing of help there either.

He plopped down in the swivel chair and tried to think.

Now what?

Finally he said, "The guy she met on the mall last week, what was his name?"

"She never said."

"Mmm." Coventry cocked his head, thought about a few other things, then found himself coming back to it. "What'd she say about this guy?"

The young man seemed to retreat to wherever it was that that memory was stored. "Let's see, they were both eating lunch near each other and somehow they started talking. He was an FBI agent, which impressed her."

Coventry raised an eyebrow.

"An FBI agent?"

"Yes," Andrews confirmed. "Oh, right, now I remember. Somehow she mentioned that she went to Ohio State University. It turns out that this man actually worked on a case of an OSU woman who was murdered back when Megan went to school there. It was a pretty famous case on campus. I guess he told her there were two other OSU women who disappeared and were never found and were believed to have been killed by the same person who killed the first one."

"Really?"

The young man nodded. "That freaked her out. Anyway, this guy made an impression on her but, like I said, it was a one-shot deal."

"Did she describe this guy, physically that is?"

"No. She just said he was nice." Then: "She would most definitely have gone out with him, if he asked."

Coventry looked at him. "Would that have bothered you?"

The young man laughed. "Me? Dude, I'm gay. I thought

you knew that and that's why you've been hitting on me this whole time."

Coventry must have had a look on his face.

The young man laughed and said, "Dude, relax, I'm just messing with you."

SUDDENLY HIS CELL PHONE RANG. Katona's voice came through. "Bryson, where are you?"

She sounded panicked.

He knew immediately why she called. The press conference had been scheduled for eleven o'clock. He looked at his watch: 10:50. "Shit," he said. "I'm on my way." Then, as he was running out of the office and down the stairs, "Do me a favor and get the number of the FBI office that covers Columbus, Ohio."

"Why? What's going on?"

"I'll see you in ten minutes."

Chapter Eighteen

Day Five
Friday Morning

———————

YESTERDAY HAD BEEN A MAJOR BITCH. Megan Bennett, during her great escape attempt out there in the goddamn rainstorm, managed to bury the front end of the Camry right down to the axle. It took two filthy hours out of David Hallenbeck's life to undo that little trick.

Plus the sex with the woman yesterday had been disappointing. It'd been like screwing a Raggedy Ann doll. The way he'd build it up in his mind over the past few weeks, she'd be fighting him off like crazy. The lack of resistance was a major frustration. Afterwards, she said, *Hope you like Hepatitis C, asshole.*

But that was yesterday.

Today, at least so far, was a hundred percent better. Megan Bennett admitted that she had just been jerking him around with the Hepatitis C comment. Also, she was the one to actually initiate the sex this morning, after he showered her. No more limp noodle. Obviously, the whole thing was just a desperate attempt to try to ingratiate herself on the hopes that he'd be stupid enough to think that she actually liked him.

He wasn't that obtuse, but still it was nice. He was already thinking about tonight. Maybe he'd look around in the kitchen and see if he could find some candles.

THEY HAD CEREAL AND MILK FOR BREAKFAST. Then, after she promised to behave herself, he tied her hands behind her back and took her out for a walk in the foothills to get some exercise. The sky was one of the brightest blues he'd ever seen. Sunlight washed over everything and the temperature couldn't have been more perfect.

As they walked he kept a close eye on her.

With her hands tied she wouldn't be able to pick up a rock or a stick or anything, or be able to climb a tree.

He didn't think she'd be stupid enough to try to make a run for it. They both knew he was faster than her, even without her hands tied.

Screaming for help was something she might try.

But it was unlikely that they'd come across anyone and even less likely that she would actually see them, with her glasses long gone. And even if she did shout, he could knock her head off within a second. If some stupid fool actually did hear her and came over to investigate, he'd handle that too, with pleasure.

They followed the stream for more than a mile and ended up sitting on a boulder. She was quiet, keeping her face pointed away from him, staring at the movement of the water. After a time she said: "I have to use the facilities."

Hallenbeck immediately pictured some grand escape plan. If he untied her, what could she do? He looked around, couldn't think of anything obvious, but still didn't like the idea.

"Wait until we get back."

She shook her head and her eyes pleaded with him. "I've

already been holding it. I'm ready to bust, honest to God."

She really did have a desperate look on her face.

Damn it.

He stood up, grabbed her under the arm and pulled her up, then walked her over to the base of a Cottonwood, in an area where there was some brush cover. He reached under her oversized T-shirt, pulled her panties down to her ankles, and held her steady while she stepped out of them.

"Thanks," she said.

He waited, a few steps away, looking the other way but keeping her in his peripheral vision.

"That's better," she said, afterwards.

"No problem."

Then she let out a nervous laugh. "I've never done that in front of a man before."

For some reason that registered with him on some emotional level.

"Yeah, well, me too." Then: "Time to head back."

Her eyes looked into his and he could see the fear in them. "What are we going to do, when we get back?" she asked him.

That was a good question and he knew why she asked. She was trying to find out if he was going to kill her this afternoon, in which case this might be her last good chance to escape, in which case she'd have to try something now no matter how unlikely the outcome.

He didn't need that.

"I'm not sure yet," he said.

She seemed petrified and he grabbed her arm above the elbow, just as a precaution.

THEY WALKED IN SILENCE, A TENSE SILENCE. "I'll do anything you want," she said after they started getting closer to the farmhouse. Her voice trembled. "Anything, anything at all. You just say what you want and I'll do it. There's no need to kill me."

Another two hundred yards and they'd be back.

He felt like the king of the world, listening to this beautifully broken woman who now cowered in his presence. He had become her God, her universe, and for the first time she'd acknowledged it in no uncertain terms.

"I thought maybe we'd exercise," he suggested nonchalantly, meaning her God had spared her life, at least for the moment.

She looked at him and he could read the doubt in her eyes.

"Exercise?"

"Yeah," he told her. "I have a whole routine I do when I can't get to the gym. You don't need any equipment."

She nodded, demurely. "That sounds good."

"You take good care of yourself," he said. "I'll bet you work out four or five times a week. Am I right?"

She nodded. "When I can."

"See?" he questioned. Then he changed the subject: "Anything," he said. "You'd do anything? You really mean that?"

She couldn't agree fast enough. "Anything you want. Whatever you say."

He nodded. "We'll see."

They were almost at the house.

She must have felt like she was getting a toehold on him, because she said: "If you let me go, I swear to God I'll never say a word to anyone. You won't have to worry about me, I promise."

He felt like a cat with a mouse.

"You promise, huh?"

"On my mother's grave."

He frowned. "But you've seen my face," he observed.

A huge fact.

And they both knew it.

She looked like two cold hands had just picked her up and shaken her. "But I won't ever tell anyone what you look like."

"And you've figured out that I'm the person who killed those women at Ohio State," he added.

"It doesn't matter."

He put on an inquisitive college professor look, and said: "So let's see if I have this straight. You want me to let you go. And then when you're in a police room somewhere, totally safe and sound, with no chance in the world of me getting to you again, not in this or any other lifetime, and the dedicated and concerned little homicide cops and FBI agents ask you all their little questions, you're not going to say a single word, because you made a promise to me." He looked at her. "Do I have it right?"

She looked frantic. "I won't say a word and that's the truth. I would owe you that, if you let me go."

"But," Hallenbeck said, as if at a high school debate, "you'd have to tell them, otherwise I'd just do the same thing to some other poor woman, and you couldn't have that on your conscience now, could you?"

He expected her to say something but she didn't.

She just looked beaten.

They were at the house now. "Well, we'll see," he said. Then, thoughtfully: "Maybe we'll be able to work something out. Who knows?"

HE OPENED THE BACK DOOR QUIETLY, stuck his head inside and listed for sounds. Nothing. Then he pulled her around to the front of the house to see if there were any cars or other signs of life.

Nothing.

Just a gorgeous spring afternoon in Colorado.

Inside, he untied her, told her to take off the T-shirt, which she promptly did, and watched the wonderful muscles in her body work while he let her make a pitcher of lemonade.

Suddenly his cell phone rang. He pulled it out of his front pants pocket and looked at the number. It was the South Beach brat, Jay Yorty.

This call could mean money.

"Okay," he told her. "This is your first test. I'm going to answer this with you standing right there. If you scream anything out, then so much for your promise."

"No problem," she said. "You'll see."

He pressed the green button on the phone, giving her a warning look.

"Jay," he said in as upbeat a voice as he could muster. "Are you saving me any of those South Beach women or are you getting them all lined up for yourself?"

Yorty sounded high on coke, but eventually got to the point. He was glad he caught Hallenbeck still in Denver. He wanted him to go back to Donald Vine's and see if he could get as good a deal on the '57 Chevy as he did on the Porsche.

It wouldn't hurt to have a '57 in his collection, if it was the right one and the right price.

Hallenbeck watched as Megan Bennett poured lemonade

from the pitcher into two glasses filled with ice. She walked over and handed one to him.

"Here you go," she said.

He took it and drained half the glass.

Yorty said, "Sounds like you're busy getting lucky, so I'm signing off, partner. Call me tomorrow with some good news on that '57. Okay?"

"You got it."

HALLENBECK PUNCHED OFF, SET THE PHONE DOWN on the table and looked at the woman. "That must have been frustrating, not knowing whether to shout out or not."

"No, I told you . . ."

"You should have," he told her.

God it felt great telling her that.

Suddenly his cell phone rang again. Incredibly, the woman jumped for it, astonishingly fast, and grabbed it just before he did.

Goddamn bitch!

She bolted out of the kitchen, phone in hand, looking at it as she ran, trying to find the right button to push.

He all but ran through the kitchen table and lunged for her.

He missed and landed flat on the floor.

Damn!

The wind shot out of his lungs and his muscles didn't want to work.

He got up by sheer force and stumbled.

She ran out the front door and shouted into the phone.

Her voice was frantic.

Help me please!

I'm Megan Bennett!

I'm in a farmhouse!

He's going to kill me!

He charged after her, his brain burning with a thousand fires.

The lying little whore just made her last mistake!

Chapter Nineteen

Day Five
Friday Noon

COVENTRY TOOK A BITE OF A SUBWAY SANDWICH, turkey with everything except mayo, as he and Kate Katona stared at the tube. The Channel 7 noon news kicked off with the Megan Bennett story, thirty beautiful seconds worth.

"That was intense," she said. "You can look downright mean sometimes, do you know that?"

Coventry shrugged.

"This is it," he said. Megan Bennett would be one of the top news stories for at least the next three or four days. Someone out there could pick up the phone any minute and give them the critical lead they needed.

Katona wrinkled her forehead. "So what was that deal with your reporter friend, Sarah Upjohn, when the press conference was over?"

Coventry looked as innocent as he could but had a pretty good idea what she was talking about. "What do you mean?"

"I saw her rubbing the twins all over you."

"That was an accident," Coventry explained.

"Oh, *please*," Katona said.

He shrugged. "The twins have a mind of their own. What can I say?"

She looked incredulous. "You know what I'd like to do? I'd like to buy her for what she's worth and sell her for what she thinks she's worth. I could use the money."

Coventry chuckled, then added, "You could retire."

"We could both retire."

SHE PUSHED A PIECE OF PAPER ACROSS THE DESK. "The FBI number you asked for," she reminded him. "Are you calling in a profiler or something?"

Coventry picked it up then dialed the number of the FBI Field Office, Cincinnati, Ohio, which had jurisdiction over Columbus. While it rang he shook his head.

"No, something else."

After talking to a short string of people, more than he really had time for, he was finally connected with someone who could actually help him, namely the Assistant Special Agent in Charge, Charles Miller. Coventry filled him in on the Megan Bennett case and the fact that she reportedly bumped into an FBI agent shortly before she disappeared.

"So the way I understand what happened," Coventry explained, "according to this coworker of Megan Bennett, is that this FBI agent was working on a case involving the murder of an OSU woman, as well as two other abductions that were believed to be related. He then manages to bump into Megan Bennett, halfway around the world, years later, who just happened to have gone to the same school where the killings took place. Shortly after that conversation she disappears. Call me skeptical, but there are a few more coincidences going on here than I'm used to."

Coventry felt a long pause on the other end of the phone.

"This is interesting," Miller said. "Very interesting. I can confirm that this office was in fact heavily involved in the investigation of an OSU student by the name of Beth Williamson, which would have been, let's see, I'm guessing about five years ago now. The person assigned with primary responsibility for the case is Special Agent Sam Dakota, who just happens to be one of our best. But he wasn't in Denver last week, or even last year."

"He wasn't?" Coventry questioned.

"No," Miller said. "He's right here in town and has been. Of course, everyone in the office knows about the case, so I'm trying to think of who else might have been in Denver recently, but, quite frankly, no names are jumping up. No one's there on assignment there out of this office, that's for sure. And as for vacations, no, no agents have been off for at least three weeks."

"Interesting," Coventry said. "But there was an actual case, though? Involving an OSU woman?"

Coventry took another bite of the Subway as soon as he stopped talking and chewed with a purpose. He was starved for some reason.

Katona, who was listening to the conversation, made a face at him, which meant he was chewing with his mouth open.

"Oh, most definitely," Miller confirmed. "This is all extremely confidential, which you already know, but here's the long and short of it. The OSU woman, Beth Williamson, drops off the face of the earth one day. The Columbus police find her about three weeks later. Someone sealed her in a 55-gallon drum, naked and without any food or water, and set her out in the woods, about two hundred yards off an old gravel road.

Nice guy that he is, he punched air holes in the top. Needless to say, she lived a whole lot longer than she wanted to."

"Jesus," Coventry said.

"Yeah," Miller said. "Exactly. The Columbus P.D. had never seen anything like that before and brought us in when they hit a wall."

"Yeah?"

"Oh," Miller said, "let me back up. The information about the drum was held close to the vest. The official statement, as far as public information goes, is that she was found in the woods."

"Understood."

"Okay, so we start working the case pretty hard," Miller continued. "We find out that the deceased was enrolled in an upper-level psychology class taught by a professor by the name of . . . ah, crap, I can't remember his name . . . but it's not important anyway. What is important is that this professor, as part of his class, had his students write a couple of paragraphs describing the way they'd most hate to die. He was going to do some kind of correlation to match the responses to personality traits or some such bullshit. It was all psychobabble to me. Anyway, what do you think the Williamson woman wrote about?"

"I think I know," Coventry said.

"Well, then you're a smart fellow," Miller said, "She wrote about being stuffed inside a drum and dumped in the woods to rot a slow death."

"Damn."

"Major damn," Miller agreed.

"So what did you come up with?"

A pause.

"Special Agent Dakota would be the best person to answer

that," Miller said. "He'll be back in the office later this afternoon, and I'll have him call you if you'd like."

"I'd like."

"The investigation was exhaustive to say the least. We also got the media involved and that generated hundreds of tips. We investigated the professor as a suspect but eventually dismissed him. The file takes up eight file cabinet drawers, to give you an idea."

Coventry was impressed. "The biggest case I ever had only took up three."

"There you go, then."

"Did you get any information on the suspect's size?" Coventry questioned. "The reason I ask is, we have reason to believe that the person who took Megan Bennett out here in Denver may be a pretty big guy, I'm talking somewhere in the six-four range."

"You know," Miller said. "I'm trying to think. Special Agent Dakota would know this better than me, but I'm pretty sure we pegged our suspect as extremely strong, based on some calculations we did relating to the movement of the drum. I'm not sure that we ever translated that to a body height, though."

"Good enough," Coventry said. "What about the other two abductions?"

"Okay," Miller continued. "Two other female students were also both from this professor's psychology class. They disappeared after the Williamson woman, in separate incidents. The first one disappeared the next semester, which would have been the fall semester, and the second one disappeared during the spring semester the next year. Neither one of them was ever found. In fact, we were never even able to identify the locations they were abducted from."

"But both had been enrolled in this professor's class?" Coventry questioned.

"Yes," Miller said. "The three cases are definitely connected. Some day their bodies will show up and we'll be able to verify it. Right now we need fresh blood to move the investigation forward."

"Well, it looks like I might have that for you. One question," he said. "Do you remember whether Megan Bennett was in this psychology class?"

"Not off the top of my head," Miller said. "But I can look it up pretty easy and get back to you."

"Any chance you could do that right away?"

"That's two questions."

Coventry chuckled. "You FBI guys don't miss a thing, do you?"

"That's three questions."

FIFTEEN MINUTES LATER THE FAX MACHINE gurgled. Coventry walked over and pulled out two pages. The first was a cover sheet from Special Agent Charles Miller.

> *Lieutenant Coventry: Megan Bennett was in fact enrolled in the psychology class we talked about. Attached please find a copy of the paper that she submitted to her professor. Looks like you have our fresh blood.*

Coventry turned to the next page and read the description that Megan Bennett had provided as to the way she'd most hate to die.

He walked back to his desk, set the fax on top of a pile of

papers and sank into his chair. Then he closed his eyes and started to work out the details of what it would be like to go like that.

Katona's voice suddenly appeared from out of nowhere.

"Bryson, what is it?"

He opened his eyes and found her standing in front of his desk.

"Picture this as a way to die," he said. "You're strapped into a chair and you have a helmet over your head, sealed at you neck. Air is fed into the helmet from a blower. As long as the blower's on, no problem, you have plenty of air. But the blower shuts off every five minutes. You have a switch in your hand, taped there, so you can't drop it. You press the switch and the blower kicks back on and runs for another five minutes. No problem. Except you sit there hour after hour after hour and sooner or later you start to get sleepy. You need to stay awake to keep turning the blower back on. Now you're up twenty-four hours, now thirty-six, now forty-eight. Now you're hallucinating and fighting like a madman to not fall asleep. But you know you can't stay awake forever."

She looked troubled.

"Sounds like something out of a Hitchcock movie," she said.

He nodded.

"Yeah. On one of his more morbid days."

Chapter Twenty

Day Five
Friday Evening

THE BASS POUNDED LIKE A HUNDRED TRIBAL DRUMS and the music bounced around inside the club like a wild animal. Kelly Parks spun her way through the middle of the dance floor, engulfed by a Friday night crowd of at least a thousand people who were partying like it was the last Friday they'd ever see. Couples, guys, girls on girls, you name it.

Raw, uninhibited, sexual energy.

Intoxicating and intoxicated.

Strippers gyrated and spread on more stages than she could count, working the crowds of catcalling men and women, in fact lots of women, drinking their beer and laying their money down.

And if men were more your style, then have no fear. Over in one corner they had a stage set up with male dancers. There must have been at least fifty women over there screaming and getting up-close-and-personal.

On the dance floor some of the women were starting to drop their tops as well, which seemed to be perfectly fine with everyone.

It was one big happy grind.

Kelly Parks made it all the way across the club to the lady's room. There were about ten other women in there already, putting their packages back into some semblance of shape. She found an empty stall, sat down, pulled her cell phone out and called Bryson Coventry.

This was undoubtedly the stupidest idea she ever had.

But screw it.

Something was either going to happen or it wasn't.

And she was in the mood to find out which.

He answered on the second ring.

She tried to compose herself so she didn't sound too drunk. "Bryson," she said, "Kelly Parks here. I saw you on the news today. You looked stressed, so I went out and had a drink for you, and then another one, and then another one. And now I'm drunk and it's all your fault."

"Oh, really? My fault, huh?" He sounded playful, like he wasn't just glad she called but *really* glad she called.

"Yes, your fault," she confirmed. "And now you owe me a drink to make up for it."

She felt the pause on the other end. "Where are you at?" he asked her.

"A place called B.T.'s."

"The strip-club?"

"Uh huh," she said. "You know it?"

She heard Coventry laugh. "The one on Evans?" he questioned.

"Yes."

"Nope, never heard of it."

She laughed. "So are you going to come down here and buy me a drink or what?"

BACK AT HOMICIDE, BRYSON COVENTRY HUNG UP the phone, looked at the clock and realized that it was 8:30 on Friday night and he was the only one there. Technically, he was reviewing, for the third time, the phone tips that came in during the day on the Megan Bennett case. So far, they hadn't received anything that really grabbed him. Someone reported seeing a large man driving a black or dark blue Camry way down south, on Santa Fe Drive, earlier in the evening, but there wasn't a woman or anyone else with him. The word was out to make contact with the car if it was ever seen again, but other than that there wasn't much more they could do about it.

And right now Kelly Parks was feeling no pain and wanting to see him.

That was fine with him, because at this point, his brain was dead anyway. Nothing of substance would be coming out of it until tomorrow morning.

He went down to the workout room, showered, pulled a pair of fresh khakis and an aqua-green cotton shirt out of his locker, slipped into them and towel-dried his hair. He didn't have a hairdryer so he just fluffed it up with his fingers the best he could.

TWENTY MINUTES LATER HE WAS AT B.T.'S, paying the cover at the door and walking inside. The music, movement, smoke and energy washed over him, and took him back to that time in his life when he used to live for Friday nights. Not more than three steps inside, a beautiful woman in classy eveningwear asked him if he wanted a beer. She stood behind some kind of cart filled with ice, like something you'd see at a company picnic except on an industrial scale.

"Why not?" he said. "Bud Light, please."

She reached down and pulled one out. "I'm Amanda," she said as she handed it to him.

"Bryson," he told her.

"Bryson," she repeated. "I like that."

He tipped her a dollar and took a swig. Damn, that was good. Almost frozen. Probably the best beer he ever tasted.

After milling around through the crowd, he finally spotted Kelly Parks seated at the bar near the far end, talking to one of the dancers.

He walked up and leaned into the conversation.

"Evening, ladies," he said.

Kelly Parks stood up, put her arm around his waist, and said to her friend: "This is the guy who wants to see my butterfly flapping, Bryson Coventry." Then to him: "And this is my friend, Jeannie Dannenberg . . . oops . . . I'm sorry . . . Oasis . . ."

Coventry felt like responding to the tattoo remark but didn't have a chance. The dancer, Oasis, had already backed into him and was grinding an extraordinary muscled ass into his crotch.

He feigned innocence and looked at Kelly. "She's very friendly."

Kelly nodded.

"Very."

He expected the woman to stop any second, but instead she turned around, put her arms around his neck, and rubbed her breasts on him. Then she put her mouth by his ear and gave him a catlike growl.

He didn't exactly know what to do. "Very friendly," he repeated.

Kelly Parks laughed and looked like she suddenly had an idea.

"Private dance!" she said.

Oasis looked at her and got excited.

Coventry wasn't quite sure if that was a good idea. He took two bills out of his front shirt pocket, tucked them in the woman's G-string, and said: "Let me get a few beers down first, then we'll see."

Oasis kissed him on the cheek followed by a slow, wet lick. "I'll be back for you later, cowboy."

When he turned to Kelly Parks she was looking at him. "She's a great gal," she said.

Coventry watched her walk away and couldn't agree more. More than a few women had turned their charms on him over the years and she most definitely ranked right up there.

Jeannie Dannenberg.

Where had he heard that name before?

"Where do you know her from?" he questioned.

Kelly Parks looked as if she didn't want to talk about anything right now. "Around," she said. Then she grabbed his belt, pulled him in close and put her arms around his neck. Her legs were spread and he was standing between them. She brought her mouth within inches of his and he felt the warmth of her breath on his face.

"I'm tired of being scared," she said. "I want you to protect me tonight."

Coventry raised an eyebrow.

"How much protection are you looking for, exactly?"

"It's not how much, it's how many," she said.

Chapter Twenty-One

Day Five
Friday Evening

MICHAEL NORTHWAY, IT TURNED OUT, lived in a Cherry Hills enclave where the houses just happened to be slightly more than mere protection from the elements. A gated community; no riffraff allowed, thank you very much. Northway's place was located on one of the primo lots, a cul-de-sac with three well-separated houses, backing to open space.

A blanket of clouds kept the night darker than dark.

Absolutely perfect.

David Hallenbeck, dressed in all things black, picked his way through the terrain towards Northway's place.

Leaving Megan Bennett alone for a few hours shouldn't be a problem. He'd doped her up real good, handcuffed her hands behind her back, laid her face down on the bed, hogtied her with more wraps than you could believe, ran a chain from the bed through her handcuffs, locked the chain, and then put the breathable gag on her.

She'd be as uncomfortable as hell.

But screw her.

That's what she gets for trying to escape.

She's lucky he didn't put the helmet on her stupid little head right then and there.

The open space behind Northway's house consisted primarily of native grasses, still laying flat from the winter. It was easier to walk through than he predicted.

Hallenbeck's heart pounded as he moved closer.

Northway's house was the middle one in the cul-de-sac. In a perfect world, there wouldn't have been gates, and he would have had a chance to drive by during the day to check things out.

But no biggie.

He could adapt.

HE COULDN'T HELP BUT SMILE at his good fortune as he picked his way through the darkness. He had that tremendous sense of relief and gratefulness that comes from having a near-miss and ending up totally unscathed. Megan Bennett's screams for help into the cell phone had been for nothing. In all the fury she'd punched the off button. A connection had never been made. It turns out that the call had been from Jay Yorty with a follow-up thought on the '57 Chevy. Hallenbeck called him back, just to be on the safe side, and confirmed that Yorty didn't have a clue. All he knew is that the connection didn't go through so he'd left a message.

That had been a near-miss of considerable proportions.

Someone or something was definitely on Hallenbeck's side.

Not that Hallenbeck believed that there was a God or higher being or any crap like that. Quite the opposite. The concept of God was for those losers and weaklings who couldn't face the thought that humans, like every other animal on the planet, were mortal. You live, you die. Period, exclamation point. When you die, the lights to out, just like when you sleep, except longer.

God? What a joke.

If cows could think and talk they'd invent gods in the form of cows, and cows would be the only living creatures to have an afterlife to go to, because they were so special.

What a crock of shit.

One thing for sure regarding Megan Bennett, there'd be no more risk-taking. Looking back on the afternoon walk, Hallenbeck couldn't help but admit just how incredibly dumb-ass stupid that had been. In hindsight, things could have gone wrong a hundred different ways.

He needed to get back to his roots. It his early days he wouldn't even think about taking the risks he'd taken in the last couple of years. Back then he planned everything to the last pathetic detail. All the risk was engineered out of the equation. He spent all his spare time reading textbooks on criminal investigation and forensic evidence. He knew what to do and what not to do. Now, shit, he probably hadn't read a single book like that in over two years. True, he gained an awful lot of real-life experience in the meantime, but that was no excuse to let the base knowledge get dull.

Success can get you cocky.

And cocky *will* get you caught, sooner or later.

In fact, one of the things he promised himself, years ago, was that he'd never get complacent. He'd always practice maximum risk reduction. But here he was, down the road, flaunting the fundamentals like he was bulletproof.

That stupid shit had to stop right now and it would.

THE OUTLINE OF A HUGE YUCCA CACTUS loomed directly in his path, a shape that was just ever so slightly darker than the blackness around it, and he avoided it. He'd fallen on one of those prickly bastards before. They were no fun. Their sole function on earth is to poke your eyes out.

Northway's house was getting closer, probably not more than two hundred yards off, although it was hard to tell exactly in these conditions. It was time to start listening for dogs. They'd be able to pick up his scent and movement anytime now.

Even this, he thought, was stupid.

There were better, safer ways to deal with Michael Northway.

But they wouldn't necessarily have the same impact or make the same statement, now, would they? There's nothing quite like having someone suddenly jump out of the shadows of your own home to get your attention in no uncertain terms. He'd seen that look before and it was always the same. It comes straight from the gut, down in those childhood recesses where the Boogieman lives, and shoots right out your eyes.

He pictured the upcoming expression on Northway's face and felt a wave of euphoria wash over him.

God, this was going to be so sweet.

So, so long in coming.

Most people, stupidly, don't keep their backyards lit up at night and Michael Northway turned out to be no exception. Hallenbeck paused at the edge of the yard and studied Northway's house, as well as the adjoining ones, looking for movement, lights going on or off, or any other signs of life or activity.

It was ten o'clock on Friday night and Northway didn't appear to be home. That much Hallenbeck could surmise from experience: the unchanging interior lights, the lack of any perceptible movement inside the house, the absence of any sounds or vibrations.

Perfect.

Plus he knew something about Northway's personality. Northway was forever the politician, forever the schmoozer, forever ingratiating himself with the powers that be. And Friday night, just about everywhere on the planet, is prime time to see and be seen. If Northway was running true to form, he was probably at some fancy-schmancy highbrow party right now eating finger-foods, sipping imported white wine and looking down thousand-dollar dresses to see if those fleshy little mounds underneath were original equipment or aftermarket.

But he wouldn't be out too late, either.

He liked to be in the office early Saturday mornings to keep a close eye on his little kingdom.

HALLENBECK PUT ON THE SKI MASK and latex gloves and then crept from the open space into the lawyer's back yard, hugging a string of Ponderosa pines near the left edge of the property. The big issue now is whether there were motion detector lights.

He instinctively padded the knife, a first-class weapon with an eight-inch serrated blade, sheathed and hidden from view under his windbreaker. It was right there where it should be.

He used to carry a .45 too, back in the early days, unregistered and unmarked, a little gift that he picked up for himself from a Chicago crack-head for a couple of hundred bucks. But carrying that around was about next to impossible nowadays. There was no way in hell you could take it anywhere if you were flying. And even having it around the house anymore was a liability. So he chucked it into Lake Erie out near Mentor Headlands two years ago and purchased a legitimate, registered unit that he kept legally at home, under his bed in a box.

He shot the new one plenty, and sometimes carried it with him when he didn't have to fly, but never used it yet in an event. It was still a virgin to that extent.

He crept towards the house.

Nothing happened that he didn't want to happen.

No dogs.

No lights.

No neighbors.

No nothing.

Before he knew it he was at the back of the house, which was an enormous structure made of designer stucco and stone, with a walkout basement. He looked in the windows and tried the sliding glass door. It was locked.

Staying low, he walked up the deck stairs from the ground level to the first floor of the house. They deposited him outside the kitchen. Again, the doors and windows were locked. There was a second story deck above him, but it wasn't connected to this level by stairs. It probably came off the master bedroom.

Hallenbeck muscled his way up to it.

As he predicted, the deck came off the bedroom. The sliding glass door was open a couple of inches, no doubt to let out the afternoon heat buildup. Oh yeah. He opened it, stepped inside and stood there taking deep, controlled breaths.

No sound or vibration came from anywhere.

There were no illuminated lights in any of the second floor rooms. He quickly checked each space just to confirm that someone wasn't up there sleeping. They were all empty.

Hallenbeck couldn't help but note how spectacular the interior finishes were. The master bathroom was right out of a magazine.

The lawyer certainly lived large.

He spent the next twenty minutes checking out the rest of the house. The place had to be at least ten thousand square feet, with all the necessities of life, including an indoor hot-tub, a sauna, a media room, bedrooms and bathrooms galore, wet-bars, a game room, fireplaces, and a massive kitchen with the obligatory granite countertops, distressed cabinets and stainless steel appliances.

He eventually settled into a chair in the study, in the dark, where he could see the street.

ABOUT A HALF HOUR LATER A WHITE MERCEDES sedan pulled into the driveway. Hallenbeck could see that Northway was alone and heard the garage door open.

A moment later he saw his target walk to the mailbox, unlock it, grab a handful of mail and thumb through it as he headed back towards the house. He wore a suit with an expensive hang to it.

Hallenbeck stayed in the den, in the sweet darkness, put the ski mask back on, pulled the knife out of its sheath and set it in his lap.

He could hear Northway in the house now. He was in the kitchen, messing with something in the Sub Zero.

A couple of minutes later Northway walked by the open double doors of the den.

"Hello," Hallenbeck said without getting up.

Northway jumped. There was just enough light on his face for Hallenbeck to see his expression.

It was priceless.

The fear.

The exploding brain cells.

Hallenbeck knew that Northway wouldn't run. Northway would feel mentally superior to just about anyone and would probably feel that his best chance was to talk his way out of the situation. But if he did run, so much the sweeter.

"Do you know who I am?" Hallenbeck questioned.

Northway didn't answer at first, but instead took off his suit jacket and draped it over his arm, and walked into the den.

"I have an idea," he answered.

Hallenbeck looked at him and felt the hate rise. "We're going to spend a little time together and decide whether you're going to live or die."

Northway nodded.

"Fair enough," the lawyer said.

Chapter Twenty-Two

Day Six
Saturday Morning

BRYSON COVENTRY WOKE TO A JET-BLACK ROOM slightly before six, flipped onto his back with his eyes still closed, and let the thoughts roll into his head while his body took another few minutes to get used to the idea of getting up.

Kelly Parks lay next to him, sound asleep on top of the covers, wearing nothing.

One thing he knew, right now, this minute. He wanted to spend a lot more time with her. He wanted to do things with her and find out all about her.

But today wasn't his.

He owed today to Megan Bennett.

He showered and dressed on the lower level so he wouldn't wake Kelly, took one last look at her, left a note on the kitchen table and headed out the door, making sure it locked.

He was at his desk, with the lights on and coffee in hand, by seven o'clock. At this point Megan Bennett had been missing fifty-four hours. Charles Miller and Sam Dakota from the FBI had been scheduled to take a red-eye into Denver last night and, if things were still on track, should be showing up sometime around nine this morning.

DETECTIVE NETHERWOOD WANDERED IN about eight o'clock, said "'Morning, darling," and headed for the coffee. Coventry walked over, needing a refill. Needing lots of refills, in fact.

"Where do I know the name Jeannie Dannenberg from?" he asked.

Shalifa was searching around the coffee area and looked stressed. "I thought you were supposed to bring donuts and bagels," she said.

Shit.

He'd forgotten all about that.

"Who delivers?" he questioned. "Anyone?"

She shook her head in disbelief. "I didn't eat breakfast this morning because there was supposed to be donuts here."

"God, I'm sorry." Which was absolutely true.

He'd screwed up.

She looked at him as if she were bailing him out yet another one. "Okay, I'm going to go get them, because I'm too starved to do anything else." Then: "God."

He pulled two twenties out of his wallet, handed them over, hugged her and told her he wouldn't trade her for two good mules. She stuck her tongue out and headed towards the door. Then she turned around.

"Remember when you asked me to find out who was in D'endra Vaughn's life a year ago, to get a lead on where that mystery money came from?"

He did indeed remember that, very well. In fact, he'd been hoping to get some time to talk to her about that.

"Yes."

"Jeannie Dannenberg is on that list," Netherwood said.

"She is?"

"Yep. Don't you remember?"

"So she was a friend of D'endra Vaughn?"

"Yep."

Coventry didn't know exactly what that meant yet, but did know that it was something big.

"Have you talked to her yet?"

"It's on my list of things to do," Shalifa said. "Why?"

"I met her last night," he told her.

"You did?"

"She's a dancer. She works at B.T.'s."

"B.T.'s the strip-club?"

"Right."

"Let me get this straight. You were on the six o'clock news, and then at a strip-club, on the same night?" She looked incredulous. "Tell me it was for work."

He grinned. "Actually, I was butterfly hunting, or vice versa, I'm not sure exactly which."

"And?"

"And what?"

"And did you get them flapping, or what?"

He shrugged. "Can't say."

"That means you did," she said, turning to leave. Then over her shoulder: "Donut man."

WHEN SHALIFA LEFT, COVENTRY TURNED ON his computer and found that Jeannie Dannenberg was in the system, with a misdemeanor charge of marijuana possession two years ago.

The interesting thing was her photo. This was definitely the woman he met last night.

Oasis.

Okay.

So Jeannie Dannenberg was a friend of the dead woman, D'endra Vaughn. And Jeannie Dannenberg was a friend of Kelly Parks, apparently a pretty good friend, judging by the events of last night.

So does that mean Kelly Parks knows D'endra Vaughn? If yes, she lied to him, back in her office Monday, when she said she didn't know anything about the dead woman.

If that was the case, what was she hiding?

One thing he knew for sure.

Kelly Parks was going to get some very pointed questions coming her way.

THE FBI ARRIVED RIGHT ON TIME, a little before nine.

Charles Miller, the man Coventry talked to on the phone yesterday, was a stately man with white hair and white teeth, somewhere in his early sixties, with the friendly air of a good people-person. He was focused and extremely interested in the case, but not fanatic, more like someone who had half-an-eye on retirement. He was the Assistant Agent in Charge of the Cincinnati Field Office.

With him was Special Agent Sam Dakota, a bodybuilder type, in his early thirties, with a hungry look in his eyes. He wasn't just here for the hunt, he was here for the catch, no doubt about it. Don't let the suit fool you.

Coventry noted that he might be a problem.

Most of the work they'd be reviewing was his. Coventry

wasn't sure how well he'd take to outsiders looking in.

The third member of the group turned out to be Dr. Leanne Sanders, Ph.D., an attractive woman in her late forties, wearing nylons over step-master legs, dressed to impress, with a wedding ring on her left hand the size of a small basketball. She clearly wasn't working for the money. She was a Supervisory Special Agent assigned to the National Center for the Analysis of Violent Crime (NCAVC) at Quantico, Virginia; a profiler, and apparently one of some repute within the agency, based on the way Miller deferred to her. Her doctorate degree was in Behavioral Sciences.

After donuts, coffee and chitchat, they got down to business. Coventry had called in half the Homicide Unit and every person, without exception, was glad to be there, even on Saturday morning. The Megan Bennett case was something new to them. It wasn't often that they had a chance to actually save someone. There must have been at least fifteen people in the room.

The meeting was designed to be a show-and-tell by both sides, a swapping of brain trusts.

SPECIAL AGENT SAM DAKOTA TOOK THE LEAD, since he was the nuts-and-bolts guy from the FBI's side of the equation.

"First," he told the group, "and some of you already know this, but just so the record's clear, we've established that the person you're looking for, and the one we're looking for, are indeed one and the same. Apparently your guy had an altercation outside Ms. Bennett's house with three other gentlemen and ended up leaving us quite a few good blood pools. You were fortunate, because this guy, in our experience, has been

199

extremely careful about forensic evidence. In our first case, the one involving the murder of Beth Williamson, we were able to come up with a few stray hair roots, and that was it as far as trace evidence goes. The DNA from the blood of your guy, and from our hair root, do in fact match. We were able to get a solid confirmation of that late last night." He added: "It really helped that you had the foresight to get that blood typified right away. That eliminated downtime."

For the next hour, Special Agent Sam Dakota outlined the highlights of the investigation that the FBI had undertaken with respect to the three OSU cases that they believed to be related. "We have reason to believe that the suspect lives within driving distance of Columbus," he noted at one point, "or at least did at that time."

"Why do you say that?" Kate Katona questioned.

"Good question," Dakota said. "The three crimes happened approximately six months apart from one another. We spent more hours than we'd like to admit obtaining and then cross-referencing airline manifests, rental car records and hotel records, to try to find the same person coming into town more than once in the relevant time frames. We were never able to find a match." He must have seen Katona about to ask a follow-up question, because he quickly added: "That doesn't mean that he isn't using aliases, of course. And it's certainly possible that he drove in every time from somewhere far away. But our better guess is that he lives somewhere in Ohio, maybe Cleveland or Cincinnati. Maybe even Columbus."

Coventry perked up. "This could be our big break," he said. "He doesn't know we've connected the Denver and Ohio cases. We need airline manifests going back—let's be overly conservative, say a month—and find out who's flown into DIA or Colorado Springs from Ohio. We need to get into the local rental car records too and find out if anyone from Ohio has rented a Toyota Camry."

"Why a Toyota Camry?" Charles Miller questioned.

Coventry filled him in on the work that led to that particular finding.

Everyone agreed that the airline manifests and rental car records should be given the highest priority. That work could lead them to a name, which, with any luck, might even lead them to a hotel room, or a photograph that they could blast all over the news.

Coventry felt cautiously optimistic.

There was a chance that a net was actually being thrown.

"Let's also get a BOLO out on a Toyota Camry with Ohio plates, too, just in case he drove out here," Coventry added. "That way we'll have all the bases covered."

SAM DAKOTA EVENTUALLY RELINQUISHED the floor to Dr. Leanne Sanders, for a summary of her profile of the suspect. "Let me just jump to the conclusions," she said, "without all the whys and wherefores, unless you want them. Male, white, twenty-two to thirty-eight, well educated and exceptionally well versed in criminal investigation and forensic science."

"Meaning a cop?" Shalifa Netherwood questioned.

"Possibly," Dr. Sanders confirmed. "It's interesting that when he talked to Megan Bennett the day or two before he took her, he told her he was an FBI agent. He wouldn't have any reason to believe, at that time, that that statement could come back to haunt him. So maybe he is, or was, one of ours, or applied to be one of ours. We'll search our files; it helps to know he's six-four or so."

Detective Richardson, who had been eying the box of donuts all morning, finally gave in and grabbed one. Coventry chuckled inside, amazed that the detective had managed to hold out as long as he did.

Dr. Sanders continued. "He hates women, deep down, that's a given." She then changed the tone of her voice from an analytical one to a hopeful one. "But here's the weird thing. Put yourself in his shoes. He's out there in the night, stalking Megan Bennett. He sees three men breaking into her house. He could have just scared them off. But instead, he attacks. And I mean he violently attacks. Why?"

Coventry could see everyone pondering the question but no one answered.

"It could be that he was protecting her," she said. "Now it's possible that he simply viewed Megan Bennett as his property at that time and wasn't about to put up with anyone messing around with what was his. But he could have done that without killing them."

Coventry raised an eyebrow.

"Protecting her so he could personally kill her, or protecting her because he had feelings for her?"

The woman wrinkled her forehead. "Either. But my guess is a little of both. I think he had some kind of bond to that woman before he attacked those three men, possibly from the meeting he had with her the day or two before. From what I understand, her coworker said that she would have gone out with him. She obviously liked him to some extent, and he would have picked up on that and liked her back. And then, after he attacks the three intruders, that bond would have become even stronger. He starts to see himself as her knight in shinning armor. She owes him her life which in turn makes his life worth more."

"So, what does this mean, to us?" Sergeant Katona questioned. "In concrete terms."

"To cut to the chase," Dr. Sanders answered, "it could mean that Megan Bennett is still alive. I'm hoping that she's thinking clearly enough to be able to tell that he has some kind of emotional attachment to her and then be able to play on that to keep herself alive." She paused, then added: "But that's temporary, at best. Sooner or later this guy is going to take her down hard. The only question is when."

Chapter Twenty-Three

Day Six
Saturday Evening

KELLY PARKS' JOB TONIGHT was to be a sexy yet sophisticated vision of nylons, smiles and Giorgio, and hang on the every word of Paul Robbins and Andrew Dinger for an hour or so over drinks.

They were two VPs from the target client, Satellite Omega, a Fortune One Hundred conglomerate in the business of providing satellite communication services.

They were in town to be schmoozed.

And Michael Northway had chosen her to be a part of the schmoozing team.

According to Michael, Satellite Omega recently lost a major antitrust suit based on predatory pricing designed to drive a competitor out of business in the expanding Arizona and Nevada markets. The company wound up on the wrong end of a fifty-nine million dollar jury verdict and was, quite understandably, in the process of severing relationships with its existing law firm. Holland, Roberts & Northway, LLC, was in a beauty contest for a good chunk of the work, meaning several million dollars in billable hours a year.

Client development.

It reminded her of a meeting that she had with Michael Northway on her second day with the firm, a long time ago. He walked into her office and closed the door.

"Kelly," he said, "I have what I call simple rules for surviving life in a big law firm. Here's one of them, for what it's worth. Every big law firm wants every client that exists.

Grow your client base.

Grow your firm.

Grow your wallet.

Lots of young lawyers who come into the established firms think their career will move forward exactly as planned by simply coming out of Harvard Law School, billing an ungodly number of hours, doing a damn good job and not crossing swords with upper management types like me. They become good little worker bees with no time for client development, and then wonder seven years into their career why everything is suddenly stalling.

Be smarter than they are.

Work hard on the work that's already in the door but work harder at getting the work in the door in the first place. Write articles, teach CLEs, get on a board or two. Get your face out there and schmooze everyone in sight. And that includes lawyers from other firms. Never forget that referrals are one of the best sources of business.

Schmooze.

Schmooze.

Schmooze."

SHE TOOK ONE LAST LOOK AT HERSELF in the bathroom

mirror, decided *Good enough*, and headed for the elevator, making sure that the door to her loft was locked good and tight behind her. She was supposed to be at the Paramount Café in twenty minutes for introductions and drinks. Reportedly the firm had a section of the bar area roped off.

The elevator bottomed out at the parking garage level, the doors opened and she stepped out, car keys in hand and purse over her shoulder. Her 3-Series BMW was parked in its designated spot over near the far corner of the garage.

Her heals clicked off the steps as she walked.

No one was around.

That made her feed good, and eerie, at the same time.

Ordinarily she looked forward to law firm events. She was fortunate in that she actually liked most of the people she worked with. But tonight, if she had her choice, she'd be spending the whole evening with Bryson Coventry. The man had some serious substance to him. This could actually turn out to be something.

Wait, that's weird.

The area over by her car was darker than usual. For some reason that sent up a red flag and she found herself still walking in that direction but a little slower now. One of the overhead lights in that section wasn't working for some reason.

She listened and looked as she approached, hypersensitive.

No one was around.

She twisted and looked behind her as she walked, to see if by any chance someone was following her.

No.

No one.

She laughed at herself for being so fidgety and thought of that stupid joke: *Just because you're paranoid doesn't mean they're not out to get you.*

A drink at the Paramount Café with friends sounded pretty good right about now.

She pressed the keyless entry and the Bimmer acknowledged with a beep. She was a little astonished at how good that made her feel. In ten seconds she'd be inside with the doors locked.

Coventry was responsible for her nervousness. He kept telling her last night not to let her guard down, that he still believed she was a target even though nothing had happened out of the ordinary yet, unless you count that guy outside the bar Tuesday night. He kept reminding her that D'endra's death had been on a weekend. There could be a good reason for that. Mister Jerko may have a job during the week. This weekend might be the first real opportunity he has to follow up.

She had backed into her parking space when she parked the car earlier this afternoon. She always did that, if there were no cars around at the time, so she wouldn't have to hassle with it later.

She walked around the front of the car, down the side, put her hand on the door handle, opened the door and started to get in. Suddenly a sound came from behind her, almost as if someone was lunging at her.

Before she could turn something happened to her back.

Something awful.

Something serious.

It was as if someone had taken a red-hot spike and nailed it into her spine.

She tried to call out.

But the pain was everywhere.

Tearing at every fiber of her being.

Then everything went black.

Chapter Twenty-Four

Day Six
Saturday Evening

———————

A STRONG WIND BLEW OUT OF THE NORTHWEST, carrying an invasive chill through the night. David Hallenbeck shivered, slipped back into the Camry while the gas pump ran, and took the opportunity to dial Jay Yorty to tell him the good news. On the second ring, Yorty's voice came through.

"Jay, it's me."

"David," Yorty said. "I've been waiting for you, man. Tell me something good."

Loud music pounded in the background and Yorty was shouting into the phone to get over it. South Beach was two hours ahead of Denver and the little trust-fund brat was obviously at a club somewhere smack dab in the middle of his next pussy hunt.

Hallenbeck smiled to himself.

"Something good."

"Screw you," Yorty countered. "Am I an owner, or what?"

Hallenbeck grinned. He loved giving people good news. "You're an owner. I just closed the deal."

"Bingo!" Yorty said. "You're the best, man, the absolute

best." Hallenbeck heard Yorty cover the mouthpiece and tell someone he just bought a '57 Chevy. *All original, primo condition, stole the little shit.* Then: "Listen, my man, good job. And, hey! I'm going to throw in a little bonus for you, next time you're down here. A little thing called Caressa."

"Caressa, huh?"

"She's going to rock your world, friend."

Hallenbeck hung up and waited for the pump to finish.

Caressa.

Rock his world.

Outside the wind howled and he could actually feel the car want to fly away under the pressure. In the back seat sat three bags of groceries. Milk and yogurt, both no-fat, vitamin fortified cereal, apples, oranges, bananas, tomatoes, wheat bread, sliced turkey, orange juice, power bars and one naughty little bag of Lay's potato chips, sitting on the top of everything where it wouldn't be crushed. He thought about breaking it open, but before he could make up his mind the pump shut off with a clank.

He pulled the baseball cap down as tight on his head as he could and stepped outside.

Damn wind.

He put a hand on his hat to keep it from blowing off, then replaced the nozzle, screwed in the gas cap and scurried inside to pay.

Always pay cash.

Another one of the many little rules.

INSIDE, OVERPOWERING FLORESCENT LIGHTS cranked out twice as many watts as they needed to, washing an ugliness over everything. There was only one cashier, a middle-aged man who obviously knew how to drink beer, in no particular hurry, hence the line.

Four people stood in front of him.

Each one held a credit card, of course.

Shit.

What the hell ever happened to money?

He pulled his hat down at far as he could over his face without looking weird and took his place at the end, shifting his weight from foot to foot. Lines equaled wasted life and pissed him off more than just about anything else on earth.

A cheap color TV, mounted on a wall bracket over in the corner, was in the process of spitting out an infomercial, trying to sell him a stupid looking car. Then the picture switched to a news update.

Suddenly Megan Bennett's face popped up on the left half of the screen. On the other half, some mean looking cop by the name of Bryson Coventry was talking to some blond reporter with a big white smile and even bigger tits.

The look in the cop's eyes was unmistakable.

Hallenbeck had seen the same thing in his own eyes enough to recognize it.

This man was serious.

He was on the hunt.

So, you want to dance?

Is that what you want, pretty boy?

He hated this Coventry cop immediately. He knew the type. A good job, a rough edge, tons of hair. Every door in his life opened oh-so-goddamned-easy. Women, success, friends, sports. Guys like him had no idea what the real world was like.

Well, if you're not careful, you're going to find out, asshole.

You're in my world now.

Megan Bennett's face suddenly disappeared from the left side of the screen, immediately replaced with a picture of a black Camry. Not his exact Camry. More like something from an advertisement.

Damn!

How in the hell did they know he was driving a Camry?

"Sir?"

The word seemed to come from a million miles away but was unmistakably meant for him. He realized that he was at the front of the line now and the beer-gut behind the cheap Formica counter wanted his money. He handed over a twenty, already in hand, stuck the change in his front pants pocket, saw that the news report was already over, and walked out.

THE WIND GRABBED HIM IMMEDIATELY and held on until he got into the car and managed to muscle the door shut.

He cranked over the engine and pulled into traffic.

So many thoughts jammed up in his mind that he had a hard time concentrating on just one. Obviously the cops knew about the Camry somehow but—and here's the important part— didn't appear to know much more than that. They didn't know his name, license plate number or what he looked like, otherwise it would have been splattered all over the screen.

He started to calm down, just a tad.

Things were definitely not as bad as they first appeared.

There were only two negatives of substance as far as he could tell. First, they somehow knew he was driving a Camry. Maybe someone saw it when Megan Bennett came out of her house that night. If that's how they knew, then no big deal. It had been raining like crazy that night and the likelihood that anyone had actually seen his face would be slim to none, and Slim just left town.

The only other bad thing was this Coventry cop. Hallenbeck wasn't afraid of him, but he really didn't need someone like that running around in his shadows. The guy was trouble. He looked fairly big, too, although not as big as he was, and no-where near as strong.

But, still, he could be an opponent if it ever came to it.

Plus he'd have a gun.

And five hundred other people on his team.

THE CITY LIGHTS STARTED TO FADE off now as he got far-ther and farther into the country, south of Denver. Santa Fe Drive turned into a measly two-lane road more than five miles back. He'd done his grocery shopping and filled up the tank not far from Donald Vine's house, after closing the deal on the '57 Chevy. That was a good location because it was more than twenty miles from the farmhouse.

Always shop and gas up as far away as you can. That way they can't triangulate you.

Okay.

Think.

The cops had some semblance of a net in place. Not much of one, but more than he was used to, just the same. The Camry was a liability at this point. He most definitely had to take care of that little fact somehow.

What were his options?

He could complete his work with Megan Bennett and get out of Dodge, even as early as tonight, if he wanted to. That was the smartest thing to do. Just get the hell out of here and jump straight down the devil's throat where they'll never find him.

Or, he could just lay low, continue the dance with Megan Bennett for another day or two or three, and then jump. This wasn't as smart a plan but was definitely the one he wanted to go with, unless he thought of a reason why it was just plain stupid.

How much risk did he want to take?

That what it always comes down to, isn't it?

He must have been thinking for some time because he now found himself on the gravel road that led to the turnoff for the house. He couldn't even remember the drive here.

Everything around him was black and he couldn't go more than thirty miles an hour because the road was so uneven. The occasional chunk of gravel kicked up from the tires and slapped against the underside of the car.

Repeated glances in the rearview mirror told him that no one followed.

He was totally safe, at least for the moment. Maybe he'd go out tomorrow and pick up a rental under one of his aliases. Something with a trunk that he could stuff Megan Bennett in if the need arose.

HE TURNED OFF THE ROAD and onto the so-called driveway for the farmhouse.

In another half mile he'd be home.

Megan Bennett.

He smiled.

Daddy's home, baby.

Get yourself ready.

When the house came in sight he immediately knew that something was wrong, but couldn't tell what. Almost by instinct he killed the headlights and stopped the car. What bothered him so much all of a sudden? Then he knew.

There were lights inside the house.

Damn!

How could that be?

Were there cops inside?

Had they found the place?

He twisted around in the seat to see if there was a caravan of cars closing in on him from behind. No, nothing. Everything around him in every direction was black.

He powered down the window and stuck his head outside to see if he could hear anything. But the wind was too strong and filled his ears with noise. There could have been a freight train running next to him and he wouldn't have been able to hear it.

Back inside.

Damned useless wind.

What to do?

He reached under the front seat and felt around until he found the leather sheath. He pulled it up, slipped the knife out and instinctively pressed his thumb on the blade, drawing strength from it.

Razor sharp.

He turned the vehicle around and parked it, pointing towards the road just in case he needed to make a quick getaway. Then he put the keys in his pocket, tightened his shoelaces, picked up the knife, and walked towards the house in the dark, briskly but not so fast that he'd be out of breath when he got there. He encountered no one and had a thought that kept nagging at him.

Maybe *he* left the lights on.

That was possible, because if the cops had found the place, the whole area would be swarming by now. And if Megan Bennett had somehow escaped, which was impossible anyway, there's no way she would be hanging around.

This could be one great big false alarm.

Or maybe the old man who rented him the place, Ben Bickerson, dropped by to see if everything was all right. If that was the case, then the little jerk just made the biggest mistake of his pathetic redneck life.

The wind whipped around like some primitive unleashed force and he could feel his tolerance for it start to seriously fade. In anther few minutes it would drive him officially crazy.

Damned wind!

HE WAS GETTING CLOSE TO THE HOUSE NOW, really close. Then he saw something that he didn't expect: the black shape of two motorcycles. Even from this distance, in the dark, he recognized them as Harleys, and not new ones either, older models with huge saddlebags, and sleeping bags bungeed on top.

Drifters.

Probably a couple of lowlifes looking for a free place to crash for the night. Maybe hiding out from the law. So they pull in here looking for a barn or something and end up finding a house with a woman inside tied up on a bed. It'd be like winning the bikers' lottery.

Hallenbeck realized that he had never stopped walking towards the house and was almost at the front door now.

Back door, he told himself.

Go through the back door.

He headed around the side of the house, towards the rear, walking briskly.

He tightened his grip on the knife and knew he was prepared.

Bust in fast and quiet and take out the closest one as quick as you can. Then go for the other one. Don't let them get you between them.

If you screwed with Megan Bennett you're going to wish to God you never turned down this driveway.

I'll rip your head off and piss in the hole.

That's a promise.

He turned the doorknob, opened the door and walked straight in.

Chapter Twenty-Five

Day Six
Saturday Evening

IT WAS EIGHT O'CLOCK ON SATURDAY NIGHT and Bryson Coventry was still at his desk, trying to squeeze the last bit of energy out of the day.

Kelly Parks should be calling pretty soon.

She'd been roped into some kind of a law firm function tonight with out-of-town clients, but she was going to break away as soon as it was politically correct. Then they were going to join forces and see where the evening took them.

He sat alone in the room with his shoes off, his feet up on the desk and his eyes closed. Everything was quiet, in fact strangely quiet, except for the hum of a couple of florescent ceiling lights that were at the wrong end of their useful lives.

Megan Bennett.

Hold on, Megan Bennett, if you can.

The day had been long and frustrating. The FBI had taken the lead in trying to obtain information from the airlines, hotels and car rental agencies. But the going had been tedious and so far no correlations had been discovered. It wasn't anyone's fault. That's just the nature of that type of investigation.

Lots of tips had come into the telephone hot line. Shalifa Netherwood had done a wonderful job sorting the wheat from the non-wheat, and allocating resources to the ones that most justified the effort. But so far nothing solid had come of it. One thing for sure, though, the Denver community was really lining up behind the investigation.

SUDDENLY HIS CELL PHONE RANG. Someone breathed into it for a couple of seconds and then hung up. He pulled up the menu for calls received to get the caller's number. It was *Unknown.*

Weird.

Very strange.

And it definitely wasn't the call he was expecting, from Kelly Parks, because his phone recognized hers.

SUDDENLY IT RANG AGAIN. This time someone was there. "Bryson? This is James, from the Carr-Border Gallery," the voice said.

Coventry recognized the voice. James was the husband of the woman who owned the gallery that had taken him in. "James, did you just call?"

"No."

"Mmm."

"Hey, listen, Picasso," James said. "We sold five of your paintings this week. We're getting low and were hoping you could bring some fresh stuff by."

"Five?"

James laughed. "Crazy, isn't it?"

Coventry couldn't believe it. "Wow."

He found himself talking art for the next five minutes, learned that the market was picking up, the pieces priced at under a thousand dollars were moving the fastest, and that summer landscapes were the hot ticket right now, which was just fine, because that's exactly what he painted. By the time he hung up he was missing the smell of turpentine and the challenge of an empty canvas.

"YOU'RE A WORKAHOLIC," SOMEONE SAID. He looked up and found the FBI profiler, Dr. Leanne Sanders, walking into the room. "I like that," she added.

She had changed out of her intimidation suit and into casual white shorts with a pink cotton shirt. He was surprised to see her, but glad. Her voice made him realize that his thoughts had started to drift.

"I have no life," he told her.

She nodded. "Me either. Nor do I want one."

Her legs were muscular and tanned and looked exceptionally good. She had really maintained herself well for her age and had to be respected for that. She must have been an absolute, incredible knockout back in her heyday.

"So what's going on?" he asked her.

She was at his desk now and sat down in a chair. He pulled his feet off so she wouldn't have to look at them.

"Nothing, just thought I'd check in." She picked up a pencil and started fidgeting with it. "So what are you working on?"

What, indeed?

He shrugged and combed his hair back with his fingers. It immediately flopped back down over his forehead. "To be honest? I've been racking my brain all day trying to think of a way to flush this guy out. I need him to call me and get a dialogue going." He looked at the woman. "I always have room for brilliant ideas, of course."

"Oh yeah?"

She seemed intrigued with the idea.

"Yeah."

He studied her face as she pondered it. "The indicators are that he's incredibly smart but his emotions can get the best of him. Take the attack on the three men outside Megan Bennett's window, for example. If you want him to talk to you, my guess is that the best door to entry is through his emotions, not his brain."

"Meaning what?" Coventry questioned. "Get him pissed-off at me? Get on the TV and say we have evidence that he wets the bed or something?"

"I don't know," she said, "I had a case in upper Minnesota several years back where we came up with plan. We captured the wrong person, one of our own actually, on purpose, and then put out a news alert stating that we caught the guy we were looking for and the hunt was off. We had great visuals of the so-called capture with helicopters and dogs and you-name-it to put on the TV. The real killer sees all this and calls us to tell us how stupid we are, which is exactly what we were going for. That started a wonderful series of phone calls that got us where we needed to go."

Coventry was impressed. "Very nice."

"Of course," she added, "when it was over, the news media jumped all over us for catching the wrong guy in the first place. We could have told them the truth, but didn't really see the need to get a public debate going as to whether it's ethical for law enforcement to provide false information to the public in the name of catching the criminal. So we just left the egg on our face and got out of town."

"Devious," he said. "I like that."

She uncrossed her legs, and re-crossed them the other direction. "So, I have question for you. How would you like to come and work for the bureau?"

Coventry hadn't been prepared for that. "Are you serious?"

She nodded. "Very. I've already talked to a few people."

He chuckled and pondered the implications.

SUDDENLY HIS PHONE RANG, not his cell phone, the one on his desk. "Excuse me," he apologized, picking it up. "This is the way my life works."

"Coventry?"

"Yes."

"This is Richardson."

The detective sounded excited.

"Yeah, what's up?"

"Give me the scoop. What's going on?" Richardson asked.

"What do you mean?"

"The phone call . . . What'd you get?"

"What phone call?"

A pause.

"Didn't someone just call your cell phone about fifteen minutes ago?"

Coventry wasn't sure which call he was referring to. "You mean the hang-up? Was that you?"

"He hung up? Okay, hold onto your seat, buddy boy," Richardson said. "Do you remember D'endra Vaughn, the dead school teacher?"

"No, who's she?"

"Bad," he said. Then: "We got a ping on her pen register about fifteen minutes ago. According to the phone company, the call from her phone went to yours. The call that you got fifteen minutes ago was from D'endra Vaughn's cell phone. Do you understand what I'm saying?"

He did.

"I want cars at two places: Kelly Parks' place and the Paramount Café. Now!"

Chapter Twenty-Six

Day Six
Saturday Evening

KELLY PARKS WAS STUFFED in something confined and tight and dark, absolutely terrified about it. She couldn't see a thing or straighten her body out. The side of her face ached from lying on some kind of hard surface for so long. The bones in her hips and knees felt like someone had taken a hammer to them. The muscles in her legs had stiffened and were threatening to convulse from being in the same unforgiving bent position for so long. Noise filled the space; the noise of an engine, sounding as if it was right underneath her. No, not an engine: a muffler. There was a muffler right underneath her.

She was in the trunk of a car.

She remembered what happened in the parking garage; the movement of someone behind her, the hot white excruciating pain in her back. She tried to move her legs, first one, then the other. They both worked. Whatever that asshole did to her back hadn't paralyzed her.

Thank God for that.

The tires whined almost as loud as the muffler. She couldn't think straight, not with all that noise in her head.

Someone was taking her somewhere.

She tried to shift around, to get her body in a different position, any position at all, as long as it was different. At first she couldn't and almost slipped into a panic attack. Then, little by little, she was able to find nooks and crannies to put the parts of her body into as she shifted around.

She managed to get on her back. That was so much better. So very much better.

Okay.

Calm down.

Gravitational forces pulled her body to one direction and then the other. The road twisted. It seemed like they might be out in the country somewhere, or maybe heading up into the mountains.

Could the trunk be opened from the inside? She felt around in the dark in the area where the latch would be. She found some kind of mechanism and pushed and pulled at it from every angle she could but the trunk wouldn't open. Her car was ten years old, probably built before that type of safety feature.

A string of five or six cars whizzed by, going the opposite direction.

She shivered.

It was freezing in here.

IF CARS WERE GOING THE OTHER WAY, maybe there was one behind them, too. Maybe if she could get to the wires for the taillight, she could flash them somehow. Or maybe knock them out and get the police to pull them over. She shifted her body to the left, towards the front of the car, and was able to get her right arm over her head, with her hand up and in the corner of the trunk where the taillight would be. The wires weren't exposed. She could feel only carpet.

Damn it!

Come on!

There had to be a way to get behind the carpet. She needed to find the edge and felt around for it. Her arm ached beyond belief and she had to consciously fight off the pain to keep from bringing it back for a rest.

Everything was so tight.

Ten more seconds.

Then she found her fingers on something that might be a seam. She gripped it as hard as she could and tugged at it. It moved. She felt the carpet pull away from the side of the trunk and tugged even harder and felt a snap open. Suddenly there was a faint red light inside the space, backsplash from the taillight. She could actually see now, not much, but some.

She twisted her head as best she could and looked up above her. She could see the back of the taillight and the wires going to it.

She couldn't tolerate the pain in her arm anymore and brought it down to her side. That felt so, so good.

She could see the latch mechanism now and felt around with her hand in that area again. But the amount of light wasn't much and she couldn't get her head close enough to really see anything.

No inside safety latch.

Just forget about it.

Forget it!

It's not going to happen!

She managed to get her arm up above her head again and was able to get her hands on the wire, but couldn't get to the end of it, where it actually plugged into the bulb. That's what she needed. If she could get to that she could connect and disconnect the wire and send out an SOS, which was dot dot dot, dash dash dash, dot dot dot, or vice versa. Anyone behind them would see it and should be smart enough to call the police.

But the wires ran through some kind of a plastic part, something like a funnel. She couldn't get her fingers through that stupid plastic part to grab the plug.

She could yank the wire out and kill the taillight if she wanted. But that wasn't anywhere near as good as an SOS. Plus she'd never be able to get to the other light, down by her feet.

What to do?

The pain in her arm was beyond tolerance again and she brought it down and let it lay next to her side, where it throbbed.

For some reason she just now remembered her purse and frantically felt around for it. The cell phone was in there, plus that emergency GPS that Michael Northway had given her.

Damn it!

No purse.

It was sitting in the car on the passenger seat. She could feel it there.

Shit!

Okay, think.

The taillight.

Maybe she could find something to break open that plastic funnel part. Maybe if she could get to the jack kit there'd be something in there she could use. But where was it? Probably underneath her in the spare tire compartment. It may as well be on Mars.

The cold gnawed at her bones and tried to get her to forget

about everything and just close her eyes. She had to make a conscious effort to fight it off.

Help!

Someone help me!

Jesus.

This wasn't happening.

She hadn't done anything to make something like this happen.

She had to think. Sooner or later the car was going to stop and someone would open the trunk. What to do? Money. She'd offer him money. That's it, lots of money. More money than he could ever imagine. And she'd never say a word to anyone. Not a word. All he had to do was let her go.

Then, suddenly, wham!

AN EXPLOSION ERUPTED FROM UNDERNEATH the car, followed by a sudden jerk to the left and the panicked squealing of locked tires. The car was off the asphalt now and on dirt or gravel or something, sliding out of control. The front end of the vehicle shook from side to side as if the two front wheels were pointed in different directions. Then the forward momentum stopped with a violent jerk.

They must have hit a rock or boulder on the road. She pictured a smashed tie-rod. If that was the case, they weren't going anywhere.

The red glow in the trunk disappeared. He had turned the lights off. Then he shut off the motor and the sound of the muffler died. Everything was suddenly eerily quiet, except for some sound that she didn't recognize coming from somewhere outside the car. She heard the driver's side door open and then the footsteps of someone walking to the front of the car.   She pictured the dark silhouette of a man up there, kneeling down to check the damage, and wondering what to do with her if he determined the car was dead.

Should she shout out?

No.

Stupid, stupid, stupid.

Be quiet.

Just be quiet.

Don't draw attention to yourself.   Maybe he'll just run away and someone will find you in the morning. You can last until he morning if you have to.

Can't you?

Then she heard the footsteps coming her way and clenched her gut.

Vomit shot up into her mouth.

Chapter Twenty-Seven

Day Six
Saturday Evening

AT FIRST, DAVID HALLENBECK thought he would bury the two biker scumbags in a single shallow grave in the barn, just deep enough to keep the animals out and the stench in. But if he did that someone would find them sooner or later. Then there'd officially be a crime scene at this location and he'd be inextricably intertwined with it because he'd scattered more forensic evidence around at this point than he'd be able to remove in a thousand years. So, instead, he emptied their pockets, threw their stinky bodies in the trunk of the Camry, drove south for thirty minutes and found a nice quiet place to dump them.

When he got back, the biker bitch, who he hadn't killed, was still hogtied and gagged on the barn floor just like he left her, except she was conscious now and watching him with wide eyes.

He wheeled one of the Harleys into the barn past her, parked it without saying anything, then went back out and brought the other one in.

Now he could relax a little.

He squatted down and checked out his new catch. She had more than enough road stink; that was for sure. Her hair was dark auburn, halfway down her back, tangled and greasy. She wore dirty jeans with a rip in the ass, and a blue flannel shirt over a tank top, with no bra. She looked to be about thirty-seven or thirty-eight. She was full of tattoos and had a defiant look in her eyes, like she'd been kicked around more than enough for one lifetime.

He pulled the gag out of her mouth and she immediately gulped for air.

"Do you want to join your two friends?" he warned.

Her eyes flashed.

"Screw them and screw you."

He couldn't help but respect her attitude and chuckled. Then he untied her legs, leaving her hands tied behind her back, and pulled her to her feet.

"Don't make me change my mind about you," he said. By the look in her eyes she took the words seriously, as she should.

HE WALKED HER INTO THE HOUSE, straight into the bathroom, and untied her hands. She stood there, still shivering from the cold outside, not making a move. He turned on the shower to get it warmed up and told her to strip off her rat-infested clothes, every shred of them, and throw them over in the corner. It somewhat surprised him that she did it immediately without even a hint of a protest.

He felt the water with his hand, determined it wasn't quite hot enough, adjusted the knob just a tad, felt the flow again and told her to get in.

She did.

Then he tossed her a bar of soap.

She caught it and said, "Hope you enjoy the show, asshole,"

and began lathering up while he sat down on the toilet and watched. Surprisingly, her body was in pretty good shape considering the neglect it must have suffered over the years. Life without TV and potato chips had kept her stomach fairly flat. Her tits were nice too, not too big or too small. But she'd ruined her skin with tattoos. They were everywhere. Some of them were higher quality but most of them were cheap junk. They ran together and bumped into one another without rhyme or reason or planning.

It was too bad.

When she was done and had toweled off, he gave her a clean T-shirt to put on and then tied her hands behind her back again. He expected her to resist and was prepared to apply some persuasion but she ended up being totally passive about it. For some reason he was almost left with the idea that she wanted to be tied if that would please him.

He gabbed her arm, pulled her into the living room and sat her down on the couch. She sank into it, spread her legs ever so suggestively and looked him straight in the eyes without saying anything.

THE STRESS OF THE NIGHT ROSE INSIDE HIM and he suddenly had a craving for alcohol.

"You want a beer?" he asked.

She nodded. "Sure. Okay."

He walked over to the fridge, keeping a close eye on her, counted the beers left, which were eleven, grabbed one and popped the top on his way back. He took a long swig and then held the can to her mouth. She tipped her head back and drained the rest of it.

Hallenbeck couldn't help but smile.

That was pretty impressive.

"More," she said.

"More?"

"More."

Why not?

He fetched another one.

"I never saw anyone fight like that," she told him. "And I've seen some shit."

He looked at the bruise on her forehead: "Sorry I had to hit you."

She nodded. "It's okay."

The woman intrigued him.

He didn't know why, exactly, but the fact remained.

She scrubbed up pretty good and turned out to be not half-bad looking. He sat down on the couch next to her where it would be easier to share the beer and organized some of the things he needed to know.

"So who are those two guys?" he questioned.

"Nobody," she said. "Nobody worth anything."

"Are they wanted?"

She nodded. "Ninety-Nine is."

"Which one is he?"

"The ugly one."

"Which ugly one?"

"The ugly one with the red shirt," she said, tipping her head back. He held the can up to her mouth and let her drink.

"What'd he do?"

She looked bothered. "Shit, I don't know, armed robbery or something. It was before my time."

"What about the other guy? Is he wanted?"

She shook her head negative. "That puss, I don't think so. He's done stuff, but there's no arrest warrant out on his ass, that I know of."

"What's his name?"

"John-Boy."

"Which bike is his?"

She tried to dismiss the question as if she'd had enough. "What is this, twenty questions?"

"No, it's thirty questions. Which bike is his?"

"The purple one. Why?"

Hallenbeck cocked his head. "Because his is the bike that's not contaminated."

She looked like she understood.

"Oh," she said.

SHE LICKED HER LIPS AND SPREAD HER LEGS even wider. Then looked him straight in the eyes. "So are you going to fuck me, or what?"

Hallenbeck laughed, a nervous laugh. He wasn't used to women like this. Things were moving way too fast and way too easy. He wasn't sure if she was trying to control him with her body.

"Show me your tattoos first," he said.

She looked genuinely interested in that. "Good idea," she told him. "Untie my hands so I can take this shirt off."

He considered it.

"Don't even think about trying anything," he warned.

"You scared of little old me?"

"I'm serious. Be good."

"Yes, master." As he untied her, she asked a question.

"Who's the bitch in the bedroom?"

"Why?"

"Because, I'll do her, if you want. You can watch."

He laughed. "You are a wild one, aren't you?"

"Who, me?"

They spent a good hour, and lots more beers, going over her tattoos. She had a story for every one of them. They were a roadmap of her life and by the time she was done he was actually starting to like them.

He found his hand in her hair, playing with it. "You know what?"

"What?"

"You'd look better with shorter hair."

"You think so?"

"Yeah, I really do," he said, which was true.

"Then cut it," she said.

The words surprised him. "Are you serious?"

"Sure, why not?"

"You want me to cut your hair?"

"Hell, it's only hair," she said. "It's been getting on my nerves anyway. Go ahead and get it the way you like it."

So he cut her hair, using his knife.

Shoulder length with some feathering.

She looked really, really good like that.

Afterwards, there on the couch, she gave him the most incredible, uninhibited sex of his life.

Then he closed his eyes, just to rest them for a second.

Chapter Twenty-Eight

Day Seven
Sunday Morning

AT THREE O'CLOCK IN THE MORNING, Bryson Coventry realized that he had now been rolling and tossing in bed, unable to sleep, for more than two hours. He was tired as hell but had two pots of caffeine in his gut pulling him the wrong direction. He was a rubber band stretched as far as it would go.

Kelly Parks had been missing now for seven or eight hours.

She'd been taken by the same sick ass that strung up D'endra Vaughn last weekend. That much was clear from the fact that the little shit had used D'endra's cell phone to call Coventry shortly after he took Kelly last night. It was his demented little way of playing with people, announcing what a clever little prick he was.

The little shit.

Coventry couldn't believe how dismal the investigation of Kelly Parks' disappearance had been so far. They went through her loft with a fine-tooth comb and found nothing. Her car was not in its assigned spot in her parking garage. A BOLO had been put out on it, but so far it may as well have spun off the face of the earth. She hadn't shown up at the Paramount Café for the law firm function. Nor was her car parked in the street, or in any of the parking garages, within three blocks of that venue. Nobody had seen or heard from her all night. She wasn't answering her cell phone, nor had any calls been made from it.

He didn't even want to think about what might be happening to her right now.

But think about it he did.

In fact, that's about all he could think about. Against his will, he found himself making up horrible little scenarios and filling in the details.

Then his phone rang.

"Coventry?" He recognized the voice as Shalifa Netherwood's. She sounded like she just stepped off a roller coaster. "Somebody used Megan Bennett's credit card at a gas station. South of town, way down south, almost to Castle Rock."

"When?"

"Now, tonight."

COVENTRY SWUNG OVER TO PICK UP NETHERWOOD, shot over to I-25 and headed south, bringing the speedometer up to 95. Exits shot by—Evans, Yale, Hampton. Before long they were through the Tech Center and then leaving County Line Road in their wake. Netherwood leaned forward in her seat and studied the traffic, visibly apprehensive of their speed.

"Want me to slow down?" he questioned.

She shook her head. "It's okay. But if you kill me I'm never going to speak to you again." Then: "I can't believe this guy would be stupid enough to use the woman's credit card. I thought he was supposed to be Mr. Careful. It doesn't add up."

"Or subtract down," Coventry agreed. "Which reminds me, to be politically correct we probably ought to give our FBI friends an invite. We owe them that much, at least, for coming all the way out here to Denver."

"You got a number?"

He didn't and tried to think where he could get one. "They're at the Brown Palace, downtown."

"I know where the Brown Palace is, Coventry. It's that place where I can't even afford to buy lunch. How do they rate the Brown Palace?"

Coventry shook his head. He never thought about it and now wondered why.

"I don't know, good question."

Shalifa nodded. "Damn right, good question. Hell, that's where Elvis stayed."

"And the Beatles," Coventry added.

She got the number of the hotel from dispatch and then talked the desk clerk into patching her through to Agent Charles Miller's room. From what she could tell, he just about popped right out of bed with a major erection for the action.

"They're coming," she warned. Then added, "Got to hand it to 'em."

Coventry chuckled. "They're hunters, those three. They're not your normal bureaucrats."

Twenty minutes later they cut off the freeway and headed west, on a winding road that neither of them had ever been on before. The lights and activity of civilization disappeared.

TEN MINUTES LATER THEY PULLED INTO A SINCLAIR gas

station, an outdated building with only two pumps. There was only one other car there, parked on the side, an old Chevy sinking low on weak springs and bad shocks, which Coventry surmised to be the attendant's.

They paused at the pumps. A credit card receipt hung there, printed but not taken. Coventry left it in place as part of the crime scene, but bent over close enough to read to name on the paper.

Megan Bennett.

Good.

This was for real.

Inside, the place reminded Coventry more of an old general store than a gas station, stocked with the obligatory junk food but also lots of real food, and liquor, plenty of liquor. One of the walls displayed a couple of hundred movies for rent, in their original video boxes, now tattered and handled. For some reason one of the boxes caught his eye, *Body Double*, and he made a mental note that he really needed to rent that again someday, if for no other reason than to watch the "Relax" scene, where they play the Frankie Does Hollywood song.

The place was huge, as if it once had old service bays that had been turned into part of the store.

THE STORE ATTENDANT TURNED OUT TO BE A KID, probably no more than a year out of high school, who was actually stocking the shelves rather than staring into space when they walked in. He had an innocent face, shaggy blond hair and eyes that, well, fixed on Detective Netherwood. Coventry had almost forgotten that she could have that kind of effect on people, he was so used to her.

"This is your lucky night," Coventry said, flashing his badge. "You get to talk to two homicide detectives, at no charge, and maybe get to say something that ends up saving someone's life."

The kid was stunned. It was all over his face. He'd even gone so far as to take his eyes off the female and give Coventry his full attention.

"What's you name, buddy?"

"Jason."

"You got a last name, Jason?"

"Windermere."

"Well, Jason Windermere, someone used a credit card here about an hour ago," Coventry continued. "For $15.22."

The kid looked relieved, like he knew exactly what Coventry was talking about. "That was at the pump," the kid said. "Outside."

Coventry nodded; he already knew that. "Did they come inside?"

The kid shook his head negative. "No."

"Okay," Coventry said. "Play it back for me. Tell me what happened."

The kid furrowed his brow. "It was a girl on a motorcycle, a Harley, I think. Major loud."

"A girl?"

"Yes, I mean, a woman. Older, you know, early thirties, maybe."

Shalifa jumped in. "So ancient, is what you're saying."

The kid laughed. "No. Come on."

Coventry pulled a picture of Megan Bennett out of his shirt pocket.

"Is this the woman you saw?"

The expression on the kid's face told Coventry immediately

that it wasn't. "No. No way."

"Okay."

"Not even close."

Coventry nodded. "Was this woman by herself or with a guy?"

"Herself."

"Herself, huh? So she was driving the motorcycle, the Harley?"

The kid nodded affirmatively. "Yeah, she wasn't having any problems, that's for sure. She was definitely a biker chick. You could probably put her in a business suit and still tell."

"So what happened? Outside?"

The kid shrugged. "Nothing, really. I mean, she pulled up at the pump, filled the tank and then left. That's about it."

"So she never came inside?"

"No."

"Did you talk to her?"

"No, I was inside."

"Watching her."

A pause. "Yeah, I guess. That's part of my job, to keep an eye on things. I would have helped her, if she needed it. But she wasn't having any problems."

"So you didn't end up going out."

"No."

"You just stayed inside and watched."

"Basically, yeah, stocking the shelves."

Coventry shifted a little, looked around the store, and then back at the kid. "I noticed a video camera outside, pointed at the pumps. It looks like a fake."

The kid nodded, obviously impressed. "It is a fake. The owner calls it a decoy, but I'm not too sure that it actually decoys anyone." He pointed up to the ceiling, at a camera pointed down at the cash register area. "That one's real," he said. "But not the one outside."

Coventry nodded. "So basically," he said, "what we have to go on is what you saw and that's pretty much it."

The kid shrugged. "I guess so." Then added: "Plus her fingerprints on the pump, I suppose."

"No one's used that pump since?"

"No."

Coventry looked outside at the pumps, momentarily excited, and then remembered that the handle would have oil residue, counterproductive to printing.

He paused, found himself about to ask another question, then changed gears and asked the one thing that had been on his mind since he walked into the store. "Is that coffee over there fresh, or is it going to hold up a spoon if I stick one in?"

"Maybe a plastic spoon, but not a real one," the kid told him.

Coventry grinned and walked in that direction. "Close enough." He took his time, pulling out a large Styrofoam cup, opening up two creamers and dumping them in, then topping it off with piping-hot coffee. He took a sip, found it a little too thick for his taste, but what the hell, then walked back over to where the kid and Shalifa were chatting.

"Fingerprinting the pump was a good observation," Coventry noted. "You're pretty smart."

The kid brightened up, as if in territory where he could brag a little. "I get by."

"You in college?"

The kid shook his head negative. "I'm saving up for it, though, that's why I'm working here. I have another job too, at a scrap yard."

"Two jobs," Coventry said.

"My mom has some health problems, so things are a little tight."

"Is that car outside yours?"

The kid smiled. "Yeah, a beauty, right?"

Coventry chuckled.

"I've had a couple of beauties myself, although, I have to admit, not quite as beautiful as yours." He pulled one of his business cards out of his wallet, wrote a name on the back and handed it to the kid. "You ever thought about going to Metro, down at the Auraria campus?"

"Not really."

"The name that I wrote down there for you," Coventry said, "Jerald Woodfield, is the head of the admissions department at Metro. He also handles some special scholarships. I'd consider it a personal favor if you would give him a call. Tell him that I sent you down. My bet is that he's going to find a way to get you into classes next semester, if you're interested."

The kid looked like he wasn't quite sure whether to believe Coventry or not. "You're jerking me around, right?"

"I don't know. I guess you're going to have to call and find out."

Coventry took another sip of coffee and looked around the store. Then back at the kid. "Which way did the motorcycle come from?"

The kid pointed to the north. "That way."

"And which way did it go when it left?"

The kid pointed the other way, south. "That way."

"Mmm."

COVENTRY SPOTTED TWO CARS outside speeding in their direction, their headlights bouncing up and down on the country road. He pulled a twenty-dollar bill out of his pocket and handed it to the kid. "For the coffee," he said. "Keep the change." Then: "The two cars coming this way are FBI. Nice people. They're going to interview you in a lot more detail than we have. Then we're going to take you downtown to meet with a composite artist. You're going to want to call the owner of this place and tell him what's going on, so you can get relieved."

The kid grinned. "He's going to crap."

Coventry walked over to refill the cup, almost empty already. "I assume you didn't get a license plate number on that motorcycle."

"No, I sure didn't."

"No reason you would have."

"It wasn't a Colorado plate, though. I don't know what state it was, but it wasn't Colorado."

"No?"

"No."

"Huh, well that's interesting."

Very interesting.

The kid cocked his head. "What exactly did this woman do?"

"We don't know yet. Maybe nothing."

"It doesn't seem like nothing."

OUTSIDE, COVENTRY AND SHALIFA intercepted the FBI at the pump, filled them in and jointly developed a plan.

They would flood the area with law enforcement vehicles, from the Denver Police Department, the Denver office of the FBI and the local police force. Everyone was to be on the lookout for not only the biker woman, but also a dark blue or black Camry. Katona would get the Crime Lab up here to process the scene. They'd alert all the major police departments up and down the interstates, on the chance that the biker woman was on the run, meaning, north on I-25 up to the Wyoming border, south on I-25 down to the New Mexico border, east on I-70 to the Kansas border and west on I-70 to the Utah border. They'd get an FBI chopper down here at the first ray of dawn, to see what they could view from the sky, or at least keep the guy pinned down a little better, if he was in the neighborhood. They'd get a better statement from the gas station attendant, Jason. If they were lucky enough to get a composite of the biker woman, Coventry would quarterback getting it on the news and keeping it there.

They'd think of more, but that was enough for now.

After working the phone outside for fifteen minutes, primarily coordinating with Kate Katona, Coventry found himself wandering back in the gas station and looking for the restroom. It turned out that it was actually outside and he had to interrupt the FBI's interview of the kid to get the key, which was attached to a horseshoe.

"This thing could break your toe," he noted.

The kid chuckled. "That actually happened once, before we took it off the horse."

Coventry grunted. "Bad."

HE WANDERED AROUND THE SIDE of the building to the restroom, went inside, and then found Shalifa Netherwood waiting for the key when he came out. He got in the car, started the engine to get the heater going, and waited for her. When she finally came over she had the FBI profiler, Dr. Leanne Sanders, with her.

"Can I join you two?" Dr. Sanders questioned.

Coventry looked at Shalifa, who didn't seem to mind, but warned her: "All we're going to do is head down the road in the direction that the biker woman came from. I don't really expect to find anything."

Dr. Sanders nodded. "Sounds reasonable to me."

They all ended up in the front seat, with Shalifa Netherwood in the middle, so that everyone could watch for whatever it was that might be out there to be seen, heading north down a country road with the bright lights on. Coventry was curious as to Dr. Sanders' take on all of this.

"Give me your theory," he said.

Dr. Sanders' started talking immediately, indicating that she'd already been working on it. "I don't believe the biker woman is our guy's girlfriend. Nor do I think that our guy is a biker himself. My best guess is that this lady came across Megan Bennett's purse somehow. Maybe she found it by the side of the road or in a dumpster. Or maybe she came across Megan Bennett's body and it was there."

"Mmm," Coventry said.

He couldn't help but note that Shalifa Netherwood's leg touched his, not pressed against it, but touching, and she hadn't made any effort to pull it away. He decided not to read too much into it, since they were, he had to admit, in cramped quarters. Either way, the touch felt nice, and he didn't do anything to pull away either.

They drove on, over rolling black asphalt, and saw nothing of interest come out of the darkness. No dead bodies. No cars parked out in the middle of nowhere. No motorcycle gangs. No six-foot-four killers.

Nevertheless, Coventry felt intense, almost as if his life force had suddenly doubled.

"He's out here somewhere," he said. "I can smell him."

Shalifa Netherwood turned her head to Dr. Sanders and said, "The caffeine just kicked in. Start ignoring him from this point on."

For the briefest of seconds, he thought he saw a red reflection up ahead, way up ahead, almost the kind of thing you'd expect if the headlights had landed on the rear taillight of a car that had its lights off.

He sped up.

Curious.

Chapter Twenty-Nine

Day Seven
Sunday Morning

DAVID HALLENBECK WOKE WITH A JOLT, more scared than he had ever been in his life. It was the middle of the night. He could tell instantly that the biker bitch was gone. The little shit had played him and he let her do it.

Damn it!

How could he be so stupid?

He called out.

No response.

He bounded out the front door to the barn, to see if the motorcycles were still there. His legs wobbled and he had to fight to keep himself upright. He remembered drinking the beer, way too many beers, which still had a solid hold on him. But he could feel down deep inside that this was something way beyond beer. The little bitch had slipped him something. What it was, he had no idea. He'd never felt like this before in his life, not even close.

When he got to the barn his worst fear came true. One of the bikes was gone.

Shit!

He never even heard her leave.

How long had she been gone?

Did she go to the police?

Were they already on their way?

Out.

Out.

Get out.

He had to get out of there.

Right this second.

He reached in his pocket and found the keys to the Camry, right where he left them. Thank God for that. He ran down the drive towards it. He remembered Megan Bennett and didn't know if she was still there, tied to the bed, or whether the biker bitch had let her go. No time for her right now.

He kept running for the Camry through the dark terrain.

He shouldn't have left the keys in the bikes.

He should have put them in his dumb-ass pocket.

He smacked the side of his head with his right hand, trying to wake his brain. He felt the impact, so intense that colored lights flashed, but the fog inside kept its hold.

When he got to where the Camry should be, it wasn't there. He ran one way, then another. Then he remembered that he used it to dump the bikers' bodies and had parked it back up by the house when he was done. He ran back, disoriented, then it suddenly popped up directly in front of him, a black blob in an even blacker night, just outside the farmhouse door. He got in, fumbled forever to get the key in the ignition, and then cranked over the engine, just to be sure the biker bitch hadn't done something to screw it up. It started immediately. Before he knew it he was back outside and running through the front door.

MEGAN BENNETT WAS EXACTLY where he left her on the bed. She must have known something was wrong because she was wide-awake and had a panicked look on her face.

He had to take her with him—that was clear. She was his insurance.

"Just give me a reason to kill you," he warned as he fought to get the handcuffs and chains off.

"I'll be good," she said.

"Damn right you will!"

He left her leg shackles on, dragged her out to the Camry, opened the truck, shoved the helmet and air blower over to the side, dropped her in and slammed the lid. Then tested it to be sure it wouldn't open.

She went peacefully.

She knew better than to screw with him right now.

Okay.

Now what?

He ran back inside, threw all his clothes into the suitcase, then the rope and toothbrushes and other crap on top of that, muscled it shut, grabbed some other stuff, and threw everything into the back seat of the Camry. There wasn't time to do much more than that.

He cranked over the engine, decided to keep the lights off, headed out to the road and made a left hand turn. He was all over the place, swerving from side to side, fighting to control the wheel.

HE SLAMMED ON THE BRAKES and skidded to a stop in the

gravel.

Shit!

There's no way he could drive where anyone would see him. The first cop he ran into would pull him over.

But he couldn't stay here either.

He continued down the road, slower this time, insanely disoriented, fighting to stay in his lane. He hadn't gone more than three-fourths of a mile when something looked familiar. It was the turnoff to the house of the guy who had rented him the place, the old man, whatever the hell his name was, the farmer with the cancer nose.

Then he remembered that the old fart lived alone. His house was way back, by the river. You couldn't even see it from the road.

He turned off and drove in that direction.

He hadn't gone more than a couple of hundred yards when a car flew up the road from out of nowhere and then disappeared just as fast in the other direction.

A cop, he thought.

Shit.

Chapter Thirty

Day Seven
Sunday Morning

THE CHOPPER RUMBLED IN with the first light of day, sounding like a thousand crazed drummers falling out of the sky. It ripped Bryson Coventry out of a sleep so deep and wide that he might as well have been dead. He jerked upright, startled beyond belief, and opened his eyes. The aircraft couldn't have been more than fifty feet away, touching down. He was in the backseat of a car and remembered climbing in there at some point during the night just to shut his eyes for a few minutes.

He tried to get his bearings.

Outside things had seriously escalated.

They had set up something in the nature of an outdoor command center in a field across the street from the Sinclair. There must have been fifteen or twenty cars parked around the area. Folding card-tables had been brought in from somewhere and maps were spread out on them, held down by rocks. Lots of people were milling around talking into cell phones. Off in the distance, down the road, several cars were being kept at bay; at least three of them were TV news vans.

He wiped as much of the sleep out of his eyes as he could,

stepped out of the car and headed straight to the Sinclair's rest-room, which had for all intents and purposes been taken over by adverse possession. Luckily the door was propped open with a rock and no one was inside. After taking care of first things first, he scrubbed his face two or three times with soap and the hottest water he could stand, then stuck his head under the faucet and let the water run over his hair until it was thoroughly soaked. Some thoughtful soul had left a tube of toothpaste, which Coventry assumed to be for community use. He squeezed an inch out on his index finger and brushed his teeth.

Then he dried his face, and his hair just enough so that it wasn't dripping, and stepped back outside, feeling a thousand percent better.

INSIDE THE STATION SEVERAL POTS of fresh coffee brewed, a far cry from the humble offerings of last night. Someone had written Help Yourself on a piece of cardboard and propped it up on the counter.

Coventry grabbed the biggest cup available, filled up and then walked over to the man behind the cash register, an elderly fellow sporting a wild Albert Einstein look.

Coventry extended his hand. "Bryson Coventry," he said.

The guy shook it. "Ted Livingston."

"You the owner?"

"That's me."

"I just wanted to thank you for the coffee. That's a nice gesture."

The guy smiled. "Not a problem, glad to help."

Coventry took a sip and then remembered more about last night. "The kid that was working last night, Jason . . ."

"Right."

"He seems like a nice kid."

"Best worker I ever had."

Coventry nodded. "He was talking about wanting to go to college some day."

"That's his plan, but between you and me, he's stuck."

Coventry nodded. "I've seen that happen."

Suddenly Kate Katona was standing beside him. She wore jeans and a sweatshirt, a hoodie, with her weapon riding on her hip. "Hey, wet head, we've been looking for you. It's time for a chopper ride. Agent Miller's already inside waiting for us."

Coventry immediately shook his head. "No way."

"Come on, you'll be safe."

He felt the need to change the subject. "Where's Netherwood?"

"She went home to crash for a few hours. She'll be back a little later."

"Did you say *crash*?"

Katona laughed, grabbed him hard on the arm and tugged him towards the door. "Come on, you big baby."

HE FOLLOWED, NOT SURE YET whether he would actually get in or not. Then he remembered that this whole thing was for Megan Bennett, thought *Screw it*, walked under the rotating blades and climbed in.

He sat next to Kate Katona and across from Agent Miller, who smiled and extended his hand.

"Kate wasn't sure she could get you to come," he said.

Coventry put on a surprised look: "Really? Why not?"

Katona hit him on the arm and told Miller, "Half the time I

can't even get him in an elevator. This guy has more phobias than some entire countries."

Then they were up and off.

The plan was to sweep the area and look for Megan Bennett's body. They were also on the lookout for a dark Camry; or any other car if it was stashed off the road somewhere or parked at some remote site.

For what seemed like a long time, Coventry found himself staring out the window, saying nothing, ostensibly helping with the search but actually concentrating on the sounds and the movement of the aircraft. After some time passed, and they still hadn't fallen out of the sky, he began to get a little more used to the idea of being up there and released his grip on the armrest.

He couldn't help but reflect on just how breathtaking the countryside was from up here. He'd always been a fan of the early morning sun and the way it amplified colors. But this morning, from up here, with the long dark shadows next to the crisp strikes of sunlight, everything was more pronounced and vivid than he could have ever imagined.

Suddenly there it was.

Coventry was the first to see it.

A body lying on the ground, splayed out, motionless.

It was about fifty yards off the road, over a crest, where you wouldn't be able to see it from a car in a million years.

"Look there," he said, pointing.

He could feel Katona take in the view and gasp. "Looks like we're too late."

Coventry kept his eyes on the body as Agent Miller directed the pilot to take them over. Then Katona said, "That's a man."

Coventry knew her eyes were better than his. Actually, he

was nearsighted as hell, and wore contacts. The left eye was fitted for distance and the right one for reading. He studied the body and, now that Katona mentioned it, he could tell she was right. It was a man.

It wasn't Megan Bennett.

"There's another one," Katona said.

True enough, another body came into view as they approached the area, lying in the long shadow of rabbit brush, with a red shirt.

"That's a man too," Katona said.

THE PILOT WAS BRINGING THEM IN for a better look when Coventry's cell phone abruptly rang. He answered it as he concentrated on the bodies.

"Coventry," he said.

It was Detective Richardson. "Bryson, we just got another hit on Megan Bennett's credit card. At a truck stop between Colorado Springs and Pueblo."

What to do?

He leaned in towards the pilot. "Have you got enough gas to get us to Pueblo?" The pilot studied the gages and wrinkled his forehead as if calculating the distance.

"A hundred miles, roughly," Coventry added.

The pilot nodded, but not all that confidently. "I suppose, if you're talking one way."

THEY TOUCHED DOWN ON THE ROAD just long enough to drop Agent Miller off with the two bodies. A heartbeat later, Coventry and Katona shot back into the sky.

Coventry was somewhat surprised that he was comfortable with the movement now and in fact even liking it, to a point. The pilot brought the aircraft close to full throttle and followed I-25 south, which snaked like a flat black river parallel to the foothills. To the left, the east, the sun rose over terrain that lay mostly flat, much of which was undeveloped and some of which was checkered with farms. To the right, the west, the foothills lifted out of the flatlands with a wave-like motion and then bumped into the Rocky Mountains, which looked like they had been pushed up with incredible force from underneath.

"You're thinking," Katona observed.

He was indeed.

"I'm thinking that our biker woman must have pulled off the road somewhere last night to get some sleep, maybe a rest-stop or something, probably because it was too cold to ride," Coventry said. "Otherwise she'd be a lot farther than Pueblo by now. If she's headed south to Santa Fe or Albuquerque, I really want to reel her in before she gets to the border."

Katona nodded.

"The two bodies, they looked like bikers," Katona said.

Coventry nodded.

That was true.

"Friends of the biker woman, I'm sure," Coventry said. He stopped looking out the window and turned to her. "Did you notice there were no motorcycles, in the area of the two bodies, I mean?"

"I did, now that you mention it."

"Bikers without bikes, what's wrong with that picture?" he added. "My guess is that this biker woman is riding one of them, but where's the other one? She's got the answers to Megan Bennett's credit card plus two dead bikers."

"The plot thickens."

AFTER WHAT SEEMED LIKE A LONG FLIGHT they spotted a lone Harley rider about twenty miles south of Pueblo, in the high-speed lane, clicking off the miles with a serious twist on the throttle. Coventry tried to get in close with the binoculars but the movement of the aircraft kept jacking him up. Finally he got it in his sight, just for the briefest of moments, but long enough to tell that the rider was a woman and that the license plate wasn't from Colorado.

"That's her," he said. "We got her. Piece-of-cake."

The pilot looked grim. "We're getting low on fuel, just for your piece-of-cake information."

Coventry scratched his head.

"How fast is she going?" he questioned.

"About eighty."

He pondered the options, then turned to Katona: "Kate, see if you can get the Pueblo P.D. on the line and get them to pull her over." He paused, then found himself thinking out loud: "The problem is, at the RPMs she's turning, it'll take them some time to catch her from behind."

"We don't have some time," the pilot told him.

Coventry felt a pressure in his forehead. "Okay, drop back, I don't want to spook her into going any faster than she already is."

Kate Katona called for assistance and explained their situation.

A few minutes later Coventry saw one of the most beautiful things in the world. A Colorado State Patrol car had come out of nowhere and was closing the gap on the motorcycle with the light bar flashing.

"That guy is flying," he noted. "He's got that sucker floored." Then: "Remind me to buy this guy a gift certificate to the Outback."

Katona chuckled.

"Coventry, you're the cheapest guy on the face of the earth, in case you forgot."

"No, I'm serious, twenty-five bucks worth. This guy's my hero."

THEN SOMETHING BAD HAPPENED. The motorcycle slowed down, bounded across the median, crossed the other side of the freeway, and was now heading due east, down a dirt road. Somehow the patrol car managed to hang with her, bouncing and bucking like a thing possessed.

They both threw pretty impressive rooster tails as they headed into the sun.

What happened next, Coventry could hardly believe. Railroad tracks crossed the road. The motorcycle slammed on the brakes, almost got rear-ended by the patrol car, made a hard right turn and took off down the tracks between the rails, bouncing violently off the timbers. The woman had to slow down considerably, and was probably doing no more than twenty miles an hour now, but the patrol car couldn't follow. The tracks pointed deeper and deeper into the arid topography of southern Colorado. She kept her speed steady, fighting to maintain control of the bike but doing pretty good so far.

"Damned impressive," Coventry said. "That bike weighs four hundred pounds, minimum." To the pilot: "Get in front of her and set down on the tracks."

The pilot said something, something about the fact that they were now flying on fumes, but Coventry couldn't even focus on him. He saw something he hadn't noticed before. From behind them, a train roared up the tracks, going the same direction as the biker woman, a freight train with three tandem engines pulling a long string of cars. It had to be going at least sixty. The biker woman obviously didn't even know it was there; the rumble of the Harley's engine would be masking it out.

Then Katona said, "She's down!"

Coventry looked and couldn't believe it. The bike was down all right, on its side with the woman pinned under it. She was trying to pull herself out, frantic. The back wheel of the bike was still in gear, spinning like a madman, not to mention the chain and sprockets.

He smacked the pilot on the side of the head to be sure he had his attention.

"Get me down there, right now!"

"Okay, there's a flat spot over there."

"No time for flat spots! Get right over her!"

Coventry somehow managed to open the door, climb out, and hang from his hands, ready to jump. The pilot was bringing him in right next to the woman. As soon as they got low enough to where he thought the fall wouldn't kill him, Coventry let go. He immediately realized that he should have waited longer.

Chapter Thirty-One

Day Seven
Sunday Morning

THE SKY HAD BEEN CLEAR of helicopter activity for more than three hours now. Still, David Hallenbeck was stuck in a spider's web with a million spiders lurking around. He knew that. But at least, right at the moment, there were no flying spiders.

The farmer's dog, a golden retriever, was named Bailey according to his collar. He tagged along as Hallenbeck climbed up the foothills, through the Yucca, rocks, and scraggly windbattered pines, to try to get a better view of what was going on at the old farmhouse, if anything.

The sky was as blue as blue could get, a warm cerulean color without a puff of buildup to spoil it. The temperature had climbed to about seventy degrees and couldn't have been more perfect.

He was a little surprised at how much he liked having the dog there with him.

He'd never had a dog before.

In fact, until today, he'd largely looked down on people who had to prop up their pathetic little lives with cats and dogs and other stupid things.

He was high enough now that he could see the farmhouse he abandoned last night. The place couldn't have been more lifeless. Now that was interesting. If the biker bitch had gone to the police, the place would be swarming by now. That means that she'd just taken off and was probably hundreds of miles away. No doubt she had enough skeletons in her own stinky little closet that she didn't need to start any up-close-and-personal conversations with the law enforcement types. The problem was, though, that if she got busted for something—which she would sooner or later—she'd try to use the information about him to leverage herself out of trouble.

She really screwed things up.

He found himself by a boulder, realized that he'd been walking for some time and sat down. The dog immediately lay down by his feet, looked up at him momentarily with big brown eyes, and then rested his head on his front legs.

From up here Hallenbeck could see only one road, the same one he'd been able to see for the last half hour, the same one that a cop car passed over every so often.

Spiders.

Spiders.

Damned spiders everywhere.

He had to get out of their web, assuming the activity was actually for him.

Of course, there was a chance it wasn't. Maybe the cops had done nothing more than find the bodies of the two dead bikers and didn't have a clue yet that they were connected in any way to Megan Bennett.

HE REFLECTED BACK ON THE LAST several hours, which had been productive. Killing the old man last night had basically been a non-event, something that needed to be done, got done, and that was the end of it. His body was up in the rafters of the barn. At some point it would start stinking and be found.

Who cares?

The cops would no doubt try to locate the owner of the other farmhouse. But the farmer didn't own it, his daughter did, and she was on vacation in Australia. The cops would eventually connect the dots and end up knocking on the farmer's door, but that wasn't likely to happen today or tomorrow.

The new place had plenty of food and hot water. All the windows had coverings. And, bless his heart, the one that no longer beat, the old fart was a gun lover. Hallenbeck picked out the best of the best, loaded them and laid them out on the bed upstairs, lined up like little soldiers.

He had the best of the lot—a 9 mm automatic—with him now, wedged in his belt, not far from the knife.

Megan Bennett had given the weapons a curious look that she tried to hide, but he'd seen it. Still, no big deal, she was overly secured and gagged in the other bedroom, with more than enough sleeping pills pumping through her veins. She wasn't about to go anywhere until and unless he let her.

The beer fog in his head had totally dissipated at this point. Last night he had been vulnerable, but today he was thinking as clearly as ever.

The Camry was hidden in the garage. The cops could fly over a million times and never see it.

The old man's pickup truck, a blue single-cab Ford F-150, was no spring chicken but looked to be in good-enough working order. Hallenbeck found the keys sitting on the kitchen counter and started it up, just for grins. No problems. The only drawback was that the stupid thing had a white aftermarket front fender and a red hood. The locals would all know it by heart and would be suspicious if they saw anyone except the old man driving it. Hallenbeck would have to have a story ready, in case that scenario played out.

THE THING THAT CONCERNED HIM more than anything else at this point was the old man's telephone. It rang this morning, on two separate occasions, five to six rings each time. Naturally, the old fart didn't have an answering machine, so Hallenbeck had no idea who was calling. It could be something totally unimportant, or it could be a friend or a relative, maybe a son or a daughter, trying to get in touch with him. If that was the case, they'd get suspicious sooner or later and end up either calling the cops or coming over to see what was going on.

So be ready for that or, better yet, don't be here when it happens.

At one point this morning, Hallenbeck decided to answer the stupid thing the next time it rang, say something like "Heating and Air Conditioning," pretend that the person calling had dialed the wrong number, just to see if he could get any information. If someone had called while Hallenbeck was in that mindset, he would have answered it.

And he would have screwed up.

Luckily they didn't.

He later realized just how stupid that would have been. The person calling might be using a phone that displays the number dialed, or they might be using repeat dial mode. Then they would know that they had dialed correctly and—not only did the old man not answer—something very strange was going on.

So Hallenbeck decided that he had no real option but to let it ring.

"Life's never easy, Bailey," he told the dog. The animal recognized his name and looked up for a second, then set his head back down.

HE COULDN'T TAKE HIS EYES OFF the old farmhouse. Was it safe to go back?

It looked safe.

He didn't see any movement whatsoever.

No parked cars.

No one walking around.

Nothing.

In all the confusion last night he forgot to grab Megan Bennett's purse. More importantly, he forgot to grab his wallet off the kitchen counter.

Maybe because the biker bitch took it, in which case he was really screwed.

Either way, he had to get back there now.

"Come on, Bailey, we're taking a little walk."

Chapter Thirty-Two

Day Seven
Sunday Afternoon

COVENTRY AND THE TWO WOMEN stared out the aircraft's windows, not talking, simply watching the earth fly by below.

The woman sitting next to him, the biker woman, Catherine Higgins, chuckled as if she'd just thought of something funny.

"What?" Coventry questioned, curious.

She leaned back and grinned at him, "Just that look on your face, when you let go of the helicopter and started falling."

Coventry tried to picture it.

"*Ohhhhh shit!*" she continued.

He grinned.

"Yeah, well, it worked," he said. "So be glad."

Kate Katona smiled and looked at him, obviously getting a visual. Then she said, "None of us will ever be allowed back in southern Colorado again, that's for sure."

That was probably truer than Coventry wanted to admit.

The Harley had been too trivial to derail the train but had been significant enough to explode under engine number two and take it out. Although Coventry hadn't personally talked yet with anyone from the train company, they supposedly weren't showing much of a sense of humor about the whole thing. They were talking about damages and delayed shipments and irresponsible police chases. That little incident was going to end up generating more than a few meetings before all was said and done.

Reportedly, the FBI helicopter was still out there too, sitting next to the tracks in the weeds and the rabbit brush, until some genius could figure out how to get fuel to it. One of the flight-for-life guys had remarked that the pilot would probably end up losing his license, for engaging in flight with an insufficient fuel reserve and taking the aircraft into the airspace of an oncoming train. Coventry resolved to get very personally involved in that little discussion should it ever come about.

THE BIKER WOMAN SUSTAINED a second-degree burn to her left arm from the Harley's exhaust pipe, in addition to several large lacerations, one of which was deep. Coventry and Katona took the flight-for-life with her to the local hospital in Pueblo and waited with her while she got treated. Until her clothes came off, she actually seemed halfway normal. Then Coventry saw all the tattoos and, for some reason, wished he could just erase them.

The good news was, she had no problem cooperating with them.

She told them how she and her two biker companions found the farmhouse while looking for a place to crash, how they found the woman tied up in the bedroom, how the big man busted in out of the blue and killed the two bikers, how he tied her up when he left to dump the two bodies.

How she escaped.

Megan Bennett was alive.

At least as of last night.

That was the most important fact, together with the biker woman's ability to hopefully identify the farmhouse from the sky.

"We're getting close," Coventry observed. "How long was he gone, when he took the bodies to dump them?"

The woman looked perplexed. "I don't know, some time."

"Ten minutes? Two hours?"

Coventry could tell she was trying to get a handle on it for him. "I'm guessing an hour, maybe more."

Coventry nodded.

"Okay, good."

If that was true then the farmhouse should be about a half hour drive from where they found the two bikers' bodies this morning.

As they started to get in range, Coventry told the pilot to take them way up. He guessed that the farmhouse would be long abandoned by now. In case it wasn't, though, he didn't want the chopper to look like it was searching. He wanted it to look just like any other aircraft peacefully on its way from point A to B.

They passed over the ground where the two dead bikers had been found this morning. "There's where he dumped them," Coventry told the biker woman, pointing. She looked and grunted, curious, but not showing any emotion. There were several vehicles in the area and a lot of activity on the ground. "That's a pretty important crime scene," Coventry explained. "Okay," he said. "See over there? That's the gas station you stopped at. The Sinclair. You came from that way, the north, right?"

She nodded. "Right."

"Okay," he said. "We're going to follow that road and you tell me when we get to the farmhouse."

About four minutes later, Coventry heard her say, "We need to turn here, follow that road, the one going that way."

They did.

Shortly thereafter, she said, "There, I think."

"Are you sure?"

She got excited, visibly excited, and he could tell that she was certain. "Yes. I remember that old rusted car on the right of the house. And the driveway was covered with weeds. And the barn was next to the house, not behind it, just like that. I don't see his car, through. His car's gone."

"It could be in the barn."

Coventry gave her a big kiss on the cheek. "You did good."

Now what?

Coventry leaned in towards the pilot, to where he would be able to hear him better. "That's the place we're looking for," he said, pointing. "Just hang right here."

IT WAS IMPORTANT THAT SHALIFA NETHERWOOD be involved in the collar. She'd been working tirelessly for a long time and had earned the right to be there. Coventry managed to get her on her cell phone and tell her his plan. Thirteen minutes later, she pulled up at the end of the driveway to the farmhouse, along with Agents Charles Miller and Sam Dakota, leading a train of black-and-whites. Once they were in place, Coventry had the pilot drop the bird straight out of the air and jumped out. The chopper immediately swooped back up, with Kate Katona on board, who would serve as the eye in the sky.

He pulled his weapon and felt the weight of it in his hand. The last time he drew like this he used it. The memory was suddenly so palpable he could taste it.

He swallowed and looked at everyone.

"Remember," he said, "if he's there he has a hostage. Okay, let's go."

Chapter Thirty-Three

Day Seven
Sunday Afternoon

_____

DAVID HALLENBECK WAS IN THE BEDROOM of the farmhouse, pissed that he was having trouble finding Megan Bennett's purse, when he first heard the rumble of the helicopter.

What the hell?

He ran to the front window and saw the aircraft, blue with a white belly. It dropped out of the sky at an incredible, almost dangerous, rate. There were several people inside.

Shit!

They were coming for him!

His senses intensified and recessed survival genes exploded.

If he got caught in the house he was dead.

Get to the barn, at least.

And get there now, right this second, before the chopper pulls back up and pins your sorry ass in the house.

He ran out the back door, behind the house, and into the barn, with Bailey by his side, almost tripping him up in fact. Jesus, the dog was going to screw up everything. His first instinct was to kill it, but he couldn't have fresh blood on the scene.

"Come here, boy," he said, kneeling down.

The dog came over, visibly hesitant, sensing danger.

"Good boy," he said, patting him on the head.

He could hear the helicopter pulling back up into the sky now. He was pinned in the barn. Whoever got dropped off would already be heading this way. He worked frantically to get the dog's collar off. The last thing he needed was for the cops to know where the animal lived. He didn't need some good-natured civil servant returning it this afternoon and end up stumbling across Megan Bennett and the dead farmer and the Camry.

He finally managed to get it off, then immediately pushed the animal away, made a violent gesture towards it, and sneered, "Go!" The animal, visibly startled, backed up, then turned and ran away.

Now what?

UP IN THE RAFTERS OF THE STRUCTURE, a good twenty feet off the ground, someone had laid down a couple of sheets of plywood, a crude ancient storage platform. There was no ladder or way to get to it, though.

Well, wait, maybe there was.

Hallenbeck ran to the other end of the barn, climbed onto the top of some old rusty piece of machinery, and then jumped up to catch a rafter. From there, he swung from rafter to rafter, like a kid on monkey bars, all the way back to the side of the barn where the plywood was. He muscled himself onto it and lay down, not quite believing he had been able to do it.

The helicopter sounded like it was right over his head.

His hands burned. He must have picked up fifteen or

twenty splinters and started to pull them out, being as careful as he could not to break them off inside. The plywood was covered with dust, dirt and pigeon shit that had to be at least twenty years old.

He managed to find a knothole in the side of the barn big enough to see through when he got his eye right up to it. Four people were running up to the house, quietly motioning to one another, with their weapons drawn. Hallenbeck recognized one of them as the cop from TV, Canterbury, or whatever the hell his name was, the hunter. Two of the assholes, an older man and a younger bodybuilder type, ran around the side of the house and disappeared. The TV cop and a strong black woman crept up to the front door, waited for a few seconds, and then rushed in.

Bailey the dog followed them.

He could hear them shouting to one another but the noise of the helicopter kept him from deciphering the individual words. There were other cops now, too, lots of them, fanning out around the property.

This was it.

HE PULLED HIS EYE AWAY FROM THE HOLE and lay down flat in the dirt and bird-shit on the plywood, with the gun on his right side, safety off, and the knife on his left. Whenever he moved the wood creaked a little. He folded his arms under his head, put his body in the most comfortable position he could find and concentrated on getting his breathing as quiet and shallow as possible.

The witching hour was here.

He'd been immobile only a short time when they enter the

barn.

The dog was with them.

He could hear it panting.

They were covering ground quickly, obviously looking for any sign of Megan Bennett, dead or alive.

He didn't move a single muscle.

His bladder had built up a pressure that was getting exponentially worse with each passing second.

An eternity passed.

Then a cell phone rang, right below him, and he heard one of the men answer it.

"Coventry."

A pause, then the man said, "They just found Kelly Parks' car. I got to go."

For some reason the dog barked.

The sound startled Hallenbeck so much that he pissed in his pants.

Chapter Thirty-Four

Day Eight
Monday Morning

———————

BRYSON COVENTRY RAPPED ON the apartment door, waited, and then rapped again, harder and longer. He knew he was waking the woman up but she'd just have to forgive him. He finally heard movement inside, peeked through the window where the blind didn't cover, and saw Jeannie Dannenberg come out of a bedroom and walk towards the door. She was in the process of throwing a long-sleeve shirt over a naked body as she worked her way across the living room. When she got to the door and opened it two buttons were fastened and that's all she had time for.

Her hair was a mess and she looked like she'd just been dragged out of hibernation.

She recognized him but was having trouble zeroing in. "Bryson Coventry," he reminded her. "Kelly Parks' friend."

The confusion dropped off her face. "Right," she said. "From the club. You're the detective." She swung the door all the way open, an invitation for him to enter, walked over to the couch and plopped herself down, yawning. "What time is it?"

Coventry shut the door behind him, looked at his watch and

took a seat in the overstuffed chair across from the couch. "Ten after eight," he told her. "Sorry to wake you." He had a thermos of coffee in his right hand and held it up, a peace offering. "Coffee," he said. "Some kind of chocolate-cherry flavor, if you're in the mood."

She shook her head negative. "I'm going back to bed as soon as you leave. So what's going on?"

"I'm assuming you haven't heard about Kelly Parks," Coventry told her.

The look on her face told him she hadn't. "No. Heard what?"

Coventry organized it, not wanting to give her too much information, but enough: "Someone attacked her Saturday night. She's at Lutheran Medical Center."

"You're kidding, right?"

No, he wasn't.

"Someone stuffed her into the trunk of her car and drove it off an embankment into Clear Creek, up on Route 6, between the second and third tunnels. Luckily the river dropped and the vehicle ended up lodging itself nose down, with the trunk up in the air. Otherwise she would have drowned."

Coventry waited while the woman processed the information and visualized the scene. She looked seriously troubled.

"How horrible," she said

Coventry nodded. "Ironically, the recovery team almost killed her getting the car out of the river. They didn't know she was in there."

"So is she going to be okay, or what?"

He wasn't sure. "They're running tests," he told her, "and have her all doped up. But she's a strong woman and that will help."

"Poor Kelly."

COVENTRY NODDED AND THEN DECIDED it was time to get what he came for. "Last weekend, last Saturday in fact, a woman named D'endra Vaughn was murdered. I'm assuming that you know about that, since you're her friend."

The woman looked perplexed.

"What makes you think that?"

"Your name came up as part of our background investigation of the victim, the Vaughn woman, that's all. You're not in any trouble or anything."

"That would be a first." Then after a pause: "Yes, I know about D'endra's death. And yes, we were friends."

Coventry zeroed in on the critical question. "And Kelly Parks was a friend of hers too, correct?"

Dannenberg immediately disagreed. "No. Kelly is a friend of mine, but Kelly and D'endra never met."

"They didn't?"

"No."

"You're sure?"

"Yes. Why would I lie?"

"I'm not saying you are," Coventry assured her. "Did you know that after D'endra Vaughn was killed, someone used her cell phone to call Kelly Parks? Did Kelly tell you about that?"

The woman wasn't particularly comfortable with the line of questioning. "Look, I don't know if I should be talking to you about all this."

"Why not?"

"It's . . . I don't know . . . complicated."

"Kelly Parks is in a hospital right now, lucky to be alive,"

Coventry reiterated. "The attack on her is connected to D'endra Vaughn. So you need to tell me what I need to know so I can get to the bottom of this." Then, after a pause: "Otherwise she's going to end up dead, plain and simple."

Jeannie stood up and paced, visibly stressed. Her shirt flapped open as she walked and Coventry did his best to not look, but wasn't quite succeeding.

"I got to think," she finally said. Then: "I'm starved. Did you eat breakfast yet?"

No, he hadn't.

She headed towards the bathroom. "Let me throw on a quick face and then I'll let you take me to Denny's. I may or may not have something to say so don't get your hopes up too far."

Coventry said, "Fair enough," and realized that he could definitely eat. He suddenly visualized a plate of pancakes smothered under whipped cream and strawberries.

JEANNIE DANNENBERG CAME OUT of the bathroom five minutes later with the sleep off her face and her hair pulled into a ponytail, wearing green cotton pants and a bulky Colorado Rockies sweatshirt.

"Meet the anti-Oasis," she joked.

They paused long enough for her to grab a mug out of the kitchen cabinet and fill it up with that chocolate-cherry coffee that Coventry had been carrying around. Ten minutes later they were at Denny's with orders already in the works and hot fresh coffee sitting in front of them. The stereo played "Girl, You'll be a Woman Soon," not the original Neil Diamond version, but the edgier one from *Pulp Fiction*. Coventry visualized the scene with Uma Thurman lip-singing it and made a mental note that he needed to watch it again.

Coventry asked the waitress to leave the pot. At first she wasn't going to but then looked at him real close and did.

Coventry had to be at least ten years older than Jeannie Dannenberg and some of the people around them were casting a glance or two in their direction. He could tell that they were thinking that he and the woman had spent the night together. He was half expecting the cook to jump out and give him a big high-five.

"Your eyes are two different colors," she told him. "One's blue and one's green. I've never seen that before. It's sort of cool." Then she closed her eyes: "What color are mine?"

Coventry chuckled. "Brown-Eyed Girl. You ever hear that song, by Van Morrison?"

She opened her eyes, blew him a kiss and rocked her head back and forth: ". . . you my-yyyy, brown-eyed girl . . ."

"Very good."

"I didn't know who sang it though."

Coventry wasn't surprised. "It came out before you were born. So let's get back to Kelly Parks and D'endra Vaughn for a second. Tell me the connection."

"It's complicated."

"So un-complicate it for me."

"It's complicated as in maybe a little bit illegal," she clarified. "If I talk to you, you can't be using what I say against me or Kelly. That's the deal."

Coventry had no problem with that. "Unless you all killed somebody or something, I don't really give a flying donut what you did."

She studied him. "She likes you, you know."

"Who?"

"Kelly," she said. "So you be nice to her. Don't go breaking her heart."

Coventry smiled. "She's lucky to have a friend like you. Now, talk to me."

OVER PANCAKES AND COFFEE, Coventry heard quite a story.

Jeannie Dannenberg had in fact been a friend of the murdered schoolteacher, D'endra Vaughn. They also had a third friend by the name of Alicia Elmblade.

In May of last year, the three women participated in a fake abduction staged at a place called Rick's Gas Station. Alicia Elmblade was the one abducted. Jeannie and D'endra were each paid $10,000 to witness the abduction and make a false report to the police, saying that they saw an Asian man drag her into a van and drive off.

Kelly Parks was also in on the deal, although she wasn't a friend of the other three women. Her part of the charade was to pull up just as the abduction was taking place, witness it, call 911 and then give the same story to the police, namely that she'd seen an Asian man.

The other person in on the charade was the driver of the van. He's the one who arranged the whole deal and paid the money. They didn't know his name at the time. However, Jeannie later found out from Kelly Parks that he was Michael Northway, an attorney in Kelly's law firm.

Alicia Elmblade, by the way, got $100,000 for her role.

She's never been heard from since that night.

After letting her get the general story out, Coventry led her back to the beginning and had her go over the whole thing again, this time filling in the million details that he needed to know. By the time they were finished, he was surprised to see that they'd been talking for over an hour.

"You done good," he told her, which was true. "I couldn't have figured this out in a thousand years if you hadn't told me."

She looked relieved that it was all out in the open. "It's off the record, though. Right?"

He nodded with agreement.

"That's the deal."

With two pots of coffee flowing through his veins, he knew what he needed to do next and was suddenly anxious to get going on it.

HE DROPPED THE BROWN-EYED-GIRL OFF at her apartment, thanked her again, then called Kate Katona and started talking as soon as she answered. "Kate, it's me, the pain in your posterior. We need a full background check on a guy named Michael Northway. He's a lawyer, lives out in Cherry Creek or Cherry Hills somewhere. Cherry something. Also, there was an abduction of a woman named Alicia Elmblade last May, somewhere in the foothills but I'm not exactly sure exactly where, at a place called Rick's Gas Station. There's a local police report on it that I need to get my hands on. Oh, I almost forgot. Good morning. By the way, this all relates to the D'endra Vaughn and Kelly Parks cases. I'll fill you in this afternoon. Love you, darling."

"You have a strange way of showing it."

"Yeah. By the way, did I say thanks?"

"No."

"I will."

Chapter Thirty-Five

Day Nine
Tuesday Morning

KELLY PARKS FOUND HERSELF coming out of a deep, drug-enhanced sleep. The first thing she saw when she opened her eyes was a dashboard and realized she was in a car, sitting in the passenger seat, reclined as far as it would go. Next to her Jeannie Dannenberg stared out at the road, driving. The car radio was turned down low, barely audible, to a country-western station. She looked out the window and realized they were clipping along at a pretty good rate on an interstate, winding through an incredible canyon of sheer rock walls with a raging river off to the left. She was most definitely not in Denver anymore.

Jeannie Dannenberg must have noticed her movement, because she said, "Good morning, sweetheart."

Kelly felt like she was in the middle of a fog that had her surrounded for a hundred miles. Then she remembered taking the painkillers this morning.

She fumbled around for the seat control and managed to get her body up to vertical. That felt better on her back. "Where are we?" she questioned.

"You don't recognize Glenwood Canyon?"

Then she did. "Yeah, okay."

"You've been out for more than two hours."

Kelly now realized why she woke up. "Bathroom," she said. "Now."

"Me too," Jeannie told her. "We need gas, anyway. How you feeling?"

Good question.

How *was* she feeling?

She remembered the endless hours of being stuffed in the trunk of her car. She recalled the ambulance ride, after they pulled her from the river, and remembered being in the hospital. She remembered being so very, very cold, and hearing the word hypothermia several times. She remembered getting warmer and warmer at the hospital and how incredibly good that felt. She remembered the X-rays and the faces of lots of strangers, telling her which way to turn, doing things to her and asking if it hurt. She remembered that every time she woke up during the night, Bryson Coventry had been there.

This morning she was feeling a whole lot better and all the news from the doctors had been good. She didn't have any broken bones and her spine hadn't sustained any permanent injury from the stun-gun. Her neck had been strained from her head bouncing around, similar to a whiplash injury, but there didn't appear to be any torn muscles. They told her the pain should go away in a couple of days and if it didn't she might need some physical therapy, but nothing to get worried about.

She remembered checking out this morning, against her doctor's recommendations, but with his authorization if she insisted. Then Jeannie Dannenberg picked her up and they swung by her loft to pack some clothes, and pick up the case file, before heading out on the road.

"Are you okay?" Jeannie asked again.

"Yeah, just groggy."

She wanted to wake up in the worst way. "Find a gas station that has coffee," she said.

Jeannie nodded and then threw a nervous glance her way. "Are you sure you're not mad at me for telling Bryson about Rick's Gas Station?"

Kelly wasn't sure, if the truth be told, one way or the other.

She hadn't talked to Michael Northway yet and didn't have a clue how much fallout was going to end up coming her way after Coventry confronted him, which was inevitable.

But it made no sense to have Jeannie feel bad about it. "No, forget it. Things were going to start busting open one way or the other anyway. If I end up unemployed or disbarred, though, I'm coming to live with you. You understand that, I hope."

"That'd be okay, but our lease has a No Lawyers clause."

Kelly smiled.

"Most do," she said.

A gas station popped up and they stopped.

TEN MINUTES LATER THEY WERE FULLY GASSED up, with a bug-free windshield, and back on the road, sipping from Styrofoam cups filled with the best piping-hot coffee that either one of them had ever tasted. Kelly felt her brain starting to return.

They were heading to Grand Junction for a one-day trial that was scheduled to start tomorrow morning in the Mesa County District Court. No one else in the firm would have been able to jump in and handle it and wouldn't want to in any event:

Kelly had taken it *pro bono*. Her client, Catherine Wilson, 23, single mother of two, was being sued by her former employer for embezzlement of company funds. The only problem was, she didn't do it, and if Kelly couldn't get a judgment in her favor, she may as well hang up any chance of ever getting a decent job again, in this or the next two lifetimes.

They were heading west on I-70 with the cruise control of the Honda set at 78 mph, three over the speed limit. It was the same car that Kelly rented for Jeannie a few days ago.

As they left Glenwood Springs behind them the terrain lost its mountain edge, turning more arid and hilly. The traffic fell off considerably and the eighteen-wheelers began to outnumber the cars. A severe thunderhead was building up in the north, twenty miles away, maybe further, looking like it would spit lightning any second. The sky overhead, by contrast, was bright blue and dotted with solid, white, cotton-ball clouds, seriously stunning.

At certain crests in the road you could see forever in every direction.

"You know what we should do?" Jeannie suggested. "After your trial tomorrow, just keep going, all the way to California and see if we can find Alicia."

She laughed. "I'm a lawyer, honey, a lawyer with a mortgage. There's more golden handcuffs on these wrists than you'd ever want to know about."

"You're a lawyer with a target on her back," Jeannie said. She wore white shorts, a tank top and sandals, and looked way too feminine. "We should go to L.A. and hire a P.I."

"We could do that from Denver."

"Yeah, but it wouldn't be as much fun. Have you ever been to La-La Land?"

"No."

"It's nuts there."

They were at a point in the road where they could only get three stations on the radio, all country. Kelly had never really listened to country before and was a little surprised to find that it wasn't all just about pickup trucks and cheating hearts.

The scenery continued to roll by. For some reason Kelly found herself mesmerized by it. It was incredibly nice being on the road.

Plus her body needed the rest.

AT SOME POINT THE COLORADO RIVER appeared on their right, running wide and brown and powerful, escorting them into Grand Junction. The interstate and the river funneled into a canyon and rubbed against each other. The road tightened and twisted and the speed limit dropped. When there were just a few miles from the first exit into town, Kelly's cell phone rang. It was Bryson Coventry. He sounded harried.

"Where are you?" he asked.

"Grand Junction."

"Grand Junction?"

"Yes, Grand Junction. I have a trial here tomorrow. You sound strange, like you're in a tunnel or something."

"A stairway," he explained. "Twenty-first floor. I'm about five minutes away from peeling back Michael Northway. I thought you should know."

Chapter Thirty-Six

Day Nine
Tuesday Noon

———————

BRYSON COVENTRY WALKED UP the twenty-five flights of stairs to the law offices of Holland, Roberts & Northway, LLC, not in the mood to mess with elevators. By the time he got up there his legs were on fire. Then he found out that the stairwell door wouldn't open on that floor from his side. He ended up having to rap on it for several minutes before someone finally opened it to see what all the fuss was about.

Shalifa Netherwood was waiting for him in the law firm's lobby, parked in an oversized leather chair, reading a *Sunset* magazine and looking like she'd been there for a while. She didn't seem overly surprised when someone escorted him into the area from behind the receptionist's desk.

"Don't even say it," he warned her.

"It," she retorted.

"Not funny."

She leaned forward in the chair but made no move to get up. "He's here and he's going to see us, as soon as the client he's with leaves."

"When's that?"

She shrugged. "When they're done, I suppose."

That was fine with Coventry. It would give the lawyer additional time to build up a sweat. The main thing is that they were invading his turf, letting him know just by their presence that the golden walls of the building couldn't protect him.

He was just about to go over to the receptionist and see if he could finagle a cup of coffee when she walked over with one.

"Shaken, not stirred," she said. "If I remember right."

Coventry smiled. "Thank you."

OVER ON THE WALL WAS A NEW OIL PAINTING, a large western scene that hadn't been there last time. Coventry walked over to it, impressed even from a distance. When he got there he couldn't believe it and waved Shalifa over.

"This is by Gerard Delano," he explained.

"Who's he?"

"He did a lot of western illustrations for the covers of magazines in the 1930s and 1940s," Coventry said. "Then he did a long serious of big oil paintings like this one, almost exclusively of Navajo Indians. This one here is worth more than my house."

She looked skeptical, but said, "It's not bad."

And it wasn't, he had to agree. It was a substantial painting, about three feet square, titled "Canyon de Chelly." Three riders were emerging from a canyon on horseback. Most of the painting was in early-morning shadow, with the exception of a bright yellow ray of light that busted through the canyon walls and lay across the desert floor like a thing of beauty.

"That reminds me," she said with a look in her eye. "I swung by the Carr-Border Gallery, when was it, Thursday I think.   The plan was to go in and pretend like I didn't know who you were and go gaga over your stuff.   But they actually looked pretty good in there, your paintings, with the white walls and oak flooring and everything.   I was actually impressed."

That sounded good, and he gave her his attention.   "How many were hanging, of mine?"

"I don't know, four, maybe.   The owner walked over, he's a horn dog by the way, and I told him you were a genius, that I wanted to know who you were so I could have your baby, blah, blah, blah."

"What'd he say?"

"He said you were an *emerging artist.*"

Coventry grinned.   "He's nicer behind my back than he is to my face.   He usually tells me to cut an ear off and see if that helps."

"That's been done."

"I know."

"I'd go for the whole head, if I was you."

He grinned.

"Make a real statement," she added.

Coventry shook his head.

BEFORE LONG, THEY FOUND THEMSELVES escorted over to a winding staircase that took them up to the top level of the law firm, where Michael Northway lived.   They walked through a fascinating space that looked like Tarzan's backyard, and got dropped off at the desk of a woman who bore a striking resemblance to Marilyn Monroe.   They waited on a leather couch for another five minutes, watching her work, until a green light flashed on her desk and she said, "He can see you now."

Michael Northway turned out to be an extremely good-looking man with an incredible energy, who greeted them warmly and openly, extending his hand and apologizing for the delay. His handshake was a lot stronger than Coventry anticipated.

"You're the ones taking such good care of Kelly Parks," he said. "Come in and sit down."

The attorney's office was four or five times bigger than it needed to be, with a wall of glass that opened up into an incredible view of downtown Denver and the Rocky Mountains. From here you could see that most of the high distant peaks were still snow-covered. Over by the wet bar sat a conference table big enough to seat ten, inundated with files and folders.

"Thanks for seeing us without an appointment," Coventry said, anxious to get to it. "You're busy and so are we, so I want to jump right to the heart of the matter. Someone killed D'endra Vaughn a week ago last Saturday. You know who she is, correct? D'endra Vaughn?"

Coventry fully expected the lawyer to deny it, or at least get a reaction, but the attorney didn't even flinch.

"Yes, I do."

"And you're not the one who killed her, of course."

Northwood laughed at such an incredible statement, and shook his head. "No, not hardly. Unless I forgot, but it seems like the kind of thing I'd remember."

"In fact, you were actually the keynote speaker at the Top Company Awards that evening, down at the Broadmoor."

The lawyer nodded. "Last Saturday? Keynote speaker might be a bit strong," he said, "but I confess to mumbling a few bad jokes into the microphone that night, yes." Then: "Although I must say that I'm a little surprised that you would even want to know that."

Coventry understood. "You start wide and rule things out," he explained. "That's how homicide investigations work."

"Same as in the law," the attorney observed. "Sometimes you hear the phrase, *pick a jury*. In reality, no jury has ever been picked. Every jury in the history of mankind has been *unpicked*. Each side takes turns throwing out the jurors they don't like and what remains are the unpicked."

Shalifa Netherwood nodded her head, and couldn't help but say, "I never thought of it like that."

Northwood smiled at her then turned back to Coventry.

"Sorry for the side trip," he apologized.

"We know that whoever killed D'endra Vaughn called Kelly Parks the next day with the dead woman's cell phone," Coventry continued. "As a warning. And we know that D'endra Vaughn and Kelly Parks both participated in that little charade at Rick's Gas Station last May."

Coventry paused to let the words sink in.

This time there *was* a reaction on Northway's face, barely perceptible and short-lived, but there nonetheless.

"Rick's Gas Station," the attorney repeated.

Buying time.

"We know about that incident from Jeannie Dannenberg," Coventry explained. "You remember her, right?"

Again, no hesitation: "Yes I do."

"By the way, Kelly Parks never told us a word about Rick's Gas Station, just so you know."

Northwood looked assured, as if that was obviously important to him, then seemed puzzled. "How did you come across Jeannie Dannenberg's name, just for grins?"

Coventry wondered if he should answer that one, glanced at

Shalifa Netherwood briefly, and saw her shrug as if she didn't care.

"Yeah, okay," Coventry said. "D'endra Vaughn's boyfriend, initially a suspect, tipped us off that D'endra had come into some mystery money. We thought that maybe she'd done something illegal, which could explain why she'd been killed, and started sniffing around to find out who was active in her life when the money showed up. Jeannie Dannenberg turned out to be on that list."

The lawyer nodded. "They were friends."

"We later found out that the mystery money was ten thousand dollars that you gave to the Vaughn woman in exchange for her participation in the charade."

"Not my money, exactly, but go on."

Coventry felt good about the conversation. It was unfolding the way he wanted and the attorney was being a lot more candid than he anticipated.

"It's our understanding," he continued, "that you set up this whole charade at the request of one of the firm's clients, who wanted to help a particular lady friend named Alicia Elmblade, who in turn wanted to fake her death and disappear."

Northway wrinkled his brow as if the question had suddenly strayed past the line. "That might be true, but I can't comment on the firm's clients," he said.

Coventry put on his most serious face. "That's a shame, because everything that's happening goes back to Rick's Gas Station, and if you can't help us take the next step down the trail then the trail stops at you."

Northway said nothing.

"So we want to talk to the client," Coventry emphasized. "What we need from you at this point is his name."

Northway looked like he genuinely wanted to help, but said: "I can't divulge that. Attorney-client privilege. And the privilege belongs to the client, not me." Then he added: "You obviously think that the client is the one who killed the Vaughn woman. He's not. The so-called trail that you're so anxious to go down is a dead-end. Take my word for it."

"Fine. He can tell me that himself and point me in the right direction."

"I'll relay the invitation," Northway said. A pause, then: "But don't hold your breath."

COVENTRY GOT UP, WALKED OVER to the wet bar, splashed a small amount of malt whisky in a fancy crystal glass, just enough to get a taste, and swallowed it.

"Smooth," he said, and then looked hard at Northway. "Here's my problem. Nobody should die the way that D'endra Vaughn did. So I told her, while she was hanging there by her wrists so incredibly dead, and with so much trauma on her body that it made me want to throw up, that I would find the person who did this to her and take him down."

Shalifa Netherwood nodded, almost imperceptibly, and Coventry could tell that she was remembering the moment.

"Then," he continued, "to make matters worse, this man, if you want to call him that, did what he did to Kelly Parks, which didn't exactly improve my opinion of him."

Northway was staring at Coventry with wide eyes, as serious as any human being could get.

Coventry motioned to Netherwood that they were leaving and she got up and stood by his side.

"You don't want the trail to stop at your feet," Coventry

said. "Believe me. So you sit back and think about all this, you hold your meetings, you talk to your client or your partners or whoever it is you're going to talk to, you have a steak and a beer, you do whatever it is that you're going to do. Just be sure you call me by noon tomorrow with something that doesn't make the trail stop at your feet."

He walked towards the door.

Then stopped and turned.

"Oh, by the way, the D.A.'s office has the opinion that the attorney-client privilege doesn't apply to situations where the lawyer and client actually conspire together to commit an illegal act, such as obstruction of justice. Then, of course, we also have the open question as to whether Alicia Elmblade ended up really dead out of all this. Rumor is, no one's seen her since that night that you orchestrated so well. On a lighter note, please say goodbye to that gracious receptionist at the front desk for us."

Chapter Thirty-Seven

Day Nine
Tuesday Night

THE THING THAT FREAKED Megan Bennett out the most, way down deep in her dark corners, was wearing the ball-gag. Every time Hallenbeck put it on her she went nuts and begged him with everything she had. She couldn't breathe properly through her nose and that the gag made her suffocate.

Right now she was curled up on the floor in the back of the Camry, her right ankle cuffed to the seat frame. Her hands were tied tightly behind her back.

The ball-gag was sitting on the front seat.

Hallenbeck picked it up and played with it, staring down at her, deciding.

"Please, no," she pleaded. "I won't say a word. I swear to you I will not say a single word no matter what happens."

Hallenbeck continued to twist it around in his hands.

Finally, he said, "I'll tell you what. I'll leave it off for now just because I'm a nice guy. But if you do anything at all to piss me off, if you try to call out or do anything stupid like that, I'm going to put it on and never take it off again. You'll wear it for the rest of your life. Do you understand what I just said?"

She nodded. "Yes. Thank you. I won't say anything. I really won't."

He took a thick brown blanket and covered her.

"You comfy?" he questioned.

"Yes, thank you."

"Good," he said. "I'm going to put a couple of pillows on top of you, just so you're hidden better."

"That's fine."

He got her concealed as well as he could, then started the engine, and said, "Okay, we're going to take off now. I have the knife right here next to me. If we get stopped by the police or anything like that, and you so much as even breathe, that knife is going straight into your face. Do you understand that clearly?"

"Yes I do."

"I hope so. I really do."

He smiled at the fact that he hadn't exactly given her all the information. If the police stopped him, he would deliver a blow to her head so fierce and so violent that talking would definitely not be an issue.

THE NIGHT WAS UNUSUALLY BRIGHT, filled with yellow moonlight so intense that it actually cast shadows.

He drove down the long dirt driveway, stopped at the gravel road, saw nothing in either direction and pulled out.

He wondered if he was making a mistake sticking with the Camry rather than taking the farmer's truck, but he didn't think so. Initially, he pictured himself escaping in the truck. But then, when he got to thinking about it, he didn't like the downside of the cops getting their hands on the Camry. Leaving it behind would be the equivalent of writing down his name, address and phone number on a piece of paper and taping it on the refrigerator door.

He brought the vehicle up to a conservative speed and held it there.

"You okay down there?" he questioned, not really sure why. She'd been through a lot. Of course, he'd put plenty of people through a lot before, but never for such an extended period, not like this.

This was something new entirely.

Virgin ground.

"Yes, fine. Thank you."

"Well, let me know if you get too hot or to cold or anything."

"Okay, thank you."

SHE HAD TOTALLY FREAKED OUT when he left for the walk on Sunday and didn't come back. But then again, he wasn't exactly having the time of his life either. He lay on the plywood up in the barn rafters hour after hour, motionless, intentionally and stressfully quiet, not able to cough or clear his throat or stand up. At one point there must have been six or eight people in the place processing the scene, taking photographs of the Harley, measuring distances, drawing field sketches and telling stupid jokes.

When they set up halogen lights and started working into the night, after he had already been up there for over nine hours, a genuine panic started to come over him and his mind lapsed into horrible little scenarios. He knew his muscles could go into spasm at any time and give him away. Plus he'd been forced to relieve himself in his pants a number of times and worried about the odor drawing attention.

And every single minute he expected someone to shine a flashlight his way and say, "Hey, has anyone checked up there yet?"

But everyone left about ten o'clock, everyone except one unlucky cop who stayed behind to guard the crime scene until the morning. Luckily, Hallenbeck had been able to get down and sneak off without having to kill him.

When he finally got back to the other house, Megan Bennett had been tied up in the same position and abandoned for over ten hours, and was almost to the point of hysteria. It took a long time to calm her down and bring her back to any semblance of normalcy. The rest of the night, out of pity and against his better judgment, he actually let her lie in bed with him without any ties whatsoever.

He held her and rubbed her shoulders and back.

That was Sunday night.

LAST NIGHT, MONDAY NIGHT, after it got dark, he set out on foot and walked all the way to the Sinclair station, to find out if any roadblocks were up. He must have walked at least fifteen miles all told, not to mention having to duck off the road more times than he would ever want to count. But he did find out what he needed to know.

There were no roadblocks.

Most likely, when the cops found the Camry missing, they surmised that he had escaped early on, right after the biker woman made a run for it, and was long gone.

WITH THE ROAD SAFE, that made tonight, Tuesday night, the escape portal.

He was feeling good.

But then something weird happened.

He couldn't have been more than a mile from the farmhouse when headlights appeared behind him from out of nowhere. Ordinarily that wouldn't bother him, even in a situation like this, except that they were coming up strong.

Damn it.

He kept the speed constant and tried to stay calm. The other car must have been doing fifty. He pictured four FBI agents inside, weapons drawn, big old hard-ons in their pants. Sure enough, the lights got brighter and brighter and were now almost right on his ass.

They were going to ram him!

At the last second he floored the car, trying to stay ahead, and braced for the crash. At the same time the other vehicle slammed on its brakes, triggering a nose-plant that made the headlights dip down for just a fraction of a second. Hallenbeck felt what might have been an impact at the rear end of his vehicle but wasn't sure.

The other vehicle shot up next to him. He could make out the silhouette of a man inside, frantically motioning for him to pull over.

What the hell?

He brought the car to a stop, warned Megan Bennett to keep her damned mouth shut, got out of the vehicle and walked back towards the other car—a late model Corvette—which had pulled up behind him. The other man was already out, looking at the front end of his vehicle.

"You got no taillights, buddy," the man said. "This accident is your fault, not mine. I hope you got insurance because I'm calling the police."

Hallenbeck looked at his lights and couldn't believe it. The guy was right. He'd been driving with his lights off. In another fifteen minutes he would have been on I-25 and, if he didn't eventually notice, he would most definitely have been pulled over sooner or later.

Damn!

He knew the world was too screwed-up to have a God but couldn't help but wonder if someone was watching out for him tonight.

"Hey," he said, his voice as friendly and understanding as he could force it to be. "You're absolutely right, it's my fault. I'm sorry. I didn't have my lights on." He walked towards the man. "I'll tell you what, you got a scrape which is maybe a hundred dollars of paint."

He reached in his back pocket and pulled out his wallet.

"Let me give you five hundred right now in cash," Hallenbeck said, pulling the money out of his wallet. "You're all taken care of and I don't get any points on my license."

The man took the money and said, "That's fine," but was now writing Hallenbeck's license plate number on the back of a business card.

"What are you doing?" Hallenbeck questioned.

"Just for the record, in case there's hidden damage or something. I should probably get your name and phone number too."

Hallenbeck couldn't believe it.

He was trying his best to let this dumb-ass live and the guy just wasn't smart enough to shut his stupid face and drive away.

Well then, screw him.

"Here's the problem," he said. "Sooner or later you're going to see my face in the news and say to yourself, *Hey, I remember that guy and, hey, I have his license plate number.*"

"Why would I see your face in the news?"

Hallenbeck felt the intensity rise to the necessary level. "We can do this the easy way or the hard way. If you want it to go the easy way, turn around and face your car and stand real still. I'll give you a moment to make your peace."

Chapter Thirty-Eight

Day Nine
Tuesday Night

THIS MORNING'S MEDICATION HAD mercifully worked its way out of her system at this point, releasing Kelly Parks' brain from the fog that held her back all day. She was still sore and achy but overall surprised at how good she felt.

And how horny.

She lowered herself down to the motel floor and stretched, no longer capable of doing the splits like in the high school days, but still plenty flexible. Her mind wander over tomorrow's trial until she confirmed that she was as ready at this point as she was going to be. No use even thinking about it anymore. The only thing left to do was to get to bed at a halfway decent hour, say ten.

The sun had just about completely set and Bryson Coventry would be showing up any time. They'd already reserved the connecting room in his name.

Jeannie was stripped down to her panties and bra, perpetually comfy, lying on the bed watching *Basic Instinct*. She hardly talked since the movie started, except during commercials. Kelly couldn't believe that she hadn't seen it before and felt a little jealous.   There are certain movies that you wished you could watch again for the first time.

Someone rapped on the door.

Jeannie was off the bed in a heartbeat and opened it up without even looking through the eyehole.

"Pizza guy," she announced, pulling him in.

The damage was $11.95. Jeannie pulled twelve ones out of her pursue and handed them to him.   Then pulled out two more and held them in her left hand.   The pizza guy, to all appearances a nice unassuming fellow, probably working his way through college or some such thing, looked confused. "You can have this tip or you can squeeze these," Jeannie told him, referring to her breasts.

"Really?"

"Sure, go on."

When he left and closed the door behind him, Jeannie smiled and said, "He'll be talking about that for twenty years."

Kelly Parks shook her head in wonder. "You know what, *I'll* be talking about that for twenty years."

BRYSON COVENTRY SHOWED UP ten minutes later, tried not to stare too hard at the Jeannie show, got situated in his room and made Kelly a proposition. The two of them ended up in his Tundra driving down offbeat roads and winding up at a small parking area by the river.

The night was blacker than black, shrouded in a low-lying blanket of clouds that totally masked any light from above. Thunder rumbled close by, giving fair warning.

No other cars were parked there.

No one was around.

They ended up walking down a path, right next to the Colorado River, able to hear the force of its power but not able to see it.

Coventry had a number of things he wanted to talk about and didn't waste much time getting to them.

"Last week, you wanted to know if someone cut off a lock of D'endra Vaughn's hair," he said. "That's been bugging me ever since you said it."

He stopped at that, waiting for her to comment.

It turned out that Jeannie Dannenberg hadn't told Coventry about the files that Michael Norway's secretary had found on his desk with the pictures of a dead woman, newspaper articles and an envelope containing hair.

So Kelly told him the story.

Ever the detective, he wasn't satisfied with hearing it just once. He kept probing her about it as they walked until he knew every bit as much as she did about it. In the end, he didn't know what to make of the fact that Michael Northway's former secretary, Sydney Somerville, hadn't been able to say one way or the other whether the dead woman she saw in Northway's file was Alicia Elmblade; nor could she remember if she saw the file before or after May of last year, when the incident at Rick's Gas Station took place.

"You only had that one photo of Alicia Elmblade to show her," Coventry noted. "I'm going to get some others and have her take another look. I'm finding it more and more interesting that no one's seen this Elmblade woman alive since the night in question."

Kelly nodded, even though he couldn't possibly see her in the dark. "Michael Northway told me that the client hired a private investigator out in California to try to locate her," she told him.

"Oh, really? Who?"

That was a good question.

"He said he'd be more comfortable keeping that information to himself," she said. "He has an obligation to protect the identity of the client."

Coventry chuckled. "He's got an answer for everything, doesn't he? You know what I'm starting to think? There is no client, there is no P.I. out in California, Alicia Elmblade is dead, and Michael Northway either killed her himself or is up to his eyeballs in it. That's why he's been trying to keep you quiet all this time and why he's trying to keep me at bay."

Kelly understood the reasoning but still didn't want to believe it, deep down inside. She'd been through too much with Michael Northway over too many years. When you have that kind of history with someone you get a sense of their fiber. From that angle, Michael Northway wasn't the person Coventry portrayed him to be.

Neither version quite fit.

She was about to tell him that when it started to rain. Only a few drops at first, but they were those big heavy ones, the kind that give you a three-second warning before they pound the crap out of you.

They turned and ran for the Tundra.

"Here it comes!" Coventry warned.

And he was right.

THEY MADE IT TO THE TRUCK and couldn't have been inside for more than a heartbeat before the whole sky fell down.

She pulled off her sweatshirt and saw Coventry fumbling

around, trying to find the right key on his key chain for the ignition. "Wait a minute," she told him.

She climbed in the back seat, a total spur-of-the-moment thing, excited by the way the rain thundered down on the roof with a thousand pings. It was solid and thick and she could tell that it wouldn't let up for some time. Being there, in the back seat of a car in the rain, reminded her of the old high school days, which got her even more excited.

She fumbled with her belt and had her pants off by the time Coventry managed to get his overgrown frame back there with her.

"Take your time," she told him. "Make me beg for it."

Chapter Thirty-Nine

Day Ten
Wednesday Morning

THE MORNING DRIVE FROM Grand Junction back to Denver was taking Coventry forever. As beautiful as the Rocky Mountain scenery was, each mile that passed represented another intrusion into a day that was already too short. The old Blondie song "Call Me" bounced around in his brain, stuck there since he heard it on the radio more than two hours ago.

The attorney, Michael Northway, Esq., called him on his cell phone just as he was climbing the west side of the divide towards the Eisenhower Tunnel. Northway reported that the private investigator in California had made significant strides in the effort to locate Alicia Elmblade and was hopeful that he would actually find her within in the next two or three working days.

Details?

No.

The lawyer wasn't at liberty to provide those.

But once Alicia Elmblade was located, Northway would have her contact Coventry directly and he could interview her to his heart's content.

"Then you can apologize," Northway added.

Most of the rest of the drive was spent on the phone with Clay Pitcher, Esq., the Assistant District Attorney for Denver, trying to talk him into getting a search warrant for Michael Northway's house. Bryson had known Clay forever. He was a slow-moving man with a barrel chest and yellow cigar teeth, who looked like he ought to be selling used cars somewhere. He usually wore a beige suit, not buttoned and couldn't be, not for two years now. He punched out at 4:43 p.m. every day and was only eight years short of retirement. In spite of all that, however, he was a damn fine lawyer when he wanted to be, and had a sense of justice that could still get him riled up at times.

Getting him to cross swords with Holland, Roberts & Northway, LLC, wouldn't be easy, though.

So Coventry had Kate Katona fax over a half dozen photos of D'endra Vaughn's dead body, so Clay could see the trauma and pain for himself. Coventry told him everything he knew about Rick's Gas Station and Michael Northway's involvement that night. He got Clay to admit that the attorney's conduct amounted to a conspiracy to commit an obstruction of justice, even if it turned out that Alicia Elmblade hadn't been killed. That meant that they had an actual crime to base a search warrant on.

Then he called in every marker he had, pleaded, begged, and had a box of bagels delivered.

Finally, Clay called him just as he was merging from I-70 onto the 6th Avenue freeway in Golden, only fifteen minutes away from the office.

"Okay," Clay said. "Come on over and we'll work up an affidavit."

Coventry slapped the dashboard with excitement.

"It was the bagels, wasn't it?"

The D.A. chuckled. "Well it was either that or your abilities of persuasion. You figure it out." Then the D.A.'s voice got more serious: "We're going to keep this low-key, though, to keep this guy's reputation intact in case we're barking up the wrong dick. That means we're going to arrive for the search in unmarked cars and do whatever it takes along the way to keep this under the media's radar screen."

That was all fine with Coventry.

THE PAPERWORK, AND GETTING A JUDGE to sign off on the whole thing, took more than two hours. By mid-afternoon, however, they were knocking on Michael Northway's front door and handing the warrant to a cleaning lady when she answered.

"He's a good man," she told them. "This is wrong."

Coventry nodded. "He's a great guy. We just need to look around a little."

Coventry couldn't help but try to put a price tag on the place. Three million? Four million? Five? He really didn't have a clue. The entry vestibule alone probably cost more than his house.

They hadn't been inside more than ten minutes when Clay Pitcher, who insisted on coming, received a call. It was Richard Ferguson, Esq., one of the senior partners at Holland, Roberts & Northway, LLC. Within the next half hour, the law firm would be filing a motion to quash the search warrant and a motion to seal anything taken. Mr. Ferguson wanted to confirm where Mr. Pitcher could be reached this afternoon for an emergency telephone conference with the judge.

Coventry watched him take the call and could tell that the

pushback had already started. Eventually, the D.A. put the phone back into the pocket of his coat, shrugged and said, "Wrong number."

Coventry smiled.

"Well that's good. From the look on your face, I thought it was the IRS."

Coventry was in the attorney's den when Kate Katona shouted at him to come upstairs.

He found her in the master bedroom. She was as usual dressed for the job below, wearing dark blue drawstring pants, a white T-shirt with a yellow smiley face, and her weapon in plain view, riding in a leather holster on her hip. The T-shirt hugged her chest tighter than normal and Coventry found himself glancing in that direction for a split-second longer than he probably should have.

"Bingo," she said, handing him a manila file folder.

He took it. The words "Attorney-Client Privilege" were handwritten on the tab. He opened it up and inside found ten large color photographs depicting a woman who was obviously and undeniably dead.

"Someone took her down hard," Katona noted.

"I'd say," Coventry agreed. He couldn't remember seeing such livid trauma before, except for maybe D'endra Vaughn.

Then, to Katona: "Do you recognize her?"

No, she didn't.

"Me either. Where'd you find this?"

"There," she said, pointing to an elegant maple cabinet over in the corner. "It was locked, but I found the key in the top drawer of the nightstand."

Coventry walked over to it, curious

"Let's see what else we have in this little fellow."

Unfortunately, the little fellow was spent. No drivers' license, no newspaper articles, no envelopes with souvenir hair, just the photos. In fact, by the time all was said and done, there was nothing else anywhere in the house.

Just the one set of photos.

Sidney Somerville, Northway's prior secretary, would need to be called down to the department to tell them if these were the same pictures she saw on Northway's desk last year. Coventry doubted they were, however, since none of the pictures depicted a knife in the woman's stomach. In fact, two of the pictures showed her midsection, both without any visible trauma whatsoever to that area.

HE EXCUSED HIMSELF FOR A MOMENT, went into the bathroom, closed the door and dialed Kelly Parks. She answered on the second ring. He could hear "Born to Run" playing in the background.

"Where are you?"

"En route back to Denver," she told him. "Why?"

"I have some photographs that I need Jeannie Dannenberg to take a look at," he said. "They're pictures of a dead woman and I need her to tell me if it's Alicia Elmblade."

"I'm sure she'll do that."

"Yeah, I know, but I want to do it now, tonight if possible," Coventry told her. "And she needs to look at them downtown, at the department, so we can get a videotaped statement. Can you ask her if she'll do that?"

He heard the two women talking.

Then Kelly Parks was back on the phone. "She will, but there are two conditions."

"Oh? And what might those be?"

"The first is, you have to take us to Rodozio's afterwards."

Rodozio's?

He didn't know the place.

She must have felt his mental gap, because she added: "It's in LoDo, by Union Station. It's one of those Brazilian places where they keep bringing meat to your table until you pass out."

"Is that the place with the rattlesnake?"

"That and about fifty other things."

"Okay," he agreed. "Done, but I'm not eating rattlesnake. What's the second condition?"

He heard Kelly talking to Jeannie again, then she was back on the phone: "Okay, brace yourself. She says the second condition is that you have to spend the night at my place, so she'll know I'll be safe."

Coventry chuckled. "Tell her no way."

More talking, then, "She says take it or leave it."

"Tell her I can subpoena her ass."

More talking. *He says he wants to slap your ass.*

"Hey, that's not what I said."

They'd just passed Vail, which meant they'd be down at the department in about two hours. That would give him time to finish up here and do the chain-of-custody paperwork.

He came out of the bathroom and hadn't taken more than ten steps when his phone rang.

It was Kelly Parks.

"Hey, I just had a thought," she said. "Take a picture of one of those photos with your cell phone and send it to me."

Good idea.

He did.

"Jeannie says that's not Alicia," Kelly said.

Coventry scratched his head. "It's not?"

"No."

"Is she sure?"

"She's positive. She's never seen the woman before and neither have I."

Coventry scratched his head.

Who are you, darling?

Chapter Forty

Day Ten
Wednesday Afternoon

DAVID HALLENBECK SET AN empty Coke can on top of the rock, then walked back twenty paces, picking up three good-sized throwing stones as he went. He fingered them, shifted the best one to his right hand and held the other two in his left. He concentrated on the can, judging the distance, and bounced his right hand up and down to get a better feel for the weight of the rock. Then he threw it with all his might. It flew horizontal through the air, easily over a hundred miles an hour, and ricocheted off the rock about two inches to the right.

He repeated the routine and threw again

This time hitting it dead-on.

Knocking it back a good twenty feet.

That was better.

Imagine that hitting you on the side of your stupid head.

He walked back over to set it up again, thinking about the TV news report that he couldn't get out of his mind. It was a short community-interest piece on the homeless assistance shelter in Denver. Some associate with the shelter was being interviewed and the interview was taking place in front of the shelter.

In the background, sitting on the steps of the shelter, with a wounded left arm, was none other than the biker bitch.

He'd recognize her anywhere.

The fact that she would be hanging around Denver for a day or two or three made some sense. She went to the cops and told them where the farmhouse was. Now, they were probably having her look through mug shots and working with a composite artist. Also, they would be putting pressure on her to be available just in case they caught their man and needed her to pick him out of a lineup.

On the other hand, it could be a trap.

One very clever little trap.

The cops knew he would be watching the news. They knew that he'd want to know if they were broadcasting a composite of his face, which they weren't, at least not yet. They also knew that he would like nothing better than to get his hands around the biker woman's filthy little tattooed neck.

So, the question was, had they set her up as bait?

Or had he just stumbled on one of those wonderful little gifts that life hands you every now and then?

Quite frankly, the situation intrigued him both ways.

With the Coke can reset in place, this time he walked back twenty-five paces and picked up only one rock on the way.

A robin flew overhead and he threw at that instead of the can, knocking it out of the sky. It landed on the ground with a thud and flapped one wing, unable to move the other. Hallenbeck walked over, watched it struggle for a few moments, and then stepped on its head.

"Wrong place, wrong time," he said.

HE WALKED BACK TO THE BUILDING, an abandoned pre-fabricated metal structure that was probably a small machine shop at one point, now gutted and abandoned.

"You're going to dance for me," he told Megan Bennett.

Five minutes later he had her naked in a standing spread-eagle position, with her arms stretched up tight and roped to an overhead I-beam. He kept her feet apart with an old broom handle made into a spreader bar.

He had her drawn tight, barely able to move.

No wiggle room for this girl.

He took off his shirt and walked around her, letting her feel his power. He ran a finger in a circle around her belly button. Then gently up her side, up her arm and back down, just a touch, barely perceptible. He grabbed her pubic hair and pulled tighter and tighter until she made a noise through the gag.

"Quite a predicament," he said.

He spotted a wooden yardstick leaning against the wall over in the corner. He walked over slowly, letting her follow him with her eyes, picked it up and studied it. Then he walked back, taunting her with in.

Then he blindfolded her.

He swung the stick and smacked her on the ass.

She jumped.

"This is for you, baby," he said. "This is to keep you from getting boring. Because if you get boring, what's the use in having you around? So my advice to you is dance like you mean it."

Chapter Forty-One

Day Eleven
Thursday Morning

———————

A STEADY STREAM OF RAINMAKERS, partners, associates, law clerks, secretaries and support staff, some whose names she hardly knew, filed in and out of Kelly Parks' office Thursday morning, glad to have her back, outraged at what had happened, pledging to do whatever they could to help if she needed it.

Michael Northway was conspicuously absent throughout it all.

She hadn't talked to him since Bryson Coventry searched his house yesterday. Coventry told her the search would be kept low-key, and it must have been, because either no one in the firm knew about it or they were exercising incredible discretion. It wasn't on anybody's lips, even the gossip queens.

Then when all the hoopla started to taper off, Michael Northway called and asked if she could meet him outside on the 16th Street Mall.

He needed to talk to her right away about something very important.

She found him sitting on a metal bench, one of those back-to-back benches, dressed in a dark pinstripe suit and a red power tie. It was actually hot today and she was glad he picked a spot in the shade. He had a large Starbuck's coffee sitting next to him, cupped in his right hand to keep it from going anywhere. She expected him to look intense and stressed following the search of his house yesterday but for some reason he was the exact opposite.

"Hey there," she said.

He hugged her, which immediately put her at ease, and said, "Hey there back."

She sat down next to him and crossed her legs. "I missed you this morning," she said.

"Yeah, sorry," he said. Then: "Here's what I want you to do. Look straight ahead. Put your eyes on that Hard Rock Café sign and don't take them off."

She looked at him, confused. "Michael, this is . . ."

"Ah, ah, ah," he said. "Hard Rock Café. Look right at the sign and don't take your eyes off it. I need you to do that for me. Come on."

She did, wondering what the hell he could be up to. "Okay. Are you satisfied?"

She felt him study her as she stared ahead. "Good," he said. "Now, don't turn around no matter what. Do you promise?"

"*Jesus*, Michael."

SHE KEPT HER FOCUS on the Hard Rock Café, feeling stupid, but at the same time intrigued as to where this was heading. She could sense him motioning to someone. Then she felt the bench shift slightly and knew that someone had just sat down on the backside of it, right behind them.

"Good," Northway said. "Now, someone has just joined us,

but it's important that you don't turn around."

"Why?"

"You'll understand in a second," Northway assured her. "In the meantime, do you promise?"

She did.

"Okay, then I guess we can begin." To someone else: "Your show."

The person behind them cleared his throat and she could tell it was a man. "I'm the client who solicited Michael to orchestrate that little charade at Rick's Gas Station," the man told her, exaggerating his voice to disguise it. Her impulse was to turn around and finally see who the mystery man was, but she didn't.

"So you really do exist?"

"I'm afraid so," the man chuckled. "Michael asked if I would speak to you so you could hear the story straight from the horse's mouth."

He paused while a shuttle bus rolled by, then continued: "Unfortunately, I somehow managed to develop something in the nature of a dark side over the years. I'm not proud of it, and things are getting better now, but there was a time not all that long ago when I wasn't a very nice guy. The fact is, I was getting increasingly obsessed with the idea of actually killing someone."

She must have turned her head a little because Northway put a hand on her knee and said, "Hard Rock Café. Remember?"

She focused on the sign again.

"I kept getting these urges, and God help me, but they weren't going away," the man continued. "There came a day when thinking about things wasn't enough. I beat a woman up. I picked her out at random and dragged her into an alley and beat the shit out of her. She was a young woman. Half of me hated myself for doing it, but unfortunately only half. That was the first of a number of other episodes like that."

The man cleared his throat.

"I was a bad person, I knew that, but I couldn't stop," the man continued. "Things were escalating. I wanted to go to the next level. At night, I spent hours on the Internet, looking in dark corners, getting into chat rooms that would scare the shit out of most people. That led to some private communications with a man. Those communications grew in number over time. He bragged that he had actually killed. At first I didn't know whether to believe him or not, but as he fed me more and more details, I knew. To me, at the time, as sick as it was, it was like a drug. I couldn't get enough."

The man stopped talking as an elderly couple strolled by, not more than a few feet from them.

Then he went on: "I ended up getting a P.O. box and he mailed me pictures of one of the women he killed. At this point, I was more than ready for my first kill. We made an agreement. For his next kill, he would not only send me pictures, but also a lock of her hair, a copy of her driver's license, and other personal stuff like that. I agreed to do the same for my quote next unquote kill. He followed through with his part of the bargain and sent me a package. Then it was my turn."

He stopped talking.

Kelly felt the need to prompt him, and said, "So you killed someone?"

"No," the man said, "I couldn't go through with it. As much as I thought that I wanted to, in the end, when push came to shove, I couldn't. The problem was, I owed this man a package. My feeling was, if I didn't give him one, he would hunt me down."

"I could see that," she said.

"Yes," he agreed. "That's when I called Michael, to see if he could help get me out of this mess. We decided to fake a death, but it had to be as real as possible, with a real woman, who really disappears, with real witnesses, with a real police report, with real news articles, etcetera."

"So that's what we did," Northway interjected. "Rick's Gas Station."

"Exactly," the man agreed. "After the incident that night Alicia Elmblade posed for some death pictures. I mailed them off, together with a lock of her hair, a copy of her driver's license and several newspaper articles. Then I decreased my communications with this man and finally ended them all together. I thought everything was done and settled at that point."

"Of course," Northway added, "It was important that Alicia Elmblade really disappear, which she did, and was well paid to do so."

"A hundred grand," the man emphasized.

Northway added: "We wanted your involvement, Kelly, to give the whole thing a higher dimension of believability. If Alicia Elmblade's two friends were the only witnesses to her abduction, someone might think it was staged. But if there was a third witness, an independent person totally unconnected to anyone else, and a reputable attorney at that, then the whole thing would rise to the level of veracity that we needed."

Kelly nodded, understanding.

Everything made perfect sense.

Northway had something else that he apparently wanted her to understand: "To get you to participate," he said, "I did stretch the truth a little. I told you the woman was escaping from something she was afraid of when in reality she was being paid. I had to do that because I couldn't tell you what was really leading up to all of this. Forgive me?"

She did.

She hugged him, keeping her face pointed at the Hard Rock Café sign.

"Okay," she said. "Let me just be sure I have a few things straight. You don't know this yet, Michael, but Sidney Somerville told me that she found a file on your desk once, with pictures of a dead woman, a lock of hair, etc."

The other man spoke. "That's the package this other man sent to me. I showed it to Michael."

Michael nodded.

"That's correct."

"Okay."

"Same thing with respect to the file that your friend Bryson Coventry took out of my bedroom yesterday," he added. "Those were the first pictures supplied by this man."

"Okay. That explains that."

The man said: "That brings us to the second phase of all this. What's going on now, to my best guess, is this. Somehow this man found out that Alicia Elmblade was a fake. How, I don't know. But somehow, he must have. He gets a copy of the police report and finds the names of three of the involved people, namely D'endra Vaughn, Jeannie Dannenberg and you, Kelly Parks. He decides to teach everyone a lesson and, hey, why not, he likes to kill people anyway and, coincidentally, you're all beautiful women and fit his profile. He starts with D'endra Vaughn. He uses her cell phone to call you, Kelly, to let you know you're next. He succeeds in abducting you last Saturday night but obviously didn't get the job done. My guess is he'll go after Jeannie Dannenberg next, or you again. He'll go after me eventually, but not until last. He wants me to experience the guilt of watching everyone else go down first."

"That's why we're paying the California P.I. firm big bucks to find Alicia Elmblade right now," Northway added. "To warn her and get her some protection. She'll be on this guy's hit list, too, if he hasn't gotten to her already."

Kelly frowned.

"I told Jeannie she was a target," she said.

The man spoke: "But not a neglected one. We've been giving her a lot of coverage," he said. "She just doesn't know it."

The comment made Kelly think back to the night she met with Jeannie at the bar on Colfax, the rainy night. In hindsight, the mystery man outside in the storm was a friend, not a foe.

The talk went on.

A while later the man—the client—got up and left.

Kelly Parks kept her word, as she should.

She didn't turn around to look.

As soon as he was away, she wished she had.

Chapter Forty-Two

Day Eleven
Thursday Morning

BRYSON COVENTRY FORCED HIMSELF OUT OF BED before the crack of dawn, took a three-mile run, did four sets of fifty pushups, crunched his abs for ten minutes, showered, gobbled down a bowl of Total cereal in his bedroom while he dressed, and was able to get downtown by 7:38.

He was inhaling coffee when the FBI called and reported they had fresh blood.

Two minutes later he and Shalifa Netherwood were headed south. Interstate 25 was thick and slow at this hour of the morning but luckily none of the cars up ahead had decided to crash into one another yet so there were no blocked lanes.

He was in a good mood.

With any luck this latest crime scene would give them the one little break they needed.

He was trying to steer with his knees, using both hands to open the thermos and pour coffee into the cup, when Shalifa Netherwood gabbed them and gave him a look that could have stopped a waterfall.

"What?" he asked.

"You know what your tombstone's going to say?"

He waited, "No what?"

"*Killed by Coffee*," she said. "You're like one of those guys who gets a fly in the car and keeps swatting at it until you end up running into a light pole."

Coventry chuckled at the thought. "What a way to go, huh? Killed by a fly."

She nodded, handing him the now-filled cup. "Ill bet it really happens."

He agreed. In fact, he'd come somewhat closer to that exact situation than he would ever admit.

"So, what did you get at the lawyer's house yesterday?" she questioned. "Anything of interest?"

He told her about the photographs of the dead woman that Katona found in Michael Northway's bedroom. That and the fact that photos were not Alicia Elmblade, at least according to Jeannie Dannenberg, who Coventry had no reason to doubt.

"Clay's not sure we'll be able to use them," Coventry added, "if it turns out that a client actually gave them to the lawyer and they end up falling under the purview of the attorney-client privilege."

"Clay's getting too fat," she said. "He's loosing his edge."

"Not his fault," Coventry said. "He's got diabetes."

"Really?"

Coventry nodded.

"I didn't know that."

"You're not supposed to and neither am I, so keep it quiet."

BY THE TIME THEY GOT TO THE SINCLAIR gas station Coventry's bladder was ready to explode. He ran straight to the side of the building, hoping the room was unlocked, but naturally it wasn't, because that's the way his life worked. So he ran inside. The kid, Jason Windermere, was at the cash register and started to tell Coventry something. Coventry waved him off, leaned over the counter, fumbled around, found the horseshoe and grabbed it.

"Be right back," he told them.

When he returned, Jason started talking almost immediately. Coventry gave him his attention, half of it anyway, while he walked over to the coffee pot. "I just wanted you to know, I called Jerold Woodfield down at Metro like you told me to. And guess what?"

"I don't know. He answered the phone?"

The kid laughed, then told him how he'd gone down to the campus to talk with him, filled out an application for this special scholarship program, and learned yesterday that he's getting a full four-year scholarship, conditioned on maintaining good grades, of course. Which he planned to do in spades.

"You'll do good," Coventry assured him.

Outside, getting into the car, Netherwood looked at him funny. "Okay," she said, "just tell me what's going on now so I don't have to pester you all day."

He laughed, as if challenged.

"You don't even know how to pester," he told her. "Now Katona, she can pester, she's a pester-professional. But you? Give me a break."

"You bankrolled that kid's scholarship, didn't you?"

"Now that's nuts," he said. "You of all people know that my money goes to coffee."

FIVE MINUTES LATER THEY CAME TO the first fresh blood. A man's badly beaten body lay on the ground on the side of the road about fifty yards away from a new Corvette. The local police department was working the scene, with plenty of FBI milling around, but Coventry didn't recognize anyone. They hung around for a few minutes and then headed two miles farther up the road, to the house of a farmer called Ben Bickerson.

They checked in with the local sheriff, a man named Russ Smith, and got access to the site. They found Charles Miller in the garage, down on all fours, studying something on the floor. He looked up when they walked in, said "About time," and stood up.

Then Miller brought them up to speed.

One of the dead man's daughters, a woman named Rhonda Ellsworth, who lives in Florida, called the local police department after she'd been unable to get her father on the phone for a few days. The locals investigated and found the body.

One thing was clear already. Megan Bennett's abductor had moved over here with his catch after the other farmhouse became compromised as a result of the biker woman's escape.

"As far as we can tell," Miller said, "Megan Bennett was tied up in the bed upstairs, and was there for quite a long time, given the amount of urine on the sheets."

Coventry frowned, picturing it.

"Probably some kind of psychological torture," Miller added. "I can just picture the little prick pretending to abandon her and then sitting back and watching the show."

A dog barked.

Miller must have noticed Coventry's expression, because he volunteered, "That's the same dog that we found wandering around at the other farmhouse. He lives here."

"So what was he doing over at the other place?" Netherwood questioned.

Miller shrugged.

"Wandered off, I guess, maybe after Bickerson got himself killed."

For some reason that explanation seemed insufficient to Coventry. He knew he had to think about that more when he got the chance. Right now he could hardly think at all. He was sick at the fact that the asshole had been right next door to them when they were processing the scene at the other farmhouse and they didn't even know it. They had him pinned and let him get away. All they had to do was drive over here and check. It would have taken five minutes.

"This guy's starting to give me a headache," Coventry said.

Miller nodded. "The only good thing out of this so far is that Megan Bennett is still alive, bless her little heart. The locals are going to double-check the area one more time to be sure he didn't dump her around here somewhere, but it seems like he took her with him."

"She has to be getting weak, though," Netherwood observed. "How much longer can she possibly last?"

Good question, indeed.

SHORTLY BEFORE ELEVEN, COVENTRY GOT A CALL from Kelly Parks, who said she needed to talk to him immediately and offered to drive out to where he was if that's what it took. He said okay, but only if she agreed to swing by a Wendy's and pick up a combo meal on the way, hold the mayonnaise and onions please. He'd pay her back of course.

She showed up about an hour later and called to say she was

down at the end of the driveway and no one would let her in.

Coventry drove down to meet her and they ended up strolling down the gravel road, he with the burger in one hand and a diet Coke in the other, and she carrying his fries for him. She wore an expensive gray suit, nylons and soft leather shoes with a one-inch heel. A Gucci purse draped over her right shoulder and she smelled like a field of flowers.

She told him the story that the client told her this morning on the 16th Street Mall. Coventry, as usual, made her repeat it over and over, and kept looking for holes or inconsistencies. In the end, however, it held together perfectly.

He didn't see a reason not to believe it and told her so.

"So you'll back off Michael Northway, then?" she questioned.

"Is that what you want?" he asked, a rhetorical question to give him time to think.

"Yes," she said. "But not just for Michael's sake, for the whole firm. It's a lot more fragile than you'd probably think. I don't want to see it get tarnished."

Coventry considered it, chewing on a fry.

Actually, he'd already searched Michael Northway's house, and hadn't found much, other than the photos in his bedroom, which were now perfectly explained. Clay Pitcher, Esq., had counseled against trying to get a search warrant for Northway's law office, which he viewed as not only too politically charged, but also on extremely shaky legal grounds given the fact that the place was a refuge of sensitive information that was truly protected by the attorney-client privilege. Netherwood was right, Clay was loosing his edge.

But, that said, there wasn't much more to do anyway. They could try to question Northway, try to make him reveal the name of the client and then talk to the client directly, but North-way could take the 5th and so could the client, for that matter. Also, if the client wouldn't show his face to Kelly Parks, there was no way he'd talk to Coventry.

"Look," he said, "I don't have any plans right at the moment to do anything that would create a public embarrassment to either Michael Northway or the law firm. This client needs to be held accountable at some point for assaulting those women, and I will follow-up on that, mark my words, but that's something for another day and another place."

He had one more thought, on a related subject: "If the story that the client told you is true, that means that the person who killed D'endra Vaughn and tried to kill you is the same person who killed the women in the pictures that he sent to the client. Right?"

Kelly obviously agreed with him, "Correct."

"You mean right."

"That's what I said, correct."

Coventry shook his head. "If someone says, right?—and it is right—then you say right. And if someone says, correct?—and it is correct—then you say correct. But you can't mix right and correct."

"Sure you can," she said, defending herself.

"No," he said, "because that upsets the balance of the universe. Right?"

She laughed. "Correct."

He shook his head, beaten.

"So," he said, thinking out loud, "maybe that gives me a foothold. Maybe I can find out who the dead woman is in the photos that I got out of Northway's bedroom and find out who killed her. That's who killed D'endra Vaughn and tried to kill you."

Kelly looked skeptical.

"That seems like a long shot," she said. "It's a whole separate investigation."

That was true, actually.

"But one that may already be done," Coventry said. A pause, then: "We also have that other file, too, the one with the hair and everything that Northway's secretary saw in his office. That's another victim of this same guy. Tell Northway that I want that file. If there really is a driver's license and newspaper articles in there, then we'll have the name of the victim and the location of the crime. That'll get me in touch with the police department who did the investigation. There's no telling what they have. Hell, they might even have a name and a picture for all we know."

She nodded.

"So, there you have it," he said. "I'm going to be nice to Michael Northway *if* he gets that file in my hands."

"I'll call him," she said.

"Do it right now," Coventry told her. "I want to know what his position is."

He sat down on a rock and picked the last of the fries from the bottom of the box while she wandered down the road to talk to Northway in private. When she came back she was smiling.

"Michael gave the file back to the client," she said, "but he's going to call and see if he still has it and would be willing to turn it over to you. In the meantime, he said he remembered the name on the driver's license. Melinda Russell. And he remembered that the newspaper article was from Memphis, Tennessee."

Coventry was satisfied.

"That's all I need, really."

Ten seconds later he was on the phone to Kate Katona.

Chapter Forty-Three

IN AN *EINSTEIN BROS* COFFEE SHOP on Sherman Street, David Hallenbeck strategically positioned his magnificent frame at a table next to the windows where he could see the shelter, and sipped coffee while he read this week's *Westword*.

He had mixed emotions about hunting down the biker bitch and still didn't know which way the scales would eventually tip. On the one hand, no one gets to screw with him the way she did, period, end of sentence. On the other hand, you don't want to let your emotions get the better of you and pull you into a trap.

What he needed to know is whether the cops had set her up as bait. And he needed to know that now, because once she drifted away from Denver he'd never see her again. She was one of those slimy little invisible people who live in rat holes and hug the dark.

It felt good to be out among people.

He realized now how much he missed the buzz and activity of crowds and how incredibly long he'd been cooped up with Megan Bennett.

Megan Bennett.

She was getting weak, familiar and uninteresting.

The initial excitement was waning fast.

Even her little pain-dance yesterday didn't help much.

Plus she was drawing an incredible amount of heat. If she was dead, the cops would still be looking for him, but not with anywhere near the sense of urgency they were now.

The end was coming with her.

He could feel it; the inevitable transition was in motion.

Maybe even tonight.

He refilled his coffee cup and refocused on the *Westword*, an alternative, edgy newspaper, but also one with articles that he found to be surprisingly well researched and well written. It clearly made its money on advertising to the fringe element, being jammed packed with come-ons for clubs, dining, tattoo parlors and, most noticeably, the escort and sex industry.

HE WATCHED BODIES FILE OUT of the shelter one after another and then, bingo, there she was, finally. The biker bitch was out of the building and walking down Sherman Street in his direction.

He adjusted his sunglasses. They were dark, oversized and cheap, something he picked up earlier this morning from a street vendor for ten bucks. He also pulled the brim of the baseball cap down so that it sat even lower on his face.

The biker bitch was on his side of the street now and would be passing by any minute. She wore oversized jeans, tennis shoes, and a black T-shirt, with those overly tattooed arms of hers hanging out. Her left arm, between the elbow and the wrist, was wrapped in gauze. Her hair was short, the length

Hallenbeck cut it just a few evenings before. It was a little choppy, too, not overly so, but enough to suggest to a stranger that the woman had probably cut it herself. She obviously hadn't sprung the ten or twenty bucks it would cost to get it smoothed out.

When she walked by down the sidewalk he held the *Westword* in front of his face. He actually felt the coolness of her shadow as she passed between him and the sun.

He turned, stood up, ready to follow her, when shit!

She was opening the door and coming inside.

Damn it!

He was back down in his chair in a heartbeat, his face stuffed back into the newspaper.

She stepped to the back of a line that was four deep, half facing him, not more than ten feet away.

His first thought was to turn his head directly away from her, get up, and head calmly for the door, just one more average Joe-Blow who had finished his coffee and was heading to work. But the movement would draw her attention; that was certain. Then she'd recognize his size, at the least, and maybe his posture. Maybe she'd be stupid enough to run over and try to get in front of his face to see if it was him or not.

What to do?

Then, shit!

Two cops came in.

He was busted!

They walked straight at him.

Then, no.

Instead of pulling their weapons, they walked past him and took a place in line, directly behind the biker bitch. One of then was older, somewhere in his forties, but the other one was young and chewing gum that made the muscles in his jaw pop. He looked like the kind of guy who wouldn't think twice about getting into a bare knuckles fistfight.

And he looked fast, like he could run.

Hallenbeck was strong but he couldn't run for shit.

The coffee for some reason was suddenly right now building up in his bladder. Ordinarily, this is where he would get up and head for the restroom.

Now the younger cop and the biker woman were talking to each other, apparently about her tattoos, because she was holding up her right arm for him to see better.

She had that come-on, flirtatious aura about her.

The one he recognized so well.

What a slut.

He kept the *Westword* propped up in front of his face and forced himself to stay as calm as he could. If everything went to hell, he would go for the younger cop first and drop him straight to the floor with a punch to the face, then take care of the old fart before he could get his weapon drawn.

With any luck the biker bitch would order a coffee to go and be out of here in the next two minutes.

Instead, she ordered a coffee and a bagel and took a seat at the table next to his, facing directly towards him. A few minutes later the two cops came over and asked if they could join her. One of them asked Hallenbeck if anyone was using the extra chair at his table, then took it after Hallenbeck forced himself to mumble, "No, go for it."

HE LISTENED, BEHIND THE NEWSPAPER, while the woman and the cops talked. She told them a story about how Bryson

Coventry, who the two cops knew well and described as "a super good guy," pulled her out from under a Harley that she crashed on some train tracks down by Pueblo. There were some warrants out for her arrest in some other states, but Coventry made her a deal, that he wasn't going to call any of those authorities provided she stuck around Denver for a while and helped him out on this big case he was working on.

There was no talk at all about anyone using her for bait.

Ten minutes later the biker bitch got up, said goodbye to the cops, refilled her coffee cup and walked out the front door.

Hallenbeck headed straight for the restroom. When he got out the trail was cold.

Chapter Forty-Four

Day Twelve
Friday

HALLENBECK WOKE IN A COLD SWEAT and looked at his watch. It was three in the morning. The world was black and quiet except for the heavy breathing of Megan Bennett who slept next to him with one foot chained to a post.

He stood up, grabbed the flashlight, walked outside and pissed in an old one-gallon plastic milk jug, now almost full. He'd take it with him when all was done to minimize the DNA.

Megan Bennett was no longer worth the effort. She had great legs, he had to admit that, and she honestly had some minor amount of affection for him on some emotional level, but that was no longer enough.

She didn't love him and never would.

That was obvious.

He gave her plenty of chances to get used to the situation and see the good side of him but she refused at every turn.

So screw her.

She hadn't earned the right to die quickly.

She made her choice and she'd have to live with it.

That was fine with him, because at least now all his hard

work and planning wouldn't be wasted. Of all the OSU women, she was definitely the most complicated so far. Beth Williamson had been a snap. All he needed was a 55-gallon drum and a nice quiet place to dump her. The next two women were equally easy from a logistic standpoint.

For Dana Frost all he had to do was bury her up to her neck, shave her head and then pour honey all over it. He went to visit her last month, surprised to find she was still right there where he left her—undiscovered. Her skull stuck out of the ground, picked clean.

The other woman, Cindy Smith, was also easy. A little rope, a bottle of acid and a good dripper was all he needed.

Megan Bennett's little nightmare, on the other hand, was complicated. Hallenbeck bought a cheap motorcycle helmet and fitted it with two holes, one to let air in from the blower and the other to let air out. The exit hole was fitted with a one-way valve so that the airflow could only go out and not back. The entry hole was connected to a blower by way of a flexible plastic tube. The blower was equipped with a timer that turned the power off after five minutes. You could turn it back on by pressing a button. Designing and fabricating all of this ended up stealing two days out of Hallenbeck's life.

But at least he had it and it worked perfect.

Right now it was all stored in the trunk of the Camry. He got it and brought it inside, quietly, so as to not wake the woman.

The time had come.

The reaper was here to visit.

In her psychology paper, Megan Bennett described being strapped down in a chair. But there wasn't one around so Hallenbeck decided he would stretch her out on the workbench instead. That would be better anyway because she wouldn't be able to thrash around as much.

He got everything into position while she lay there sleeping.

Luckily there was still power at the outside junction box to the building and he was able to rig up an extension cord for the blower.

With everything in place, he unchained the woman's leg from the post and then picked her up and carried her over to the bench as she woke up.

"What's going on?" she questioned.

"Nothing much," he said. "We're just changing positions."

She fought with her last ounce of strength but it did no good. Within five minutes he had her securely racked on the bench with the helmet on her head and the blower going.

He sat back and watched her for an hour.

It was so cool when the blower shut off.

It startled the woman, every single time.

The way she jerked when it happened was so cool.

She punched the switch immediately, usually three or four times, just to be sure.

Then the blower kicked back on and she got quiet again.

Finally he got bored with the whole thing and went back to sleep.

She'd be a lot more fun to watch in the morning, after she'd been at it for a while.

Chapter Forty-Five

Day Twelve
Friday Morning

BRYSON COVENTRY WAS DOWNTOWN at his desk by 5:30 in the morning, which was 7:30 Memphis time, dialing the direct number of Corey Peterson, who was the detective in charge of the Melinda Russell investigation. Coventry naturally got the answering machine again, for the umpteenth time, hung up and walked over to refill his coffee cup.

Before he could do that his phone rang. He weighed his options for a second, then ran to his desk.

"Coventry," he said.

"Coventry, huh? Well, I thought I'd better get back to you first thing, before you wear out the ringer on my phone."

Coventry was excited.

"Hey, listen," Coventry said, "thanks for getting back to me. We have a killer in common, namely the one from your Melinda Russell case. We have reason to believe he's out here in Denver and that he murdered a young woman named D'endra Vaughn. It's a long story and I'll fill you in, but let me ask you one thing, what's your file like on this case, good, bad, ugly or what?"

"Our file sucks. We got nothing, basically."

Ouch.

"That's not good."

"No forensics, no eye witnesses, no motive, no nothing."

Coventry paused.

"Could we look at it anyway?"

"Sure, but you're wasting your time."

"I'm going to fly someone down there this afternoon."

"Whatever. I'll be here."

"Thanks," Coventry said. "By the way, do you guys still have all those blues clubs down there, on Beal Street or wherever it is?"

"Let me put it this way. Do you guys still have all those mountains out there?"

Coventry chuckled. "Touché. Listen, this person I'm sending down, his name is Richardson. He loves that stuff, just for your information."

Coventry spent the next half hour bringing Detective Peterson up to speed as to what was going on in Denver. Even with that, Peterson couldn't think of anything in his file that would help.

After he hung up, Coventry pulled out photocopies of the dead woman obtained yesterday from Michael Northway's bedroom. He spread them out on his desk and studied them.

Who are you, darling?

If he could find out her name, he'd be able to track down yet another case file to look at. Somehow he had to get some direct face time with Northway's client.

But right now he had the Megan Bennett case to worry about. Yesterday, FBI profiler Dr. Leanne Sanders made a comment that Coventry couldn't get out of his head. She'd suggested that extended abductions, like the one involving Megan Bennett, followed a modified bell curve. The abductor's interest initially rises fast as things start off fascinating and intoxicating, then holds at a steady level for a time, and then falls straight down when everything turns dull and familiar and high maintenance. Right now, in her opinion, they were standing at the edge of that cliff, if they hadn't fallen over it already.

He called her about nine-thirty.

"Leanne," he said, "it's me, Coventry. I'm starting to panic here. Are you free for lunch?"

She was.

"I just want to pick your brain, one on one," he explained, "without all the group dynamics to worry about."

That wasn't a problem with her.

BY MID-MORNING, COVENTRY HATED HIS DESK, and found himself heading outside and taking a walk on the path next to the South Platte River, dodging inline skaters, dog walkers and homeless people pushing shopping carts. On the Megan Bennett case, he thought about going back to the two farmhouses and revisiting the crime scenes, on the chance there was a neon sign he hadn't seen before, but in the end he wasn't convinced that was the best way to spend the day.

The morning's coffee propelled him further than he intended, then he remembered lunch with Leanne Sanders. When he got back his office it was already 12:10 and Dr. Sanders was sitting at his desk, waiting for him.

"I am *so* sorry," he apologized.

She ignored it and instead picked up one of the photographs from his desk, the ones he obtained from Michael Northway's bedroom. "Where did you get these?"

Her voice was tense, as were her eyes.

"Why?" he questioned. Then: "I have another case going on, involving the murder of a woman by the name of D'endra Vaughn. We have reason to believe that the person who killed the Vaughn woman also killed the woman in these photographs."

"Do you know who this is?" she questioned, waving the picture.

"No."

"No?" Dr. Sanders said. "Then let me tell you. This is Dana Frost. Remember when we were taking before, about the two OSU students from the psychology class who disappeared after Beth Williamson, but were never found?"

Coventry remembered, but vaguely, and tried to bring it to the surface. Beth Williamson was the OSU student who had been stuffed into the 55-gallon drum and left out in the woods to rot. She had been in a psychology class and had described the barrel as the way she'd most hate to die. Two other girls from that same psychology class later disappeared, one six months later, and one about a year later. Neither of them had ever been found. Megan Bennett has also been in that psychology class. It was the FBI's theory that the person who killed Beth Williamson also killed the two missing students and is the same person who abducted Megan Bennett. In fact, that's why the FBI was out there in Denver right now, trying to find Megan Bennett's abductor.

"Yeah, I remember," he told her.

"Well," Dr. Sanders said, "This dead woman is Dana Frost, who is one of the two OSU students who disappeared and were never found. So where did you get these photos?"

Coventry waved her off for a second. He had to think. There was only one conclusion he could reach and when he did he was flabbergasted.

The Megan Bennett case and the D'endra Vaughn case, which he had always viewed as separate and distinct, were actually connected.

Whoever the OSU killer was—the one who abducted Megan Bennett—he was the same person who killed D'endra Vaughn.

Coventry looked at Dr. Sanders.

"We need a task force meeting immediately. We have a new wrinkle. A big new wrinkle that I need to fill everyone in on."

Chapter Forty-Six

Day Twelve
Friday Afternoon

DAVID HALLENBECK FOLLOWED THE biker woman down Lincoln Avenue, sixty steps behind, wearing dark sunglasses, a Colorado Rockies baseball cap, jeans and tennis shoes.

She needed to die.

He'd follow her all day if he had to but she'd be dead by midnight, guaranteed. She'd be sorry she ever screwed with him. Unlike Megan Bennett—who was in the death process even at this very moment—she actually deserved to die, and die she would.

Today.

Maybe even in the next ten minutes.

Then he was going to get out of this old cow town. Get away so fast and far that no one would ever find him again in a million years. In fact, he wasn't even going to go back to Cleveland. Screw that place and screw his entire previous life. He was going to go to California and get a whole new identity. He could find more than enough work in the car business to keep the rent paid until he was able to build up a new network of clients.

Yes, a clean break.

That's exactly what he needed to do and exactly what he was going to do.

He hung back as the biker bitch stopped to buy a late lunch at a hot dog cart at the corner of Lincoln and Colfax, across the street from the Colorado State Capital. From there she walked west on Colfax for a block and then headed into the Civic Center Park, eating as she walked.

He felt the excitement rise.

She was finally getting out of the crowds and into more grassy and garden type areas. This is the place he would take her down. He started closing the gap, walking past bums curled up asleep under trees.

Squirrels scampered about everywhere, millions of them.

The biker bitch wandered around the grounds. Hallenbeck lost sight of her now and then but was always able to pick her up again without too much trouble.

He closed the gap even farther.

Then he slipped the knife out of its sheath. He cupped it in his hand, upside down, with the blade pointed towards the sky, hidden between his forearm and body.

He would stick it as far as he could into her head or heart or back, all the way up to the handle if he could, and then twist.

He lost her again.

No big deal. She'd show up.

He swung around to the right.

She wasn't there.

Where are you biker bitch?

He was trolling now.

Looking everywhere.

Hoping he wasn't going the wrong way.

He came around a small utility building at a half trot. Then, bingo, right in front of him, five men sat on a concrete ledge and the biker bitch was standing in front of them with her shirt lifted up, showing off her stomach tattoos.

She looked straight at him.

Then screamed.

"Get that guy!"

Chapter Forty-Seven

Day Twelve
Friday Afternoon

FIFTEEN MINUTES BEFORE THE task force meeting was scheduled to begin, Bryson Coventry filled Shalifa Netherwood in on the fact that the D'endra Vaughn and Megan Bennett cases were related. Both women were victims of the killer from OSU that the FBI had been hunting for years.

She scratched her head.

"And he's the one who kidnapped Kelly Parks, too?"

"Exactly."

"And you say that because . . . ?"

"Because he used D'endra Vaughn's phone to give her a warning call the next day. Whoever killed D'endra went after Kelly, that's clear."

"So one person did *all* this, is what you're saying?"

"Right."

"Wrong."

The word startled Coventry.

"What do you mean, wrong?"

"Think about it," Shalifa said. "Kelly Parks was abducted last Saturday night at about eight o'clock. That's the same time the bikers got killed at the farmhouse, if you believe Catherine Higgins."

Coventry instinctively walked over to the coffee machine and filled up, his brain racing.

"She didn't give us an exact time," he said. "It still fits."

"No it doesn't," Shalifa insisted.

"Why not?"

"Okay," she said, "play it out. You're the bad guy. You abduct Kelly Parks about eight. You drive all the way up Clear Creek, which is what? A good twenty miles west of here? You break a tie-rod and then push the car off an embankment into the river. Now you're out there in the middle of nowhere with no car. You got to get from there all the way back to the farmhouse, which is a good twenty-five or thirty miles south of Denver, to kill the bikers. Even if you hitched a ride off the mountain and got picked up right away, you're talking about some serious travel time."

"But . . ."

"Hours," she added.

Shit.

She was right.

Now, suddenly, it didn't make sense again.

Damn it!

He looked at his watch. Two minutes until the Task Force meeting started.

He drained the coffee cup and then refilled. "Okay," he said. "What am I missing here?"

She shrugged. "I don't know. But something, that's for sure."

SUDDENLY HIS CELL PHONE RANG. He answered it, pissed at the distraction when he needed it least.

"God, I am so glad I got you!" someone said. He recognized the voice, a woman's, but couldn't quite place it.

"Who is this?"

"It's me, Catherine Higgins," the woman said. "I just saw him! He was following me! He was going to kill me! He has a knife! Five men chased him but he got away!"

"Where?"

"At the Civic Center Park."

"How long ago?"

"I don't know, five minutes maybe. I had to find a pay-phone to call you."

"Which way was he headed?"

"Towards downtown."

"What was he wearing?"

He felt her pause, trying to get a better visual, then said, "A baseball cap, sunglasses, jeans, a long-sleeve shirt—blue—and tennis shoes."

"Where are you right now?"

"Outside a Subway store, on Lincoln, near Colfax."

"Get inside the store and stay there. A police officer will be there to get you."

"Okay."

Then: "Did the baseball cap say anything?"

"I don't know, maybe."

"Okay, stay there."

Thirty seconds later Coventry busted into the task force room, drawing the startled stares or twenty or more people.

"He's just been spotted!" Coventry said. "He's somewhere downtown, right now! Pay attention because I'm handing out assignments."

A BOLO WAS IMMEDIATELY SENT OUT to every Denver cop with a description of the suspect. All officers not performing essential duties were directed to report immediately to the downtown area and sweep the major streets, especially the 16th Street Mall, 17th Street, Lincoln Avenue, Colfax Avenue, Broadway and LoDo.

Patrol cars were rushed into position to watch every major corridor out of the city with instructions to stop every black or dark blue late model Camry that went by.

Notifications were sent to Amtrack, rental car companies, Yellow Cab and DIA. The chopper—Air One—was positioned over downtown.

A team was dispatched to start with the shelter as the center of a circle, and search the surrounding parking lots and side streets, looking for a parked Camry.

Shalifa Netherwood was assigned to interview Catherine Higgins, as soon as she was brought in, to find out where she had been walking prior to the encounter, in an effort to locate any video cameras that might have recorded her stalker.

People scattered.

Forty-five minutes later, Richardson called. "Bryson?"

"Yeah, talk to me."

"We have a black Camry parked in the lot at Broadway and 20th," he said, obviously excited. "It's a rental. We can see some rope on the floor under the back seat."

"Okay, good," Coventry said. "What company?"

"Avis."

"All right, here's what we need to do," he said. "Call Avis

and get the location where he rented it. They should have a copy of his driver's license. Get that faxed down to me. The biker woman's here and if she identifies him, we'll have his picture up and running on every TV station in minutes."

"Done," Richardson told him.

Coventry slapped his hands together. "Oh, yeah, baby!"

He paced back and forth in the war room, a spider frantically weaving a web, knowing that if this guy did manage to escape then Megan Bennett was a dead woman. The little asshole would either abandon her in-place to rot to death or he would kill her as baggage that he could no longer afford to carry.

Either way she was dead unless they nailed his ass quick.

This was it.

Chapter Forty-Eight

Day Twelve
Friday Afternoon

HALLENBECK HAD TO GET THE HELL OUT of downtown!

He took 16th Street east to Logan and then cut north, walking as fast as he could without looking like a freaking maniac on the run. He dumped the baseball cap in a first trashcan he came to, then peeled off the long sleeve shirt and the knife sheath as he continued walking, getting down to a red T-shirt underneath. He found an abandoned newspaper, slipped the knife inside and carried it in his right hand. He dumped the long sleeve shirt and the sheath in the next trashcan.

Helicopters flew overhead

Cop cars were everywhere, billions of them.

Every time one came by he would duck in a building, or look in a storefront window, or bend down to tie his shoe, or do whatever else he could.

The main thing at this point was to get back to the Camry and then weave out of downtown using the secondary streets.

He was almost at the car now and starting to calm down.

Then, damn it!

Some dickhead was standing right in front of it talking into a cell phone. Now the jerk was taking out a small spiral note-book and writing down the license plate number. Now he was back on the cell phone again.

Damn it to hell!

He needed a refuge.

Someplace safe.

A corner where he could hole up until it got dark.

Then he had an even better idea.

He turned and walked south down Logan, away from the Camry, pulled his cell phone out of his front pants pocket and called Michael Northway.

"It's me, now listen very carefully," Hallenbeck told him. "I'm downtown and have a bit of a situation going on. Where is your car parked?"

"Why?"

"Don't screw with me!" Hallenbeck said. "If I go down, you're coming with me, I guarantee it. Where is your car parked?"

The lawyer paused, but finally said: "In the building."

"I know that. What parking level?"

"P-3."

Hallenbeck sighed, okay, P-3.

"All right, good. Go down there right now and wait for me by the elevator. And bring whatever cash you have, including whatever you got in your safe. Do you understand?"

"I do."

"I should be there within five or ten minutes. Don't try anything fancy. Remember, you've got a shit-load of a lot further to fall than I do."

Chapter Forty-Nine

Day Twelve
Friday Afternoon

KELLY PARKS DIALED MICHAEL NORTHWAY'S extension and got transferred to Lori Chambers when he didn't answer. "Hey, Lori, where's that Michael dude?"

"He just left."

"You're kidding." She looked at her watch. It was only three-thirty. "Already?"

"Something came up."

"The Friday Afternoon Club?"

Lori sounded negative. "I don't think so, but something not on his calendar. He looked stressed. Why, what's up?"

"Our brief in the Anderson case," she said. "Our filing deadline's Monday and Michael made me promise that he'd have a hard copy of our draft in hand before he left today, ostensibly so he can quote *read* it this weekend, meaning totally rewrite it."

"I remember that now." Then, in a brighter tone, "Hey, you know what? He hasn't been gone for more than a few minutes. I'll bet you can catch him at his car before he leaves. I can call him on his cell phone, if you want, and tell him you're on your way down."

"Bingo, do that."

She grabbed the papers in one hand, her cell phone in the other, and headed for the elevator banks. The up and the down elevators both arrived on her floor at the same time. A cop got out of the up elevator just as she stepped into the down one. Inside, she faced the front and tried to not stare at some poor slob who was unfortunate enough to be wearing the worst toupee ever made. It looked like an orange cat crawled on top of his head and died.

Just as she was getting off on P-3, Bryson Coventry called her.

"Hey there," she answered.

Coventry sounded tense: "Have you heard the news?"

"No, what?"

"We have a major manhunt going on, right smack downtown," Coventry told her. "This is the guy who killed D'endra Vaughn and abducted you, among other things. There's a chance, one in a million, that he could decide to make another play for you, if he felt totally trapped and decided to go out in style."

"You're kidding, right?"

"So we have an officer coming over to the law firm to keep you company," he said.

"Yeah, I saw him," she said.

"You're breaking up."

"I'm in the parking garage."

Kelly spotted Michael Northway at the far end of the structure, talking to a man, a big man, in what looked to be an intense discussion. She walked towards them, waving the brief in the air as she went.

"Hey, Bryson, I have to talk to Michael Northway for about

ten seconds, but don't go anywhere, just stay on the line, I need to tell you something."

"Lori said you were coming down," Northway said as she walked up.

Something was wrong.

Dreadfully wrong.

The big man looked around, as if searching for witnesses. She looked at Northway and started to say—*What's going on?*—but never got the words out. Instead a burst of colors exploded inside her head.

Chapter Fifty

Day Twelve
Friday Afternoon

AFTER THEY GOT KELLY PARKS' LIMP BODY into the trunk, David Hallenbeck told Northway to take off her pantyhose and tie her hands behind her back. He expected Northway to give him some pushback and try to minimize his involvement, but that didn't happen.

Hallenbeck smiled as he watched his accomplice work.

"Welcome to the dark side."

The lawyer looked up at him, hard. "Just don't get caught."

Hallenbeck felt the need to remind him of just how fortunate he was. "I'm doing you a favor, counselor. The cops are going to think that whoever took her the first time took her this time too. I'll kill her tomorrow around noon. You just be sure you have a solid alibi when that happens. Then you're home free."

The lawyer looked straight into Hallenbeck's eyes. "So, what, we're even, then?"

Were they?

Hallenbeck had to think about it for a second.

Northway at least *tried* to kill Kelly Parks before, even

though he didn't quite get the job done. And today's help was invaluable. Still, the lawyer hadn't actually taken a life yet. He still hadn't delivered a package with real pictures.

"We're even for a while," Hallenbeck said. "But you still need to perform, eventually."

Hallenbeck wasn't sure, but it looked like Northway was actually relieved that he hadn't been let completely out of his deal.

"Okay, fair enough."

Hallenbeck removed the keys from the trunk, slammed the lid and walked to the side of the car. This was it.

"Remember, have your cell phone with you all the time," Hallenbeck said, "in case I get pulled over and need you to verify that I have permission to use the car. When I get to California I'll call you and make arrangements to get the vehicle back. No one will ever know."

"Just don't get caught."

Hallenbeck contemplated it. "I shouldn't, everyone's looking for a Camry. But if I do, I'll keep my mouth shut and you get me a lawyer. Then we'll think of something that gets me bail and keeps you out of it. I owe you that much."

The two men shook hands.

"Take care."

"I'll be in touch."

Chapter Fifty-One

Day Twelve
Friday Afternoon

BRYSON COVENTRY COULDN'T STAND IT anymore, told Shalifa Netherwood that she was in charge of everything until he got back, and took the steps two at a time up to the sixth floor to see how Paul Kubiak was coming along in the forensics lab.

Not knowing what happened to Kelly Parks was driving him crazy.

He'd been smart enough to hit the record button on his telephone when he started picking up distant voices from Kelly's cell phone, then gave the tape to Kubiak to see if he could enhance it.

But that was more than an hour ago.

When he walked into the lab three or four people sat around a computer arguing about whether a particular phrase was "take care" or "take her." They were playing it over and over and Coventry could barely tell that it was a human voice, much less what the words were.

"Sounds like ducks fighting," he said.

Kubiak looked up at him, and said, "Come over here and

look at this," referring to the screen of a second computer, a laptop. It turned out to be a transcript of a conversation between Voice 1 and Voice 2.

He scrolled through it and couldn't believe his eyes.

"Print me a copy of this, please and thank you."

As he grabbed the paper from the printer, Kubiak warned him, "It's just a work-in-progress, don't take it to the bank."

"Keep working on it," Coventry said. Then: "Did I say thank you?"

"Yes."

Coventry walked out, "Well there, you have it twice."

Within five minutes they had a BOLO out on Michael Northway's car, a white Mercedes sedan, Colorado license plate number CKM 994, possibly heading to California, with a hostage in the trunk. The suspect should be considered armed and extremely dangerous.

FIFTEEN MINUTES LATER, COVENTRY AND NETHERWOOD were in the nosiest helicopter in the world, following I-70 west into the Rocky Mountains, on the hunt for a vehicle that had, at this point in time, an hour and a half jump on them.

The sky was gray and a light rain dripped out of it.

As he studied the cars on the interstate beneath them, putting the binoculars on every one that was white, he remembered the lawyer, Michael Northway, and called back to headquarters to get an arrest warrant out for his ass; on a charge of aiding and abetting the abduction of Kelly Parks, for starters.

"If this guy's smart, he'll pull over somewhere until it's dark," Shalifa commented at one point.

Coventry nodded.

"My fear is that he going to drive back to wherever Megan Bennett is, take her and Kelly Parks out, pick up his stuff, wait until dark, dump the bodies somewhere, and then take the back roads out of the state," Coventry said. "That's what I'd do."

Lightning flashed directly outside their window and Coventry couldn't have jumped higher if he had been plugged directly into it. Netherwood laughed and said, "You should see your face."

Then the aircraft abruptly dropped, straight down, and bottomed out on a floor of air with a spine-compressing thud. Netherwood's face was a lot more graven now.

"Got some chop," the pilot said.

No shit.

Coventry looked straight ahead out the pilot's window. The sky was charcoal-gray, swirling and totally insane.

Chapter Fifty-Two

Day Twelve
Friday Evening

KELLY PARKS HEARD SOMEONE put a key into the trunk lock, coming for her, and braced.   A second later the pitch-black world turned to light.   She closed her eyes and then opened them a slit.   Someone grabbed her hard and yanked her out forcefully, a man, the big one from the parking garage who had been arguing with Michael Northway.

"Get your ass out here," he told her, waving a knife back and forth in front of her face, not more than a few inches away.

He looked insane and his voice sounded vaguely familiar.

He grabbed her head hard, held it like a vise in one hand, and ran the blade down the side of her cheek, drawing a line of blood.

Then he pushed her away and stared at her.

"Walk back, good, good, now stop, right there. Spread your legs, wider, wider, good. Now stay just like that, stay absolutely still. Do you hear me?"

"Yes."

She stood there, with her hands tied behind her back and blood dripping off her face, while he lowered himself until he was sitting on the ground. He leaned back against the car and stared at her.

SHE LOOKED AROUND. It was dusk and they were in some kind of an old mining field.

Lunar looking mounds of yellow mine tailings dotted the landscape for as far as you could see, each one marking the location of an old abandoned vertical shaft. Roads snaked through the area, no doubt once used to cart away underground treasures. It didn't look like they had seen any activity for a long time, though, based on the weed infestation. She guessed that the old mine tailings contained heavy metals that the rains leached into the rivers below. So there was a good chance this was a Superfund site and, if so, it was probably well posted as a no trespass area.

No one would be coming around.

She sensed that he pulled in here to hide until it got dark.

KELLY TURNED HER ATTENTION BACK TO THE MAN and was awestruck by his muscles.

"I'm not the one who abducted you before, in case you're wondering," he said. "That was your Michael Northway friend who rolled you into the river." He paused, then laughed. "Life's a bitch, sweetie."

"He wouldn't do that," she said.

He picked up a rock and threw it, then said: "I came real close to taking you and your little friend out that night when you two were getting drunk in that stupid little dive on Colfax. But then I came up with an even better idea. I decided to pay a little visit to Mr. Northway, who still owed me a kill, and make him an offer. We ended up having a little talk in his study. I gave him a choice to kill either you or the other woman, Jeannie Dannenberg. If he did that, I'd call it even. If he didn't, everyone would die, including him. He thought that was fair, and chose you."

Kelly didn't believe it.

Michael Northway would never kill anyone.

Especially her.

They were friends.

"Bullshit," she said.

The man grinned. "He choose you over Jeannie Dannenberg and I'll tell you why. I already used D'endra Vaughn's cell phone to send you a warning message. Your lawyer friend just happened to have an alibi the night that I took the Vaughn woman out. Northway wanted me to give him that cell phone. Then after he abducted you, he used it to call your friend, Bryson Coventry. That way Coventry would think that whoever took you was the same person who killed the Vaughn woman, which in turn meant that it couldn't be the counselor. So, with you he gets an alibi. With Jeannie Dannenberg, he doesn't. So don't take it personal."

The man shook his head, in apparent respect.

"You got to hand it to the man," he went on, "he's got a knack for this shit."

She was confused. "But Michael Northway's not the one who owed you a kill. It was his client."

The man laughed. "There is no client, honey, there never was a client. Your lawyer friend *is* the client."

No, that couldn't be true. "You're wrong. I spoke to the client myself, yesterday."

The man smirked. "You spoke to *me*, bitch," he said, using the same exaggerated voice that the client had used. "That whole thing was a charade, just one more fancy-ass trick concocted by the good Mr. Northway to get you to put pressure on your detective friend to back off." Then he laughed. "From what he tells me, it worked too. Like I said, the guy's a genius."

He stopped talking and studied her, picking up pebbles and flicking them with his thumb.

"Are you the one who abducted Megan Bennett?"

He laughed.

"Brave enough to ask a question," he said. "I like that. Megan Bennett? Yes, I'm afraid that's me. In fact, she's the reason I came to Denver, that plus a little business I needed to get done for a client. While I was here, I decided to pay a visit to D'endra Vaughn and the rest of you."

"So where is she?"

"Wow, now there's a question." He looked at her, almost sympathetic. "I hate to tell you this, sweetie, but you need to worry a little more about you and a little less about her."

HE STOOD UP AND SHE SAW SOMETHING in his eyes that wasn't there before. He came up to her, his face within inches of hers, reached around behind and unzipped her skirt. Then he slid it down her legs and had her step out of it.

Then he ripped her panties off.

He reached down and raked his fingers through her pubic hair.

Then he grabbed her head, like before, and ran the knife down the other side of her face, drawing another trail of blood, even deeper this time.

"I'm not going to kill you until noon tomorrow," he said, "but that doesn't mean we can't have a little fun right now."

He grinned, insane looking.

"Now run! This is your chance! Run!"

Chapter Fifty-Three

Day Twelve
Friday Night

———————

THEY WERE ON THE GROUND IN VAIL, waiting out the storm when Bryson Coventry got the phone call. Thirty minutes ago, just after dusk, a hiker spotted a man chasing a half-naked woman with her arms tied behind her back. This was at the old mining site just northwest of Idaho Springs.

He found the pilot inside the hanger sipping coffee, and said, "We got to go, now!" Moments later they were swooping up into a turret of rain, into a dark and ominous sky, directly into the meat of the storm. Coventry put both armrests into a death grip and stared straight ahead.

Lighting exploded around them, so close that the sky actually shook.

Coventry expected a direct hit at any second.

One that would take them down to a fiery death.

After what seemed like a long time, Shalifa Netherwood shouted, "Look!"

Coventry forced himself to look out the window and said, "What?"

"There, the car."

Then he saw it; a white car, sideways on an old mining road, apparently stuck in mud, illuminated by the chopper's search-light.

"Get us down there!"

They let the chopper touch all the way down this time before jumping out. The pilot kept it on the ground, blocking the car, just in case.

Coventry ran over to it, weapon drawn, with Netherwood two steps behind. No one was in the car. The keys were gone. He saw the trunk up and ran back there to look. No one was there. He ran up front and shot both of the tires, startling Netherwood who didn't expect it.

He fought his way through the rain over to the helicopter.

"Get off the ground, I don't want him using this thing as an escape vehicle. Keep your spotlight off us. Call for backup."

The chopper lifted off and everything turned instantly black

A lightning bolt ripped across the sky. Coventry saw mounds of mine tailings everywhere.

"Watch your step," he warned Shalifa, getting his voice up so she could hear it over the pounding of the rain. "If you fall in one of those bastards you can kiss your ass goodbye."

Suddenly something whizzed by his head.

A rock.

It must have been going a hundred miles an hour.

He whirled around but didn't see a thing.

Damned rain.

Then suddenly something blacker than the night struck him. The gun flew out of his hand, and he landed so hard on the ground that the breath flew out of his lungs. Fists of iron pounded on his head and face from out of nowhere.

A gun fired.

It was Netherwood, not firing at them, but using the gun as a light.

Again.

And again.

And again.

The barrel flashed each time, like a slow, eerie strobe light. Shapes came into focus. Before she could fire again, the force pounding the life out of Coventry jumped off and disappeared into the night.

Netherwood fired in that direction.

Bam!

Bam!

Bam!

They didn't hear anything.

Seconds passed.

Then more.

Then more.

Then, from out of the blackness, they heard a scream.

Chapter Fifty-Four

Day Twelve
Friday Night

DAVID HALLENBECK, TO HIS UTTER DISBELIEF, found himself pinned in a shaft, at least twenty feet down. Both arms were locked immobile at his side. He tried to move, desperate, and realized decisively that that was not going to happen. Blood poured into his eyes. He tried to shake his head, to get it to change course, but it did no good. He was in water up to his chest.

He called out for help, in a panic.

It felt like his right knee was broken. The pain was terrible, shooting up his spine and straight into his brain.

He called and called and called.

Then something happened.

He heard a man's voice, far above and faint, but definitely a human voice.

"Where is Kelly Parks?"

He shouted back, "She escaped. She's safe somewhere. Get me out of here."

"Where is Megan Bennett?" the voice questioned.

He slipped down further in the hole, bringing the water even closer to his head. He could hear the rain wash down the sides of the shaft.

"Where is Megan Bennett?"

"She escaped."

"Bullshit! Where is she?"

"She escaped, that's the goddamned truth!"

No more shouting came from above.

"Hey, are you up there?"

No answer.

He called, again and again and again.

For at least two minutes.

Still no answer.

The water was definitely rising. He was certain of that now and struggled with all his might to free his body.

Damned rock!

Then a voice came from above. "Here's the deal. You're going to tell me where Megan Bennett is. Then I'm gong to send someone out there to verify it. If we find her and she's alive, then I'm going to call a rescue team in here to get you out. If you don't tell me where she is, or if she's dead, then you can rot in there. My report's going to say you ran off into the night and we had no idea where you went."

He screamed.

"Get me out of here!"

COVENTRY PACED ABOVE THE HOLE, then kicked rocks into it.

He got on his hands and knees, like a dog, and shouted in: "Last chance, asshole. You tell me where Megan Bennett is, right this second, before I start dropping rocks on your goddamn head!"

A pause.

"Get me out first. That's the deal."

He picked up a rock the size of a golf ball and threw it down with all his might.

"There's your deal!" he said. "How do you like it, huh? Is that good enough for you?"

"Bryson, stop!" The words came from Netherwood, who shoved him hard in the chest. "Don't do it! He's not worth it."

Coventry knew she was right but didn't care. He pushed her to the ground, picked up another rock and threw it so hard that his arm hurt.

"Talk!" he shouted into the hole. "Where is Megan Bennett? Where is Megan Bennett? Where is Megan Bennett? Do you hear me? Where is Megan Bennett?"

A pause, then, "Okay, stop, I'll tell you . . ."

"Tell me now!"

"Okay, calm down, she's south of Denver . . ."

Coventry got Kate Katona on the phone and fed her the directions, staying on the line as she tore down I-25 at well over a hundred miles an hour.

"How you doing?" he questioned.

"Two miles to the turnoff," she said. A short time later, "Okay, I'm getting off."

"Good," he said. "Head east for about two miles . . . you should see a gravel road on your left . . ."

"What marks it?"

"Nothing . . . it's just a road . . ."

"Got it," she said.

"Two hundred yards, on your right, a metal building . . ."

"Bingo, there it is!"

The vehicle slid to a stop in the gravel, so loud that Coventry could hear the wheels locking. "The back door should be open," he said.

"I'm heading around." Then, after a moment, "Oh my God!"

"What?"

Katona's voice disappeared, and Coventry could tell she was running, then the phone clanked, as if she dropped it on the ground.

"She's strapped down to a table," Katona shouted. "There's something on her head, a helmet or something . . . she's moving! She hears me! Come on baby, hold on, let's get this thing off . . ."

Seconds passed.

Someone gasped for air and choked, as if they'd just broken the surface of the water.

"You're okay baby, breathe!"

More gasping.

"Bryson, we got her," Katona said. "She seems okay . . ."

Coventry slapped his hand on his thigh.

"We got her!" he told Netherwood.

Chapter Fifty-Five

Day Thirteen
Saturday Morning

BRYSON COVENTRY AND A TEAM of ten other people, armed with flashlights, frantically searched the area all night long. The rain never let up, not a bit, and instead just got colder and heavier. Then the wind kicked up and pushed it sideways, keeping the chopper planted even more firmly on the ground. Kelly Parks didn't show up anywhere.

They found her skirt and her panties but not her.

The prevailing theory was that she went down a mineshaft, either at Hallenbeck's hands or at her own misfortune trying to escape.

Then he found her, just after daybreak, way off the beaten path.

She was in a sheer walled pit about thirty feet deep and ten feet wide, more bloodied and bruised than he'd ever seen anyone in his life.

He waved until he got the attention of one of the other men, then jumped down, splashing into chilly water about a foot deep.

He untied her hands, took her in his arms, gently, and held

her.

"Baby, you're okay now," he told her. "We're going to get you to the hospital."

She cried.

For a long time, neither of them said anything. Then she said, "It was so horrible. I jumped in, because I knew he couldn't follow, but he threw rocks at me. Every time he threw one, he told me exactly where it would hit."

Coventry held her, picturing it.

"I couldn't protect myself." A pause: "Then he left. He could have killed me but wanted me to rot to death instead. He knew no one would ever find me in here."

"Yeah, well, don't worry about him, he won't be bothering you anymore."

They held each other, there in the water, while the paramedics scrambled above, rigging up a stretcher and ropes.

Then, at one point, she moved ever so slightly, and said, "What about Megan Bennett?"

"We got her," Coventry said. "She's at Lutheran Medical Center right now, which is where we're going to take you. Maybe you two can be roommates."

She squeezed his hand.

"That would be nice."

Chapter Fifty-Six

Day Forty-Three
(One Month Later)
Thursday Evening

———————

"GET READY FOR THE BEST FIVE MINUTES of film ever made," Coventry said, sitting up straighter on the couch. "Courtesy of Brian de Palma."

Kelly Parks sat next to him, a glass of wine dangling from left hand and a transcript of today's trial testimony sitting next to her, unread and unmarked. She hadn't touched it since Coventry put *Body Double* in the CD player forty-five minutes ago. She'd never seen the movie and was hypnotized by it, especially the haunting music.

"You're a bad influence," she said.

"Yeah, but that was in the fine print when you signed up."

"Who said I signed up?"

"Hold on," he said. "Here we go."

The Frankie Does Hollywood song—"Relax"—poured out of the surround sound speakers and Coventry cranked up the volume and sang along. "Relax, don't do it . . . "

A heartbeat after the scene ended his cell phone rang. "Told you," he said to Kelly as he picked up the phone. "Best five minutes ever, period."

"If you like weird stuff," she said.

The person calling turned out to be Jeannie Dannenberg, who he hadn't spoken to for over two weeks. "Bryson, I need to talk to you, right away," she said.

Bar sounds filled the background.

"Why, what's up?"

"You'll see. I'm down at B.T.'s, on duty tonight. Can you come down?"

He looked at his watch: 9:42 p.m.

"I don't know . . ."

THIRTY MINUTES LATER HE PAID his six bucks at the door and pushed his way into the strip-club. The place was mobbed, something he didn't expect on a Thursday, until he realized it was amateur night. Jeannie Dannenberg—Oasis—was working one of the stages, stripped down to a barely-there thong and spreading her strong, tanned legs. Coventry looked for an empty chair at the stage, found none, stood there until he got her attention, threw a five-dollar bill by her feet and wandered over to the bar for a beer.

Jeannie came straight over as soon as she finished her set and gave him a warm, sweaty hug; then a wet kiss on the lips.

"Thanks for coming," she said.

"Yeah, so why am I here?"

Another woman wandered over and leaned in. She held a half-empty bottle of beer in her right hand and wore street clothes—shorts, a tank top and sandals.

She was stunning and seemed familiar somehow, but he couldn't place her.

"Coventry," Jeannie said, "meet Alicia Elmblade." He must have had an expression of shock on his face because she added: "See, I told you it'd be worth the trip."

"So you're alive," he said to the woman.

The woman looked at Jeannie, said "He's so formal," then put her arms around Coventry's neck, pulled him in and planted a big kiss on his lips. "I understand you've been watching out for me," she said. "Is that true?"

Coventry shrugged.

"I can't believe you're alive," he said. "I thought for sure Northway killed you right after Rick's Gas Station."

"Apparently he didn't," she said.

Jeannie grabbed Coventry by the arm and started to lead him off. "Come on, you. You're going into the back room for a couple of lap dances, on the house." Alicia Elmblade grabbed his other arm and fell into step.

He found himself in the dim-lit back room, seated in an oversized chair with a six-foot high back, a private unit shaped like a Tilt-A-Whirl, pointed towards the wall. The women stripped down to thongs and turned their powers of persuasion on him.

"So tell me the story," he said.

Alicia Elmblade shook her head negative and gently rubbed his crouch. "Not until you get hard first," she said.

It took thirty-five or forty minutes for them to tell him the story, grinding on him the entire time. They were back there so long that one of the bouncers poked his head in a couple of times, just to be sure nothing illegal was going on.

TWENTY MINUTES LATER, DRIVING BACK HOME, Coventry

reflected on the lawyer, Michael Northway. So, it turns out that he really did try to sever himself from Hallenbeck in the beginning by setting up a fake death. Still, he let himself give in to his dark side, eventually, which was too bad. There was no excuse for rolling Kelly Parks into the river.

Michael Northway, Esq., the fancy-schmancy lawyer.

Now just one more dumb-ass fugitive on the run.

When he got home, the house was dark and Kelly was in the bedroom lying naked on top of the sheets, breathing heavy and steady. He watched her as he stripped down to his T-shirt, and then climbed in, trying not to wake her.

"You smell like perfume," she mumbled.

"Oasis."

"Yeah, right. What did she want?"

"I'll tell you in the morning."

"Umm," she said, rolling to her side.

Because if I tell you now that you didn't participate in an actual murder, he thought, you'll be too excited to sleep. Then your ass will be dragging in court tomorrow.

And we can't have that.

He leaned over, kissed her, then laid his head down and closed his eyes.

Then he opened them.

"Oh," he said. "Jeannie gave me a lap dance, just for your information."

"A good one?"

"Nah. I hardly even noticed, to tell you the truth."

A pause.

"Is that your last lie of the night?"

He chuckled.

"I certainly hope so."

"Okay, good. See you in the morning."

ABOUT THE AUTHOR

Jim Michael Hansen, Esq. is an attorney practicing law in the Denver, Colorado metropolitan area. With over twenty years of courtroom experience, he represents a wide variety of corporate and individual clients in civil matters, with an emphasis on civil litigation, employment law and OSHA. He often speaks on legal topics. Visit him at www.jimhansenlawfirm.com.

TO ORDER

For information on how to order *Night Laws* or any of the other novels in the *Laws* series, visit the author at www.jimhansenbooks.com. Contact the author at jim@jimhansenbooks.com.